To kulvinder
with love
Peter

'Imagination is more important than knowledge. Knowledge is limited. Imagination circles the world'

~Albert Einstein

The Fate Book: The Emperor's Tomb
By Peter Van Minnen
Published 2017 by Your Book Angel
Copyright © 2014 Peter Van Minnen

All rights reserved. No part of this publication may be reproduced, stored in or introduced into a retrieval system, or transmitted in any form, or by any means (electronic, mechanical, photocopying, recording, or otherwise) without the prior written consent of the publisher.

This book is sold subject to the condition that it shall not, by way of trade or otherwise, be resold, hired out, or otherwise circulated without the publisher's prior consent in any form of binding or cover other than that in which it is published and without a similar condition including this condition being imposed on the subsequent purchaser.

Printed in the United States

Edited by Keidi Keating

ISBN: 978-0-9975727-5-9

THE
FATE BOOK
The Emperor's Tomb

***** <u>Peter Van Minnen</u> *****
# The Fate Book
The Emperor's Tomb

Acknowledgements

The Fate Book: The Emperor's Tomb was originally published in 2014 by Pegasus Publishers simply titled *The Fate Book*.

It has now been revised and skilfully re-edited by Keidi Keating and republished by The Light Network with a lovely new cover, and it is the first book in *The Fate Book* series. The second book: *The Fate Book: The Tiger's Nest* will be released by The Light Network in early 2018…

The characters in this book bear no direct or deliberate resemblance to any persons factual or fictional, living or dead.

Hopefully.

A big thank you to my kind and long-suffering friends and relatives who were patient, appreciative. and really encouraging when I read them some early sample chapters from this book, and didn't fall asleep on me. Thanks guys! You know who you are!

And last but never least, my thanks to All That Is for guiding my pen…

To my wonderful wife and muse, Debra, who has stood by me and urged me with her unflagging enthusiasm and support throughout this creation.

To my dear parents, Ernie and Ethne, whose sense of fun and craziness fuelled this book.

To you, Rex and Jim: thanks, dear wordsmiths. It's the 'words' that got this going!

Episode One:
The Portmanteau

Professor Clarence 'Stinky' Kalikaloos wiped his sweaty brow with an already soaked handkerchief.

The Cairo Museum was a veritable treasury of antiquities but was seriously let down by an inadequate air conditioning system. Though the antiquities were properly cooled within their sealed glass display cases, today the viewers were not. Stinky, now living up to his nickname, made a mental note to complain about this to his colleague Professor Wadji Wadjiwadj, curator of the Cairo Museum.

In fact, why wait? He would do that right now, he thought, wrenching his gaze from a first dynasty nose pump, artfully displayed among a range of mummification tools. He waddled purposefully through the main gallery into one of the narrow corridors winding up to the curator's offices, now feeling even more stuffy and airless.

Cameras mounted on the ceilings followed him, and he allowed himself a tiny smile knowing that Professor Wadji would now 'surprise' him with a cup of tea, all the while knowing his bulky friend was wheezing his way up the corridor. Cameras had their uses!

Finally, he found himself outside the door to Professor Wadji's offices and let himself in. Even though he had visited here countless times, Clarence was subjected now, as always, to the scrutiny of Professor Wadji's secretary, the formidable Mrs. Kofi, who sat behind a large ornate desk in the reception area.

Without looking up, she ran a long finger through Professor Wadji Wadjiwadj's appointment book, clearly failing to find Clarence in it.

She was a strikingly attractive woman: tall, slim, and dark-skinned, with almond-shaped eyes, thick black hair, and high cheekbones. She was always immaculately dressed and made up with deep blue eyeshadow, red lipstick, and false eye lashes, with not a hair out of place.

Clarence always thought she bore a remarkable resemblance to Cleopatra, though her looks were not helped by an almost constantly severe expression.

Clarence had once, he thought helpfully, suggested prunes.

'Now look here, Mrs. K; it's just me, old Stinky, wanting a word with me old friend, Wadji. I promise I won't keep him long, old girl. It's about the air in this place. It's ruddy well stinking in these parts!'

At this point, Mrs. Kofi looked up and fixed Clarence with a withering stare, which made him feel like he was being pinned into a display case like a helpless insect.

How did she *do* that? How *did* she manage to make him feel like an impaled moth?

'Please Professor, you will *not* use that kind of language here. And I see that you *do not* have an appointment with Professor Wadji Wadjiwadj. He's extremely busy today cataloguing some new finds, although I shouldn't be telling you that. Please call me later and I shall see when he's available.'

Clarence rolled his eyes and chuckled. He was used to this kind of treatment from Mrs. Kofi and had always suspected she was a little jealous of his friendship with Wadji. There were persistent rumours that she and Wadji had been close as students, though neither of them ever talked about it.

She did everything for the professor: arranged his meetings, flights, and conferences. She even bought his clothes, ordered his groceries, and paid his bills.

And she was an amazing techie: she replaced light bulbs and rewired plugs in the office, plus she updated and rebooted computers.

And so *of course* she would take his complaint about the air-conditioning personally.

Clarence had also noticed that whenever he dropped his voice to share something confidential with Wadji, there she was in a flash with her clipboard, on the pretext of needing to discuss some urgent matter or other. She was quite clearly an inveterate eavesdropper. But Clarence always used one simple and effective technique to bypass her:

He started whistling.

This drove her nuts. It was his way of getting his old friend's attention. And today it worked yet again, much to her annoyance. She looked up and glared at him.

Then she slammed the appointment book shut and stalked down the corridor.

'Magnificent!' Clarence thought, watching her walk away.

Wadji, as emaciated as his colleague was rotund, greeted him at the door to his office, ushering him in with the effusive welcome peculiar to Egyptians. He was tall, dark, and handsome, his abundant hair grey-white and combed back. He had a hawk-like nose and bright penetrating eyes, tempered with good humour and a generous mouth. Now he stood in his doorway, welcoming his old friend.

'My dear Clarence!' he cried. 'Welcome, welcome, welcome!

Come in, come in, come in... I won't ask you to pardon the mess; you know that the place is always like this! Please, please, please, my dear old friend. Allow me to pour you some mint tea, freshly brewed by the lovely Mrs. Kofi, who it seems, has just slipped out of the office.'

'Wadji my old chap. Look old boy, I'll get straight to the point; you've got to do something about the ruddy air conditioning. It's bloody well melting me!'

He noticed there was very little in the way of floor space: the entire room was covered in antiquities, some labelled, some piled up in crates, and others awaiting classification.

In a nanosecond, his trained eye had scanned every object in sight. He greedily peered about him, taking in the labelled artefacts and relics, placing them within the paradigms he knew so well; ignoring his skinny friend's invitation to a bowl of dates, and by now forgetting the heat he had come to complain about.

Clarence dropped his portmanteau as he took in this treasure trove, not noticing an almost identical one nearby, which had been pasted with red stickers emblazoned with the skull and crossbones.

By now, Clarence had even forgotten his sticky stinkiness.

History opened up before him, as Professor Wadji Wadjiwadj eagerly pointed out the latest unlabelled finds, some of them freshly excavated.

The son of a Greek philosopher and an academic Irish mother, Clarence was something of a polymath, not only understanding every branch of archaeology, but also its associated sciences. He was fluent in thirty-five languages and held doctorates in Mathematics, Ancient History, Chemistry, and curiously, the Liberal Arts, which he would have all too shortly to call upon... But for now he took in the excited chatter of Wadji who had lapsed into Coptic as he swept his hands about like windmills, enthusiastically describing and cataloguing the huge array of dusty items in the vast room.

What he didn't notice during this tour was that his portmanteau had started slowly vibrating in time with the stickered one, and that at some point in this weird waltz of the suitcases it inexplicably vaporised into the hot dry air, as the stickered one shrugged off its stickers and assumed the appearance of the professor's!

Meanwhile, after exchanging pleasantries and receiving his Egyptian colleague's assurances that the air conditioning would be dealt with, Clarence reached for his portmanteau, which now seemed strangely heavier, blew the crotchety Mrs. Kofi a kiss as he passed her desk, and waddled down the corridor, with Professor Wadji bowing and smiling for as long as his colleague was still visible to him.

Finally back in his pleasantly cool hotel room, Clarence closed his eyes and sighed with the sheer relief of the cool air, shut the door on the world, and heaved the portmanteau onto his bed.

There was a sudden metallic click, then a whirring. and an almost human sigh.

Clarence stared.

It was coming from the portmanteau.

Feeling ridiculous, he tiptoed up to it. It was, after all, his old companion suitcase. He was never without it. His whole world lived in there: reference books, clothes, medicine, equipment... everything!

With a chuckle at his own silliness, he clicked the catches and threw the lid open.

There was a bright blinding flash, a puff of white smoke, and a long cry, as if all the pain in the world was expressing itself. The professor fainted, but not before he caught sight of a small, fierce figure of a man, wrapped in a blue cloak and turban, with bulging eyes and bright gold teeth. The man's expression, if indeed he was a man, was inscrutable. It was not quite malevolent, but certainly did not seem to have anyone's interests at heart.

Meanwhile, at that precise moment, Professor Wadji Wadjwadj was trying desperately to reach his fat colleague in his hotel room, not knowing he was unconscious.

'My God Clarence, answer the phone, answer the phone! You've got the wrong suitcase, the one we recovered from the tomb. You don't realise the danger you could be in!'

Epsisode Two: The Djinn

Professor Clarence 'Stinky' Kalikaloos was having the loveliest dream:

He was Morris dancing in a sunny English glade, his bulky body incredibly light and agile. He was somehow not surprised to see his friend, Professor Wadji Wadjiwadj, dancing alongside him, smiling broadly and looking attractive, Clarence thought, in a manly sort of way. They were dressed in traditional costume and with every step, bells attached to their arms and legs rang out with a rhythmic sound, while around them a ring of bright maidens clapped in time.

Clarence suddenly woke up.

The phone in his hotel room was ringing. He was lying on his bed and beside him was the most beautiful woman he'd ever seen, dressed only in a shimmering blue cloak and a turban.

He sat bolt upright. This was most irregular, he thought.

He definitely hadn't rung room service, and certainly not for, well, not for...

She smiled, batted her eyelashes, and said,

'Don't bother answering that phone, you darling boy; it's only skinny little Wadjiwadji making sure I'm looking after you. And I am, aren't I, Billy boy?'

'Billy boy...?' Clarence squeaked. Looking down at himself he realised that somehow he had been magically outfitted as Billy Bunter, a comic character he had loved as a boy. He blushed to see himself in those self-same schoolboy shorts and cap, and now she reached an arm out to him, touching him and causing all kinds of things to happen in places he'd forgotten about.

'Anything you want darling, you just say!'

'Erm... you're a succubus?' Clarence blurted, beginning to recover himself, but was then astonished to find he was now in a skintight latex suit!

'Of course, darling...' she purred, moving snakelike down the bed. Clarence leapt up and onto the floor, realising what was happening, and fumbling for the protective talisman he always kept hanging round his neck.

'Looking for this, Clarence baby?' she demurred, her lips suddenly huge and moist. She held up a tiny Egyptian ankh on a leather thong. She looked at once innocent and triumphant. In her magical hand, the talisman suddenly gave out a rasping pop and turned into a blue plastic smurf! Clarence felt small in spite of himself and now felt a little afraid. This woman was formidable, he decided.

He glanced over at the door, and looking back at the

bed, found the siren had now disappeared.

In its place sat the little man in the blue cloak and turban he had first encountered before he fainted.

Bowing slightly, the Djinn flashed a set of bright gold teeth and said quietly,

'At your service, Professor!

I do apologise for the theatrics and the excessive show of magical and theurgic power, but you have no idea how boring it can be, locked in a frigging suitcase for two thousand years! Do let me explain. You see, old chap, this very portmanteau you see as yours, is not yours at all.

Or rather, it is yours, but not yours as you know it!

In fact, this very suitcase belonged to your very own ancestor thrice removed: the good Professor-doktor Heinrich Friedrich von Kalikaloos. He never did like his Greek ancestry and he did his best to wallpaper it over... poor chap. Anyway, thanks to him, I'm here now! You see, due to a little indiscretion on my part, I found myself sealed in the pyramid, defeated by the magic of those far more advanced than me. I am ashamed to say it, but say it I must. Some centuries back, I had a part to play in raiding the very tomb your ancestor entered. Back then, I was summoned up by the court vizier of the all-conquering silly sultan of the time, to help him break the seal on the pyramid; which back then was still intact and unassailed: a jewel of the ancient world and one of its seven wonders!

The greedy sultan felt sure there were treasures beyond imagining in that sacred place, and he wanted in.

He wanted in and he wanted in bad.

So, summoned I was.

And using my arts, I cracked the code and found my way in. But I didn't allow for the far superior arts of those who had built the pyramid in ways you can have but an inkling. Believe me, dear professor, I'm but a novice compared to them! Anyway, once in, I was immediately enchanted by their enchantments. I could not leave, whatever I tried. Though I am indeed a spirit, there are spirits higher in the order of things than me.

So when your great great great but then again not so great grandfather arrived and opened the door, I escaped into this very portmanteau the old explorer brought into the pyramid some two hundred years ago, and I concealed myself in the mechanism of his watch, until I substituted his bag with yours, and here I am now, at your service!'

'You're not… oh my god, you are, you're, yes yes, you're…' Clarence was so excited he couldn't get the name onto his tongue. He knew who this was!

He had studied the ancient Sufi manuscripts kept in the secret vaults below the market in Istanbul, where this magical shape shifting hermetic being had been repeatedly referred to under so many names: sometimes a trickster, sometimes a bandit, or even a hermit.

He cropped up in almost every ancient culture.

Even the gods themselves had been tricked and humiliated by him.

'Wassup muthafucka! You got my handle bitch! You dig my slave magic, dude?' he boomed out with unnecessary force.

Clarence had to smile at him now: shape-shifted and standing there in a kind of album-cover pose, blinged to the extreme in sparkling diamonds and gold chains like a rapper.

Clarence softly applauded his effort.

The rapper held up his hand in modesty.

Then he shape-shifted back into the familiar figure of the little man in the blue cloak and turban.

'Whoever you think I am, isn't important, dear Professor. What is important, is that I'm free and now I owe you one. Dude, as long as you're alive, I'm at your bidding.

'Forget the three wishes. Wish all you want, old boy, I'm yours.

'But first let me tell you how your erstwhile ancestor, the said but dead Professor Heinrich Friedrich set me on the path to freedom.

'Make yourself comfortable, dear sir. Lie back upon those cushions of silk and satin and allow me to entertain you with a description of it all.

'Imagine the scene, some two hundred years ago, our man has found his way, with the help of guides and hirelings, to the door of the tomb, the self-same tomb in which I had been sealed for all those dark and dreary years.

'Unlike your own esteemed presence, this professor-doktor is, with all due respect a dilettante, and doesn't know a pharaoh from a feather duster.

'So he has reached the sealed door, and without magic or much knowledge at all.

'He coughs on the dusty air, mixed with the choking smell of the creosote torchess guttering in the still dead air, for a moment losing his monocle.

'Our man now stands in an intensely dark stone corridor.

It is narrow, with high ceilings disappearing into the gloom.

'He is in every way a Teutonic carbon copy forebear of you, his great-great-great-grandson Clarence.

'Meanwhile the good professor-dokter is examining a cartouche at the entrance to this first dynasty tomb, muttering to himself, his skilfully waxed moustache vibrating like an antenna. He's dressed inappropriately for this climate and place, in an aristocratic German traveler's outfit, resplendent in khaki jodhpurs and a cloak, which he keeps in his leather portmanteau.

Behind him stand a scruffy group of Egyptian peasant

assistants trying not very hard to take their job seriously while the good professor-dokter consults with the heavy hieroglyph decoder, which he also keeps in his portmanteau, and which has been freshly printed by the enthusiastic French under Napoleon.

'He turns to glare at the scruffy help, who are of course giggling at this big fat book held by a big fat man.

One of them has said:

'"Oh Ahmed look at the big fat infidel, looking in his big fat book for the address to the tomb!" They all fall about, slapping their skinny legs.

'And so suddenly, the professor-dokter has found what he is looking for. He stabs at the book with a podgy forefinger, trying in vain to share his triumph with his bored indigents...

'"Silence! Fools! Look! You see zis? Zis cartouche is trying to tell us to vatch it! Ja! Zay are saying zat ve are in mortal danger here, zay are saying... (he adjusts his monocle for effect), zay are saying ve are dead meat if ve are vonce entering in here!"

'He chuckles irreverently, shrugging off this deadly warning with the nonchalance of one who typifies the age of reason and who has not seen any Hammer films. He turns to his helpers to demonstrate his indifference, but they have legged it. No curse of no mummy will keep them there they've decided. Underpaid and underfed is one thing, but dead is another.

'Undeterred by this sudden desertion, the professor-dokter pushes firmly on the cartouche, and with a bitter groaning sound, the stone door slides slowly and heavily along into the wall. As the sound echoes into the deeper space ahead of him, he pauses for a moment in the dense silence, then stretches his flaming torch into the vaulted chamber; stiffens, and immediately drops dead to the ground.

'He has, seemingly, been struck senseless by the curse of the mummy and its daddies, but really, his ailing heart has attacked him, and sadly, his bones won't be discovered for another two hundred years; for behind him the stone door groans and slides back into place, but not before a tiny turbaned figure (namely, me!) has leapt out of the cloistering darkness through the tomb door into the abandoned portmanteau and hidden itself within the attractively gravity-defying tourbillion mechanism of the dead professor dokter's Breguet watch. There's a whirring sound, a click, and then silence falls on the scene like a heavy cloak.

'And so it is that this very portmanteau will one day find its way to his own great-great-great but not so very great grandson, you; my dear Professor Clarence 'Stinky' Kalikaloos, whom surely we all know and love.

'Well, what do you think of my story Professor?

'Of course, the key thing is that your ancestor died before I was able to serve him and thus receive my freedom from him, and so I was then obliged to wait a further two centuries before the portmanteau was retrieved and I could stand before you as now I do.'

He bows now with exaggerated finesse. Clarence isn't quite sure what to say. After all, there is no guidebook on conversing with a Djinn, particularly one with such an informed demeanour.

'Extraordinary! And so... well... here you are then, at my... er... service?'

'Precisely, professor! At your service, indeed! For it's only in serving you that I shall in turn be set free... Now, please, it's time you told me all about yourself; I want to know absolutely everything about you, dear sir. Your century is certainly an interesting one, if not a little bewildering to me; for you have magic of every kind at your fingertips, and yet, I dare say, you don't seem to know your own minds.

'Oh, please pardon me for saying that, dear sir. I am but a traveller in these lands, you see.'

Clarence has recovered himself now, and is not quite so daunted by the Djinn, who seems quite civilised and altogether grateful to him for his freedom.

What harm can it do to have a little chat? he thinks. *After all, the poor chap knew my relative, even though it was for a very short time. As long as he doesn't try shape-shifting into something quite so... er... saucy again!*

Episode Three: The Affair of the Condor

In Professor Clarence's wonderfully cool hotel room back in Cairo, things have calmed down.

Over a large overtly ornate silver pot of mint tea, he and the shape-shifting Djinn, who is for the moment content to appear as the small turbaned man, (though in the ensuing conversation he has the disconcerting tendency to turn himself into whatever the professor is reminiscing about) have covered some considerable ground together.

Finding himself in the company of one with equal or greater intelligence, he is rapidly describing his early years under the skilful tutelage of his friend and mentor, Professor Wadji Wadjiwadj, who patiently taught him everything he knew about the secret history of the world.

Together they traveled the world to the ancient sacred sites, placing them within the context of this arcane science, handed down the millennia from adept to pupil.

Some of these places revealed terrifying mysteries beyond the comprehension of the mind.

In fact, that was their purpose!

Yet somehow, Clarence was undaunted. He seemed to have an endless capacity for adventure, despite his horizontal challenges.

He tells the Djinn that on one of these occasions they visited the initiation-centres of Macchu Piccu, where the poor professor came close to a coronary, climbing the steep mountain tracks in the rarified air, and was saved only by a stiff shot of twelve-year-old malt suffused with essence of maca root and something sticky, which Wadjiwadj refused to discus

He tells him that, on this same trip, condors, which probably thought their eggs nesting in a nearby eyrie were being targeted, unexpectedly attacked them. The huge birds, with wingspans easily exceeding the ten feet normally recorded, swooped down upon them, just as Clarence was taking a dump on the edge of a precarious escarpment.

With his trousers around his ankles, he was no match for them. The larger male condor gripped Clarence's quaking shoulders in its talons and with considerable effort, began to lift him away into the air.

Again, his good mentor Wadji saved his sweaty bacon by neatly distracting the angry birds with a pretty good rendition of a sacred Peruvian bird dance, squawking and hopping about with his arms gyrating.

At this point in the professor's story, the Djinn has shape-shifted into a laughing condor.

Clarence was dropped quite suddenly by the distracted condor, from a height of around ten feet and landed on a soft but surprised lama, which doubled up as dinner that night.

After they had both bathed and cleaned themselves off in a mountain stream, Wadjiwadj made a fire and prepared the unfortunate llama for roasting. He spoke long into the night, after they had feasted on roasted lama washed down with highland beetroot wine.

He told Clarence of the Incas, the ancient people of these mountains and their mysteries; of the role of the virgin priestesses, who lived in the precincts of this mountain citadel and channelled sacred information to the people who ruled this huge kingdom. These maidens, it was said, channelled the voices of the gods who guided humanity and advised the populace on every aspect of their lives and, considering they did not yet have the wheel to help them out, they did pretty well, and in relative peace. Back then, you could worship whatever you wanted and people lived in harmony with nature. For a time.

Clarence tells the Djinn that in those days, Professor Wadjiwadj was an extremely athletic man, before his body became wasted by a mysterious disease contracted from the rare Himalayan cave bat, whilst searching the area for the entrance to the Kingdom of the Immortals.

Famously, he could hold his breath underwater for around thirty minutes or more; a feat which saved him when he was forced to wrestle a Nile crocodile to the death, when he fell off the back of a boat whilst engaged in an amorous moment with a willing tourist.

He tells the Djinn that what passed between teacher and pupil on these adventures is not something he can easily describe, and the Djinn nods, for he knows the secret history of the world cannot be revealed to the uninitiated.

He then describes these adventures, some of which are covered in this very book and more importantly, tells the Djinn that on one of these trips, Professor Wadji Wadjiwadj passed over something incredible to him:

The Fate Book!

Episode Four: The Fate Book

Sitting at the campfire that night in Macchu Piccu, the two friends reminisce.

They have pitched their large tent on the summit of the mountain. Normally that is not allowed, but as the two men are archaeologists and are well known to the Peruvian authorities, they are allowed to come and go as they please.

The beautiful rarified Andean sky is a huge field of stars above them. The destiny of every man, beast, plant, and stone is written there, thinks Wadji, and he is moved to break the companionable silence between him and Clarence.

'You know, my dear friend, I was just thinking: it's been almost thirty years since we first met at Trinity College in Dublin. Then, if you remember, the following year you came to visit me in Cairo... and then of course, years later, when you got that job at the British Museum, we started seeing a lot more of each other.'

Clarence smiles, nodding as he remembers that first meeting, but still he says nothing. He knows Wadji has more to say, and he watches his old friend across the dancing campfire intently.

'I suppose, by now, my old friend, you know as much about me and my work as practically anyone on the planet.'

'That's certainly true, old chap... and the same applies to me,' Clarence answers and nods, looking deep into the dancing flames, as if to find those memories in there. He is also feeling the contentment following a good meal and the deep calming embrace of the mountains.

He just hopes Wadji doesn't spoil things by getting too sentimental now. That sometimes happens when he's had a few drinks. And the beetroot wine certainly has a kick to it.

In his earlier days Wadji was very much the lady's man; something which had often created problems.

He and Clarence went back many years. They had first met as post-graduate students. Wadji had travelled to Trinity College in Dublin to deliver a paper on his studies in papyrus and its place in Egyptology. Clarence was fascinated and together they spent long hours in the university day rooms or in the pubs of Dublin, where he extracted everything he could from Wadji's formidable mind.

Later, Clarence found himself employed by the British Museum, and rapidly made himself indispensable there with his encyclopaedic knowledge of archaeology and all of its associated branches of history. But he was rather more interested in exploring and finding new pieces, finding that being restricted to the dusty rooms in the museum made him restless.

So, he soon developed a reputation as a pathfinder and explorer extraordinaire, following up on clues from ancient documents and maps, constantly challenging his colleagues on their inherent need to catalogue and fix history into convenient pigeon holes.

He felt that history was cyclical rather than linear.

There was also ample proof, so he felt, that certain civilisations simply appeared out of nowhere and vanished just as mysteriously... what some archaeologists called the stair-step evolution.

This made him both notorious and popular, whether it was for fearlessly upholding new theories or challenging the establishment.

He developed close ties with other museums worldwide, but especially with the Cairo Museum, where he would share new information with his friend, Professor Wadjiwadj. They would visit each other as often as they could and regularly shared assignments and even archaeological digs together.

Wadji loved Ireland. He loved the absolutely opposite kind of weather there from his home in Cairo, its humour, and the warmth of its people. He was equally fascinated with local folklore and fairy tales, and the magical and peculiar history of the island.

Wadji continues now, a slight slur in his words

confirming Clarence's suspicions about the effect of the wine.

'Yes, we certainly have shared some wonderful times together, my dear Clarence, and I've shared with you everything I know about the secret history of the world. And that, as you know, is a very big subject indeed.'

Clarence nods in agreement. He has lost count of the number of sites he has visited with Wadji, and the number of conversations they have had about them.

'I know I'm going to sound maudlin, perhaps, and you'll have to find it in your heart to forgive me for that. I know you'll be sitting there thinking, Oh God, Wadji's had a drop too much of the beetroot wine, but you'll just have to get over your Britishness and hear me out, old friend...'

He pauses for a moment, and the silence surges around them. The crackle of the fire fragments that silence and Wadji continues.

'As much as I love my life and I am of course still enjoying every moment of it, I do feel that the clock is ticking, and as you know, Clarence, I haven't been in the best of health lately.'

He stands up now, stretches his arms, and stares into the night sky. Then he walks slowly over to Clarence, who feels himself tensing a little.

What the hell is Wadji up to? he wonders. What's got into him? He is not one to sit easy with this kind of emotional stuff.

'So Clarence, because you now know so much about the secret history of the world, and as we've shared the sacred sites together, I feel it's now time to pass something else over to you. Something quite special. I've been consulting the stars and I'm told that this is the right time...'

He stands over Clarence, who, feeling more than a little embarrassed by this sudden outburst of sentimentality, looks away for a moment.

Suddenly a small leather bag drops at his feet, and as he looks back, Wadji is already at his place opposite the fire, staring intently first at him, then the bag...

'Open it, Clarence. It won't harm you,' he says, his voice now a little husky, as if what he had handed over in the bag is stirring his feelings, which indeed it is. Clarence opens the soft leather bag and draws out something, which is carefully wrapped in silk.

A book.

But this is no ordinary book.

It is The Fate Book.

Professor Wadji Wadjiwadj has been its custodian for around forty years, having received it from its previous custodian, Morkabalas the mystic.

Morkabalas received it from someone much earlier, that person having received it from one before him.

And so The Fate Book follows a paper trail which vanishes into the twilight of human history.

And so now Professor Wadji Wadjiwadj, curator of the Cairo museum, is about to hand The Fate Book over to his lifelong friend, Professor Clarence.

It surprises Clarence, who has known him for so many years, that he has never spoken of it before.

Not once.

He now feels the weight of the book and its strange energy and he passes his hands over its smooth surface. There is something very familiar about it. Something friendly even. It is warm to the touch, as if it has life. Its cover is beautifully inlaid with precious stones. They are large brightly coloured crystals, highly polished and carved in unusual geometric designs.

He notices now that one of the crystals is missing, or rather there is a place where a crystal should be. It is impossible to say, in the dancing firelight, what kind of material the cover is made from, but it isn't leather and it isn't stone or wood. And yet it feels warm, strong, and substantial. Though it is clearly very ancient, strangely, it does not show signs of wear, almost as if it is a living, self-maintaining thing.

Clarence shudders; he doesn't know why; perhaps it is the cold night air. He can feel Wadji's eyes on him, inviting him to carry on, willing him to open the cover of the book.

So he does.

In the instant he opens the cover of The Fate Book, he finds himself suddenly rushing down a shimmering tunnel.

It is the strangest feeling, as though he is traveling at enormous speed, yet he feels very calm and still and safe.

Wadji, the campfire, and indeed Macchu Piccu and the starry night have all disappeared and Clarence is now quite on his own. He knows, somehow, that from here on his life will change forever.

He rushes down the tunnel, which now twists and expands and reveals vistas along the way; living scenes from the past. It is like an interactive archive, a library of all the events in time. But at the same time, it is alive! *Really* alive: as he focuses on any particular event, it immediately responds and opens up to him, and he then sees the events from that particular time played out before him, in the most exact detail.

He has heard of this phenomenon and in his heart of hearts has always suspected its existence. It is known to some as the Akasha or the Akasha Chronicle. Perhaps even, the Book of Life.

Now he truly understands what that means. As much as human beings would and could distort history to suit their needs, the gods who created us and this sublime world we live in, made sure that the true history of events would be kept forever safe and secure in this living library!

This he now understands and marvels at the wisdom behind it all. This is what Wadji has been telling him all these years. He can hear his voice even now, though he is not present: *'Clarence, there is a dream that is dreaming us....'*

Perhaps it is the pull of his analytical intellect or perhaps the gods have decided he'd seen enough for now, but the next thing Clarence knows, is that he finds himself suddenly back at the campfire at Macchu Piccu. As if he has woken from a long dream.

The Fate Book lies open just where he had left it. The campfire is burning just as brightly, as if he has not been gone from there for more than a minute or two.

But of his erstwhile friend and mentor Professor Wadji WadjiWadj, there is no sign.

He has completely disappeared.

Episode Five: Morkabalas

Long before factories and mass production and paper money, computers or electricity, or even the invention of the wheel or the telescope, there was a man called Morkabalas.

A most unusual man.

First of all, his eyes were different colours.

One was bright yellow and the other was pale violet.

One looked inwards, the other out.

One eye saw the future, the other the past.

From his early youth, this set him apart from others.

His parents always felt he was not of this world.

His mother had dreamed, on three separate occasions, that she would give birth to a rather special son.

Fortunately for the infant Morkabalas, people in those ancient times set great store by their dreams.

Not only that, but the couple were visited by a holy man before the child's birth, and he told them that their son-to-be was going to be a special kid who would fulfil a special fate, and that he, the holy man, would return for him when it was time, and instruct him in the secret ways of the mystic.

The holy man said their lad was going to be instrumental in bringing something quite special into the world.

What could they do?

What would you do with a boy with eyes like that?

Morkabalas lived somewhere in the Middle East before it was divided by culture and religion into the many countries it is now.

Not that Morkabalas would have cared too much about all of that anyway, because by now he was a hermit.

A kind of holy man or mystic who had chosen quite freely to withdraw from the world, in order to study and chart the windings and turnings of his mind, and somehow, in this way, to leave a map for others to follow; for it is said that what one person accomplishes he makes easier for those who follow.

This, as you know, is true of many things....

Anyway, let us take ourselves to this time before too much was known of the world as we know it now.

Let us join Morkabalas on a very special day.

The day he received The Fate Book.

Morkabalas claimed to have been given The Fate Book

by an angel after a period of sustained meditative practice.

He says the angel came in a disguise, pretending to be a travelling door-to door nougat salesman, who knocked on his door, disrupting his deep trance state.

Somewhat rattled at being disturbed from his reveries, Morkabalas stomped angrily to his door, threw it open, and said something like:

'Yeswhatthefuckisit!'

In Coptic, of course...

The tiny nougat salesman responded with a huge grin, as if verbal abuse were quite normal and just as effective as a cheery good morning.

He flashed a marvellous set of bright gold teeth and bowed deeply, simultaneously balancing a shiny silver tray of fresh nougat on the tips of his fingers, his blue turban almost touching the ground.

Before Morkabalas could stop him, the nougat man stepped nimbly under his arm and slipped into his house.

He set down his tray and immediately started humming *ommmmmm*...

This mantra immediately calmed Morkabalas down and put him back into the deep trance state from which he had been disturbed. His arms dropped to his sides, he found his eyelids drooping, and in a moment he collapsed like a starched tablecloth into a chair, helped carefully by the nougat man, who looked at his sleeping face for a moment, said something magical over him, moved the silver tray of nougat to a table close by him, and almost as an afterthought as he left, pulled an ancient book from the folds of his pale blue cloak, and gently and respectfully left it there alongside the sweetmeats.

He then slipped out and slammed the door hard, snapping Morkabalas awake.

He stared around him as if seeing the place for the first time. Then he saw the tray of nougat on a side table and it all came back to him and he remembered his mysterious visitor; he rushed to the door, slammed it behind him, and stuck his head into the street.

There was no one in sight. Not even a dog or a cat or a camel.

'Mmm... how unusual' thought Morkabalas, who walked straight into his closed door, bumping his head and swearing, before stumbling back into his house still muttering and rubbing his head.

It was then that he spotted the book on his side table, alongside the silver tray of nougat. How could he have missed it? And there was something else, which hadn't been there before: a faint smell of frankincense.

The house wasn't really a house; it was more like a simple hut with small rooms set around a larger central area. It was made of mud, with a plain mud floor and a roof made of reeds. Quite clean, but shambolic.

In the central space, which also accommodated a small stove with a chimney coming out the back and going out through the roof, were a few simple chairs and tables.

On one of these tables was a bowl of herbs and some scrolls of parchment, tied with colourful ribbons.

The walls were decked in tapestries and hangings, which seemed to be covered in a lot of symbolic script, and there were animals going in circles and spirals everywhere.

And there were stars amongst the animals, but it all made sense somehow, and there was a story unfolding in the script, in a symbolic language not spoken outside of this place.

Clearly this house lacked a woman's touch, for it was untidy and it didn't receive any visitors. But it was clean.

Morkabalas noticed the book on the table, where the nougat man had left it, alongside the tray of nougat.

He slowly circled around it, like a cat with a mouse, as if it might try to escape. The book was unusual, like no book he had ever seen before. The truth is, he had never seen a book before, because in those days books hadn't yet been invented. There were scrolls of course, made of papyrus or leather, but books would not appear for many centuries.

So Morkabalas had no idea know what this object was.

Was it a small box?

Was there a treasure inside?

Was it dangerous?

And why was it even there?

As he pondered these questions, Morkabalas thoughtfully ran his fingers through his scraggy beard, his head cocked first to one side, then the other.

Several times he reached forward for it, and then drew back. Then he slowly picked up a piece of nougat and put that in his mouth, clamping it between his teeth to let the sugary taste spread.

His eyes widened.

It was delicious...!

In fact, it was probably the tastiest morsel that had ever passed his lips, he thought, greedily reaching for another, then another.

Then another...

Strangely, the more nougat he ate, the more appeared back on the little silver tray. It was as he reached for his twelfth chunk of nougat that he realised this incongruity, and as the thought reached him through a sugar-softened mind-scape, he dropped the twelfth nougat morsel suddenly as if it was a rotten egg.

One hand held his throat; the other stretched out in front of him, like it was stopping the traffic of morsel travel.

The more he ate, he realised, the more he wanted!

Of course! he thought, as only a mystic could:

It's a sign! Perhaps the angel has been trying to tell me something! But what?'

For a long moment, Morkabalas stood frozen, searching his mind.

Then he connected the two things:

Nougat-book, book-nougat.

Sooooo, if the nougat could magically replace itself, what could that thing do ...? Then he had an idea.

Taking his old carved walking stick from its place by the door, he held it out in front of him and very carefully edged the heavy cover open. This wasn't easy, as it had a golden catch securing it, which had to be eased open first.

As the cover flipped over, he leaned forward, and his eyes nearly popped out, because the words on the opening page were alive.

And with them were moving pictures, and one of

them was the face of the nougat man, staring out directly at him, as if it could see him!

This was too much!

He slammed the book shut.

Morkabalas paced around the room, his fingers laced in his beard.

Pondering.

What *was* this?

What did it *mean*?

Was it some kind of demonic magic?

Was he being tested in some way?

Was he now being sweetened up with nougat of the never-ending-variety, only to fall under the spell of that other 'thing' over there? The thing that had words that could move and a face that could see him. What could the thing *tell* him? (He didn't yet know it was called a book...)

Morkabalas was a mystic. He had been studying the Kabbala and hermetic magic for most of his life. He knew the properties of plants and herbs, those that could harm and those that could heal. He knew their relationship to the planets, and he knew how they could even affect one's mind and change one's mind from one state to another.

Lying on the flat roof of his house, he had watched

the stars at night, observing their movements and their effects on one another.

In addition to all this knowledge, he had tried to live a simple and righteous life, eating and drinking sparingly, and though he was sometimes bad-tempered, he had tried to be kind and considerate to others.

Was *this* his reward?

What were the Gods now *saying* to him?

Were they toying with him, after he had spent a lifetime fasting, meditating and praying?

He was allowing himself to become annoyed!

And so his anger was getting the better of him!

And this was clouding his judgement.

So, he sat down and took a few deep breaths, clearing his thoughts, relaxing his shoulders and neck. He allowed himself a moment or two of peace, having now emptied his mind.

It was then that he *really* got it!

He realised that his mood was influencing the way in which the book was revealing things:

'You are what you see' or *'you see what you are.'*

Both of these axioms applied.

He realised he needed to approach the book in a neutral state of mind, otherwise he would only see his own projections.

He stood up and calmly approached the book, this time without the carved walking stick.

He reached out and slowly opened the cover.

This time, the letters reappeared with no sign of the nougat man, and as the letters danced and moved, he could hear, clear as a bell, a voice *inside* of himself. The voice which was neither male nor female said:

'GIVE UP HOPE ALL WHO ENTER HERE!'

Whereas most people would recoil in fear, seeing this as a warning, Morkabalas was not like most people. He was a hermit and a mystic: he knew his own mind, he had worked through its inner windings and turnings. He had mastered what masters most men: Their thoughts.

He had wrestled these thoughts within the labyrinths of his mind; he had met his fears head on, and subdued them so he understood precisely what was being said.

For him, the words meant hope was redundant in those who truly know, in those who have the requisite knowledge; which is rather like having a map to find your way.

And then, as he watched, the first page of that book slowly open...

In that very instant, Morkabalas stepped *through* the book and into another reality.

You could say that, at this point, he took a virtual tour of everything he had spent his life studying and meditating on, only now, it was like looking at someone else's life and in full colour, including smells, tastes and all the other senses.

Along with anything experienced by anyone else through engaging with him in that life.

This part wasn't too intense for Morkabalas, as having been a hermit most of his life, he had very little contact with anyone else anyway... well, apart from that time when he chased a hungry dog from his door.

So now he had to feel the hunger of that dog, and his own anger as experienced by the dog.

He was also shown highlights from his own life, and he was informed that he was now the custodian of the book and that it was called The Fate Book. He would have to pass The Fate Book on to the next custodian at some point, and that new custodian was even shown to him: A certain Professor Wadji Wadjiwadj, curator of the Cairo Museum. His custodianship wouldn't be for some time yet. Several centuries.

You guessed it: Morkabalas was going to have a very long life.

Episode Six: A Letter from Uncle Clarence

Jess is lying on her bed sulking. Her mom has just grounded her for not tidying her room… again. She wondered what the big deal was. She knew where all her things were, and it was only a few clothes. So what if yesterday's pizza was lying under it all?

It wasn't fair! *And* she couldn't go to the concert tonight with her brother Josh.

Dammit!

She was fourteen and being treated like a kid. Well, she would show them!

She jumps up and stomps downstairs, heading for the front door. As she is about to open it, a letter pops in through the letterbox, and lands on the carpet. She stops, her hand still on the front door handle, and glances down at the letter.

Mmmm… who could this be for? she wonders. ,

It is a chunky letter, and as she picks it up, she smells a faint odor coming from it …mmm, a churchy kind of smell. Frankincense perhaps?

It is addressed to *her and Josh!*

Oh my God! How exciting! She *never ever* gets letters!

She turns the letter over. It is heavy and the sender's address is on the back:

Prof. C. Kalikaloos

She smiles. Uncle Clarence! They haven't seen their mom's only brother for a year or two now. Cool! Uncle Clarence is fun!

On his last visit, he brought them some weird stuff from Egypt. Bits of papyrus and tiny clay statuettes of gods with animal heads and some very old bones and boxes made of alabaster. He told them exciting stories about tombs and mummies and ancient history.

She liked him because he didn't try and be something he wasn't and he didn't talk down to her, unlike Mom.

She is tempted to open the letter *immediately*. But Josh will be upset if she does so, as the letter *is* addressed to both of them, after all.

She goes into the kitchen to make herself a sandwich, tossing the letter onto a table.

Her mom works in the city library. She is the chief librarian there, which means that she and Josh have loads of books to read, anytime they want them. Not that she's really that keen on reading, aside from romantic stuff that involves vampires.

Josh is keen on science and astronomy, and sometimes they look at the stars through Josh's telescope in their tree house and Josh tells her about some of the stuff he's been reading.

They bring their own food and flasks of hot chocolate, and sometimes they talk for hours without being interrupted. On summer nights they even sleep up there sometimes.

Josh is like the world's best brother. He never gets angry with her. If they fall out or don't agree on something, he just shrugs and leaves the room then comes back minutes later as if nothing has happened.

And he knows what she is thinking long before she says it. She so is proud to have him as a brother. Even though he is only a year older, he feels so much older and wiser.

During one of their late nights watching stars in the tree house, she said to him that it felt like they had known each other in another life. Josh looked at her for the longest time, and smiled slowly. The smile said:

Yeah, I know. I feel that, too.

As Jess is making herself a sandwich of cold chicken with plenty of mayo, she hears the front door open, and Josh walks in. She quickly puts her sandwich down and pretends she's eating the letter instead. Josh giggles and comes over to hug her. Then he picks up her sandwich and really does start to eat it.

Taking a large bite, he takes the letter from between her teeth and looks it over.

'Mmmmm, interesting, sis. It's a letter addressed to both of us. Now there's a first! Mmm... I wonder what these odd markings are on the edge: they look a bit like teeth marks.'

'Yeah, weird, huh? Hey! They aren't mine, really! I was only pretending. It's from uncle Clarence... come one now, quick, Joshy, open it. I know it's gonna be something really exciting!'

Josh takes the letter to the kitchen table and they both sit down, Jess fidgety with expectation as Josh takes a knife and slits open the envelope. He removes the letter, written on quality paper and reads it out:

Dear Josh and Jess,

I am sorry I haven't been in touch for some time. I'm sure you'll understand how much I travel and how little time I have to write, and lately, I've been working in some places that have no post boxes, telephones or even roads for that matter...

For the last few weeks I have been engaged in some rather unusual work. Some of it involves archaeology, but as you will soon discover, much of it is a mystery, even to me! But more of that later; it will all keep until I can see you both...

Now, here's the thing. Sadly, I have only very limited computing skills, and as I need to gain some very quickly to keep up with the new cataloguing system at the British Museum, I thought of you two, as someone said: if you don't know about computers, ask a teenager! And I haven't got time to go and do one of those tedious courses where they make you feel like an idiot...

Anyway, I do hope you'll agree to my plan, which is this: as soon as I can tie things up here in the Andes, I would like to come and stay for a while and spend some time with Mara and you two, and you can teach me a few tricks on the old cranial keyboard, and in exchange, I will share a few of my stories.

Does that sound like a fair exchange?

I have written a separate letter to your mom at the library, and she has responded and seems to be fine having me over there, as long as I don't mind going on your next camp out, she says.

Oh, and Josh, there are a few details about the Lalibela site in Ethiopia and its correspondence to the Pleiades that Professor Wadji was telling me about recently. It's rather fascinating information really, so I would love to see the Northern starry sky through your telescope. That's if your tree house can bear my weight! Mind you, I think I have lost a few pounds lately; trekking through the Andes has made sure of that, I can tell you! Nearly got carried off by a gigantic bird too, but more of that when I see you. Much to tell you and I'm sure you'll have a devil of a job believing some of it!

Looking forward to seeing you in a couple of weeks.

Toodle do!

Best regards,

Uncle Clarence

P.S.: the slight mark on the envelope is where a monkey got his teeth into it. Ruddy things are all over the place here!

Josh and Jess laugh at this ending to Clarence's letter.

'Cool! That should be fun!' says Josh as he takes another bite from Jess's sandwich.

'Yeah, right! And it'll also get Mom off my back while he's here. Can you believe it Joshy... she's grounded me *again*! I mean... come on, what's the deal, huh? Just because my room got a bit like, *informal* for a while, she's *grounding* me, *tonight?!* Like duh? It's the **green-eyed beans** concert! I mean, shut up!

Josh holds up a hand, both reassuring her and holding her back from erupting into anger. Something he noticed she was doing a lot of, these days.

'Okay okay, relax Jess. It's gonna be okay. Really. Mom will be fine. I'll talk to her. She doesn't know how important this concert is to you, to us, right? I mean you and Mom are so alike, but neither of you can see it. She's too worried about doing the right thing to notice what's really going on with you. And you're too angry to see that she's struggling to let go of you as a kid, and coming to terms with you becoming a person with her own special needs... or whatever. Or maybe you're just too full of shit!

Jess pretends she's going to wallop him and he holds up a hand in defence.

'Hey! Don't worry. It's sorted, sister. Sooooo, how about we just like slap your room into shap? Tell you what: You can put your stuff away and I'll like supervise or something... okay? Perfect! Or even better, I'll make you a sandwich cause I've eaten most of yours, *and* I'll make us some really cool banana and strawberry shakes. What you reckon? Then, when Mom comes home you can show her what an effort you've made, and if that doesn't work, maybe I can remind her that she like owes me for all the firsts I got graded last semester... time to cash them in, huh?'

Episode Seven: Mara and the Waterfall

Mara is not what she seems. If she was standing in a crowd you wouldn't see her. Perhaps you wouldn't see her even if she was right in front of you, and if you did, you wouldn't remember her. This is something deliberate on her part; she is quite pleased about it, after all, it's something she's worked at perfecting over her life:

The art of being invisible.

Mara is a librarian, in a large municipal library in Dublin.

She has been there for over twenty years, and though she is popular with the staff, she keeps her distance.

She doesn't connect with them outside of her work.

That's the way she wants it.

For a reason.

Actually, two reasons: Jess and Josh.

Mara has raised them on her own.

They do not know their biological father. Even her

early years growing up in Ireland are sketchy. Jess and Josh sometimes quiz her about this but she has incredibly creative ways of fending them off, and she has made sure they have never needed anyone but her in their lives.

She is a tireless researcher, so if she needs to know something about parenting, or baking, or the planting cycle of courgettes, she'll find out, in whatever way she can.

She'll google it, take books home, consult with experts, do whatever it takes.

That doesn't mean she is a theoretical parent. Being Irish, she's never out of touch with her imagination and this is what Jess and Josh love the most about her.

She will think nothing of trekking into the wild with them, sleeping rough and sometimes taking them places most parents would think irresponsible. Like the time she took them bungee-jumping over the Victoria Falls on a trip to Africa they will never forget.

Mara has only one relative left in her family: her brother Clarence. Professor Clarence 'Stinky' Kalikaloos.

They are close, but rarely communicate. They share academic interests, they both graduated from Trinity College in Dublin a few years apart; but what really connects them is Jess and Josh.

And their love of mysteries.

When Mara was nine years old, she felt no fear.

She followed the fairies who led her on a narrow track towards the waterfall.

She trusted the fairies, who are still respected and honoured in Ireland today. She had made friends with them a while back on one of her many walks to the river. She sat quietly on the grassy riverbank watching the water vapour curling up from the base of the waterfall, and where it met the sunlight, rainbow colours danced. And in these dancing rays of colour, she saw The Little People for the first time.

And as everyone knows, the Little People can only be seen if they themselves allow you to see them.

So they allowed Mara to see them and they had their reasons, as you shall soon discover.

Over time, she gradually made friends with them, and she often came to visit them.

They were playful and loved to play tricks on her, sometimes shapeshifting into little bunnies or frogs, and then suddenly disappearing and re-appearing as fairies again as she approached.

Mara loved them as her only friends and talked to them endlessly about her life. And they told her secrets about the forest and the things that lived and grew in there.

She was quickly making her way along the track that vanished under the waterfall.

She was being chased by her stepfather.

He was in another of his frequent drunken moods.

He would get drunk and violent and beat on her or her mother, but for some reason he never laid hands on her brother Clarence. Most likely because Clarence was always out looking for insects or buried in a book somewhere. She could hear her stepfather stumbling among the rocks lower down the river, where it bent away sharply out of sight of the falls. Just as well, because he was shouting and cursing angrily and falling over a lot and calling out for her.

This is where the fairies decided to step in and help this little human child.

They knew, as fairies do, that the nine-year old Mara would one day play an important part in their world, so they didn't want to see any harm come to her.

She hesitated for an instant looking right up the curtain of water rising above her, and as she heard her stepfather coming around the bend in the river, she quickly stepped right through it. For a moment, she was drenched as, then she stood dripping in the cool dark interior.

The Little People flew all around her, just as excited as she was. She heard her stepfather's voice, closer now, shouting out her name:

'Mara, where are ya?

Damn youse girl!

You're gonna get what's coming to ya!

D'ya hear me now!'

This time he was angry because she'd forgotten to lay out his dinner for him, as her mother, who usually had the job, was out working in the fields all day with the harvesters.

Weirdly, she could see his watery outline on the other side of the falls. She knew he couldn't see her, as it was much darker here on the inside of the waterfall, and she felt incredibly safe. He shouted and stumbled about for a while, and for a moment Mara thought he was looking through the curtain of water right at her, but then turned away and shuffled off, and out of view.

Looking around, she was astonished to see how many of the little folk were gathered here. As if they were expecting her, which they were.

Mara had never been this close to so many of the little folk and the space behind the waterfall was much larger than she could have imagined. It was like a huge cave hollowed out of the rock, and this entire space was filled with fairies.

In the centre of the circle they had formed around her stood a regal and incredibly beautiful couple who must have been their leaders, for indeed, they wore crowns.

Suddenly, Mara was aware that she was being spoken to by these leaders.

But she 'heard' them inside her head.

It was the strangest thing, but it seemed perfectly normal. They told her she would one day, be working with books, and though they had no interest in books, there was one *very special book* that was important to them. One day, Mara would come across this book. When she did, they would like to know about it. Then they were quiet.

They all looked at her with their wonderful shining faces, and she got the sense that they had been waiting for something for a long time, and with that she began to see what they were seeing.

A picture of what they were picturing formed in her mind.

They were showing her the cover of a book.

An ancient book.

She could see that if you opened this book you would know something about your life and everyone you knew would be in it, and you would understand the connections.

Stretching both forwards and backwards. And everything about everything was in it. Remember, she was only nine then, and she didn't have the vocabulary yet to say more.

Years later, she would have quite a vocabulary, and she would see the Book of Kells at close quarters, whilst expanding her knowledge and vocabulary at Trinity College in Ireland. And when she did see it, something about the sinuous interlinking Celtic forms brought to her memory the time she had spent behind the waterfall with the fairies.

Though the Book of Kells was not the ancient book the fairies had shown her back then, it was somehow related.

The fairies wanted her to see that ancient book.

And so, as Mara brought them into her mind, quite suddenly she could feel them close again, as if she were with them again.

Then, again, in the eye of her mind, she sees the interlocking forms of Kell dancing like the little folk at the waterfall.

Mara told no one of her friendship with the fairies. And I suspect the fairies, knowing this would be so, were in turn so free in showing themselves to her.

The little folk knew things about the future. They knew back then, when she was but a small child, that she would one day bring Jess and Josh into the world. And somehow, they had given something of themselves to Mara, in the way in which Josh was able to see the world.

Because they saw the world in the same way he did. And so they have become a part of this story as you shall soon hear.

Episode Eight: Monkey Business

Hacking their way through the dense undergrowth of the jungles of Central America are three figures. One very large man, and two teenagers (a brother and sister).

The large man, though dripping with sweat, is muttering encouragement to his two young companions and forging a path ahead with enthusiasm. Though they are in the middle of nowhere, he seems to know where he is going. He has serious tracking skills.

Now, if you were a monkey in the top branches of the fifty metre trees high above, you'd be able to look down and see them making slow progress. And if you could tear yourself away from grooming the tasty insects out of your brother monkey's fur and looked ahead of these three noisy humans, over the treetops, a few hundred meters ahead, where the trees thinned out into a huge clearing, you'd be able to make out, right in the middle of that clearing, the overgrown shape of a vast ancient monument.

A kind of stepped pyramid of sorts…

If you were a monkey in the top of the tree canopy, you'd see that, and you'd also see someone sitting on the top of that monument, waiting for the three people who were approaching:

A skinny man with dark parchmenty skin.

But, knowing the ways of monkeys, it's likely you would be more interested in the fat juicy insects on the backs of your brother monkeys, than in the affairs of three tired and sweaty humans, and the skinny one with dark parchmenty skin who waited up there on the pyramid for them.

'How much further, Uncle Clarence?' Jess asks for the umpteenth time.

They have been travelling through the thickest part of the jungle, a two day walk from Guatemala City, where the plane carrying them from Dublin had landed, some hours ago now.

She still can't believe her mom allowed her and Josh to come on this expedition with Uncle Clarence.

Normally, she would at least insist on coming along herself, or just say no.

This time she just shrugged when Clarence put the idea to her, and said okay.

They had all packed quickly before she had time to change her mind and they left early the next morning when she was still asleep. Though Jess sensed that Mara would have loved to come too, she went quiet like she does when she's having her own thoughts about something.

Her uncle Clarence is renowned for his tracking skills, and she trusts his sense of direction and his experience in places like this. But a rest round about now would be great, she thinks and an ice-cold coke would be even better, and she is feeling so tired now.

It's so tiring just being on the lookout for things. I mean, she thinks to herself, *like everything around here just wants to bite you and sting you and eat you, for God's sake; like what is it with jungles...?!*

She has tied up her long hair and kept it tucked under a floppy hat so as to not provide a home for a hitch hiking insect.

How much further?

She knows her uncle's response will be the same as always: 'Just a tad, my dear! Just a tad!'

Her brother Josh doesn't even ask. He knows it isn't much further. And he doesn't really care; he just accepts it. Josh is like that. He is a hunch kind of a guy. He just knows stuff. Some might call him an intuitive.

But if you were a monkey in the treetops of a certain Central American jungle, you *would* turn your attention, reluctantly, away from the juicy insects on your brother monkeys back. Because if you glanced down at the three figures forging a path through the undergrowth, you'd now see something you hadn't noticed before; something just there, a little distance from the trio, following them and hiding in the dank warm shade, watching their progress.

And, believe me, you *would* be interested, because right there, in a quiet huddle, crouched a small group of local indigenous people.

And you'd be a scared monkey now, as well as interested, because these people were armed with very long blowpipes, and they were made for one purpose only: for hunting and bringing down monkeys.

And seeing that, you'd have no choice now but to leg it! And, of course you'd make as much noise as you possibly could to warn all the other monkeys up there in the treetops!

And so that's exactly what the monkeys did right then!

They screeched and chattered and swung away seeking safety in the highest branches. They didn't stop to look back once, but if they had, they would have seen two of the Indians breaking away from their group, and dragging Jess away from her companions into the opposite part of the jungle, one of them having tied a length of cured banana leaf around her mouth...

Down there on the forest floor Clarence pauses in mid-machete stroke and looks up at this sudden eruption of monkey mayhem high in the treetops ahead of him.

He is glad to rest for a moment, dropping his hardworking machete to his side and wiping the sweat away from his face with one of his huge handkerchiefs. Though never one to complain, he is being bitten alive by all kinds of crawling and flying insects, many of them bigger than anything he has seen before.

'Ruddy monkeys! Making fun of us, eh Josh?' he chuckles and he takes a swig from his canteen, glancing back at Josh, who is a few paces behind him, and who has been preoccupied with checking his compass.

But Josh suddenly feels uneasy. He looks up. Something isn't right. Something has startled the monkeys.

What is it?

He turns to say this to Jess, but Jess isn't there.

Oh my God!

Where is she?

He looks around for her, in a full circle.

But there is no sign of her!

Josh suddenly turns cold in spite of the heat and runs back down the track the professor has carved out, calling out for her:

'Jess, where are you? Come on, Jay! Where are you hiding?

Are you taking a leak, sis?'

Nothing.

Not a sound.

Just the chatter of the monkeys, who have now fled to a safe place in the treetops, much further in the distance.

Episode Nine: The Scene in the Clearing

Jess has been having a bit of an ordeal.

The most shocking part was when she was taken completely by surprise by the Indians. One moment she'd been checking her lippy in her compact, and the next thing she knew, two small near-naked painted men, with porcupine quills through their noses, appeared from nowhere and were bundling her strongly and silently into the depths of the jungle.

There was no time to even cry out, and when she got back her breath to do that, she couldn't shout because they'd put a banana skin gag over her mouth.

Weirdly though, they were smiling at her, as if this was a game to them! That made her really mad!

Like, who did they think they were...?

Struggling was useless, and even if she could break free, she was miles away from the others by now.

So instead, she closed her eyes and thought of Josh; she knew he'd tune in on her and find her.

But, what if they ate her before Josh and Uncle Clarence found her?

She certainly hadn't heard of cannibals in this part of the world, from the stuff Uncle Clarence was telling them on the plane on the way there, but she would just have to trust.

She opens her eyes now as the men suddenly stop walking.

They are in a kind of open glade. A few more of the painted men are standing there, waiting for them. They jabber excitedly amongst themselves.

One or two of them stand right up close to Jess, and she defiantly sticks her tongue out at them.

This makes them fall about laughing!

They are smiling and nodding a lot. What can it mean?

Is she perhaps some kind of mythical white queen to them?

Suddenly her eyes widen with real fear. As all the men are facing her, they can't see what she is seeing. They cannot see the huge anaconda quietly unwinding its massive body from the branches in the tree just above the men, it's tongue flicking noiselessly in and out.

Still, they don't see it!

Should she warn them or not?

Before she can decide, the great serpent has dropped down and coiled itself around and around and around the leader of the Indians.

She guesses he is the leader, as he has more tattoos adorning his body and he seems to say less. The anaconda quickly wraps itself around him, so only his head is visible now, and it starts lifting him up into the tree!

To Jess's surprise the other men suddenly drop to the ground, their faces glued to the earth. They seem to be worshipping the serpent!

Oh my god! thinks Jess.

What the flipping heck is going on here?

She finds herself wishing she were back home in the safety of her untidy room. She would rather be grounded forever in her room at home, than be here right now with a sodding great snake and a bunch of near naked weirdo serpent worshippers.

This is beginning to look like some kind of off-Broadway production of *The Jungle Book*, she thinks...

Where are you Josh, for god's sake?!

Come and get me out of here, bro!

Should she run away now, while she has the chance, she wonders? She realises she has suddenly been forgotten in all of this chaos: everyone is either staring at the ground or at the snake. If she runs away now and hides in the forest, would they ever find her? But then, even if they didn't, what else would be waiting out there in the jungle to eat her?

She is about to take her chances with that, when...

Suddenly a tall skinny man walks, seemingly out of nowhere, into the glade. Without hesitating, he steps right up to the snake and stares into its yellow eyes.

The anaconda is now as still as a statue, staring right back at the skinny man, eye to eye. The only sign of movement from it is its flicking tongue. Its like time is standing still.

Then, just as quickly as it had arrived, the snake breaks away from the skinny man's gaze, uncoils itself from the slightly squashed chief, and slips away into the trees!

The chief falls forward, gasping for breath, then immediately shows his gratitude to the skinny man by holding him by his shoulders and spitting in his face.

The skinny man then walks up to Jess and smiles putting his hand on her shoulder. He has an immediate calming effect and Jess can't help but burst into tears.

He hugs her as she cries on his shoulder, while the Indians dance about shouting and laughing their joy at having their chief back in one piece.

Before Jess can ask him who he is, the man turns to the chief and the two of them get into an animated conversation. The skinny man seems to be fluent in the indigenous language, and it is clear from their frequent pointing at Jess, that she is the main subject.

It also seems from his body language that the chief is apologising and that they've made some kind of mistake in kidnapping her.

The chief then summons his men and with the newcomer at her side they all move back into the forest, back the way they came before they grabbed Jess.

The skinny man gives her a kind, reassuring smile.

She feels safe with him.

Meanwhile, Clarence and Josh have got over their panic at losing Jess. They have manned up and pooled their resources. Clarence is a brilliant tracker and can pick up the smallest clue: a bent twig, a loose leaf, a hair, or even the faintest footprint. From bits and pieces, including the compact that Jess dropped when she was grabbed, he quickly works out that there are two men carrying Jess and five others accompanying them.

One is heavier and probably the chief, and he has gone on ahead. The others have followed with Jess.

Josh has a different tracking system, though it is just as effective: He simply closes his eyes and tunes in on Jess. He finds her very quickly, as her emotional energy is radiating out like sparks on bonfire night. He can see what the professor cannot:

He sees the scene in the clearing.

He sees what Jess has just seen.

He sees the anaconda dropping down from the trees and winding around the chief, then his men falling on their faces and the skinny stranger arriving.

He sees the man step up to the snake and out-stare it and then the chief being suddenly released as it slips away into the trees and disappears.

He sees all this is because he can be Jess's eyes.

He can see what she's seeing.

He can feel what she is feeling.

Intuitively.

Without saying anything to each other, Josh and Clarence now walk purposefully into the jungle, heading in the same direction. They know where to go now. Each has his own guidance system. Clarence is tracking, Josh has soul-nav!

But, after only covering a few metres, they stop and listen.

They can hear something.

Something is coming towards them.

Fast.

They hear a crashing through the undergrowth which is so loud it seems like a rhinoceros. Josh is feeling Jess very strongly now, and suddenly there she is.

Behind her is a group of small fierce looking half-naked men with porcupine quills in their noses. Alongside Jess is a tall dark skinny man whom he doesn't know, but it seems that Uncle Clarence does. He gasps with astonishment, and cries out:

'Wadji! Wadji my dear old friend...

My God man, I thought we'd lost you!

Where the bloody hell have you been all this time...?'

Professor Wadji Wadjiwadj runs forward and the two men embrace like long lost friends, for that is what they are! Remember, Clarence has not seen Wadji ever since that night in Macchu Piccu, when he had become custodian of The Fate Book.

When, with the help of The Fate Book he had taken a trip down the time-tunnel and returned only to find Wadji gone.

Clearly there is much explaining to be done, but right now, there are more urgent things at hand; they have to think about completing their journey before nightfall.

The monument lies ahead of them and the natives are restless. To them, Wadji is now some kind of a demi-god.

He has faced up to the serpent god and sent it packing, and he has saved their chief from being its lunch. And perhaps he has also saved Jess from being their lunch. They want to repay him and a feast is suggested.

Wadji tactfully stalls them. He tells them they have a journey ahead of them, they need to reach the pyramid before nightfall so they will have to forgo their feast for now. So they then offer themselves as guides and protectors. They know every part of the jungle. It seems peevish to turn them down, even though Wadji has already found his own way to Jess from the monument.

And this is how he found her:

From his high perch on the pyramid, Wadji knew his friend's arrival was imminent.

The Fate Book had informed him of that.

Even though he had passed it on to Clarence, he was able to still read it inwardly; it had become a habit of soul, as he liked to call it. Anyone working with The Fate Book for long enough would find that.

It became intuition, and that was the lesson it offered all who carried it: it was rather like an inner map, which though it could be read with the outward eye, needed to be filled in with the living content of the inner eye.

And so Wadji had found his way to this ancient Mayan monument with exquisite timing.

No sooner had he climbed the stepped sides of the pyramid, and taken a rest on its summit, admiring the view out over the forest treetops than he saw the normally still and calm tree canopy twitching with the loud flight of the alarmed monkeys, and moving in his direction.

From this he knew two things...

One: the Indians had found the monkeys, and...

Two: the Indians were not chasing the monkeys, for they were far too skilful at hunting monkeys to let them get away!

And if the monkeys had escaped from them, it could only be because the Indians were distracted from the monkeys because they'd encountered Clarence and co.

And now his inner eye was confirming just that!

Just like Josh, Wadji could see Jess being taken away. Though he didn't yet know her, he sensed she was connected with Clarence.

He had to act fast.

He knew this tribe. He had researched and collected ancient artefacts here before, and over the years had formed a trust with them, helping them in every way he could to preserve their tribal identity in the face of creeping exploitation from industry and sheer western curiosity.

The rest we know. Professor Clarence is delighted at having been reunited with his old friend and mentor at last.

For years he had been making persistent inquiries as to his whereabouts, annoying the irascible Mrs. Kofi and the Cairo Museum staff with his regular calls. He had also spoken to all of their mutual friends, including a global network of archaeologists, academics and scientists.

Nothing.

No one knew anything.

Not since his disappearance in Peru.

Not since he handed The Fate Book over to Clarence. Which only you and I were, of course, witnesses to. You will perhaps also remember that Clarence slipped away into another dimension on opening The Fate Book, and when he returned from that, his first ever spiritual journey, Wadji had disappeared.

Now, without warning, he reappears in the Guatemalan jungles, hypnotises a giant anaconda, and persuades it to let go of its prize meal. He has dazzled Jess and Josh without uttering a single word, and he has caught up with his old mate Professor Clarence, not yet explaining his sudden absence. And he has, of course, won the undying loyalty of an entire tribe by rescuing their chief from the coils of the snake.

Impressive.

All in a day's work for an ephemeral professor who happens to be in the right place at the right time. Sooner or later he will have to reveal all and explain to us how, what and where.

Episode Ten: The Pyramid

It is pitch dark here in the depths of the ruined pyramid. There is an overwhelming smell of decayed vegetation and underlying it, the stink of bats. Jess has been fighting the urge to run screaming from that place and never return. It's not just the dark, the smell, and the thoughts of bats. There is something truly creepy about this place. A sense of being watched.

Several times on this slow journey down into the bowels of the pyramid, she has looked over at Josh, hoping for some kind of reassuring wisecrack from him. But Josh has retreated somewhere inside of his own self and she knows nothing will draw him out once he's in Josh-world. And if he's in there it can only mean one thing: Fear The only thing keeping Jess together now is the company of the two professors.

Uncle Clarence and the mysterious professor Wadji have sustained a constant and undiminished enthusiasm for this fearful place from the moment they started their descent into its Stygian gloom. Once the tribe had guided them to the ruin, they all started singing and chanting and dancing. Their chief went over to Wadji, stared him in the eyes, and spat in his face again. He didn't flinch. Then the whole group turned and vanished into the forests without looking back. Clearly they were not happy to be there one minute longer than they had to be, and their job was now done.

Now Jess looks over at the two professors, who are eagerly discussing a painted figure on the wall of the abyss they are descending. They seem totally fearless, these two men, which somehow comforts Jess. She knows she can trust them. After all, if a long lost friend of Uncle Clarence can step out of nowhere and save her and the chief of the Indians from certain suffocation, anything is possible! She steps closer to hear what they are saying.

'...yes, I believe it's probably some sort of an early Mayan reference to astronomy, Clarence.

'You see there?

'Look here at these stars, see: there and there!

'And just there... can you see it? Ah and I can see that there's even an astrological reference just there, oh and it looks like it's referring to water... Mmmm... Look at these wavy lines inscribed just here, ahead of the figure. What do you think, Clarence? Aquarius?'

Wadji holds up his paraffin lantern, and Clarence eagerly follows the brown pointy finger his friend is using to describe this ancient marker.

They all now look at the carving, all except Josh, who is looking away, down the slope of the passage. Suddenly, he raises his hand to call for silence, still staring into the dark. He is listening intently. Now they all turn toward him and listen. Now they can hear it too. It's the sound of fast running water. And it's getting louder.

They turn to run.

Only Jess has noticed that the carved figure on the wall is now moving about, and is looking directly at them.

As they rush away, back up the slope they've come down on, she glances back, not believing her eyes.

It has winked at her!

There is no time to confer with anyone else.

Whether they saw it or not, the sound of running water is now much louder; in fact, it's all they can hear now, and they have to shout to make themselves heard.

Then, Josh stops right there, in mid-flight!

The others almost don't notice for a moment.

They're too locked into fight-and-flight mode, but Jess spots him behind them, stopping as he's about to fade into the dark.

'Josh! C'mon!

What are you doing standing there? We need to get out of here, man!'

The professors stop now, and Wadji runs back to

Josh, who astonishes everyone by standing there, smiling. The next thing, he is laughing hard. Has he lost it?

Professor Wadji seems to have got the joke now too.

The two of them are laughing like hyenas, prompting Jess and Uncle Clarence to walk back to join the hyenas.

'It's just a trick, Jess!

It's just a trick to scare people away!

Can you feel the breeze now?'

Sure enough, Josh is right.

The sound of the water is, in fact, not the sound of water at all. It is the whooshing of air, passing through some clever device, creating the illusion of running water...

Now Jess understands why the carved figure attracted her attention and winked at her earlier on! Cheeky bugger!

Clearly these things are stalling tactics on the part of the pyramid architects. They are saying:

'Are you sure you've got the bottle to be down here?

Have you got what it takes?'

Josh, who before this has been taciturn and withdrawn, is now suddenly the leader of our little group.

Wadji catches Clarence's eye and smiles.

Clarence shrugs in a told-you-so way.

'Look guys, I mean, like if there's so much air suddenly wafting this way, it can only mean that we're heading for somewhere that has a fresh supply.

Right?

And if that's so, it must be some kind of habitable place rather than a tomb...

Right?

I mean, I reckon that's why these guys have done their best to scare folks away.

There must be a reason...

Right?'

The professors nod. They cannot fault his logic.

They turn around now and head back downwards. The air is indeed fresh and to Jess's great relief it is blowing away the fetid smell of decay which had been so overpowering.

Weirdly, without any discussion, Josh has now become their undisputed leader. He is showing a new confidence which is both exciting and unnerving, especially to the academics in the group. Suddenly, he stops dead and turns around to look back up the slopes.

Everyone can see it there.

A small shadowy figure is standing just outside of the light from their paraffin lamp. Wadji holds it up, and the figure now steps toward them.

It is the tribal chief!

In the semi-darkness his white teeth smile back at them. He seems very glad to join them.

Episode Eleven: The Chief

The arrival of the chief surprises everyone. He has managed to evade even Josh's radar!

The little man now runs up to Wadji and chatters away excitedly, his little arms describing something, his eyes flashing what he feels about it all.

Clarence steps in a little closer to hear the conversation too and now the chief's eyes are out on stalks, as he now realises, with Clarence's interjection, that he too, can speak the chief's language.

What kind of gods are these? he wonders, noticing also that Josh, a mere child, has become their leader.

Clarence turns to Josh and Jess and quickly translates the chief's excited words, keeping his eyes on his lips.

Meanwhile, Wadji has stepped away from the little chief, just far enough to avoid a third spittle drenching, in case it should come.

Clarence is translating. 'The chief is saying that he wants to be here with us. Mmm... he says his shaman has sent him back to accompany us, insisting that he's a part of this... mmm... and there's something about a prophecy being fulfilled... yes, an ancient prophecy from the grandfathers... the shaman says that fair people from afar have come to unlock a mystery.

Yes... He's saying that there are four of these fair-skinned people. Two men and two children.

One man is... erm, large, and the other is... erm, thin.

The two children are from the... erm... large man's tribe.

One of these children, the boy, is erm...the star child? Mmm... It's hard to translate this: he says he's the eye of a star.

No. That's not right. He says he's the one who *sees* like a star... That's it, yes... *sees* like a star!'

Jess smiles. She understands the shaman's message.

Josh has always seen things that no other person is seeing; he kind of lights up a dark place. Sees like a star. She gets it all right.

Josh, meanwhile, has now lost interest in the little chief, and is looking back toward the long slope downwards. He seems impatient to set off again.

But the chief isn't done yet. He reaches up, removing a skin bag from his shoulder, and out of it he draws a thong, from which is hanging a small pouch containing something magical the shaman has concocted. He holds this up to Josh, who allows the chief to gently, even reverently, pass it over his head. Josh smiles. He feels the warm energy of the offering, it's protective embrace.

Next, the little man brings out several small parcels, which he gives to each of them. The parcels are meals wrapped in banana skin.

To everyone's surprise, Wadji eats his with no hesitation.

Clearly he knows what this is, he has had it before, and he relishes it. His brown eyes flash, wordlessly urging the others to eat theirs.

Jess is a little hesitant. Naturally enough. After all, she has been dragged about the jungle by the chief's men, and doesn't fully trust him. And she's a teenager. But then she sees Josh swallowing his, even greedily looking over at hers, so she shrugs and eats it.

It is delicious! Both fruity and meaty at the same time, there is something about the morsel that is sustaining and gives instant energy.

Clarence is now slightly unnerved, but not by the snack.

For just one moment, looking at the chief, he thinks he has seen a flash of gold teeth; but then, as he does a double-take glancing back, he meets the chief's eye. The chief winks back at him... *Surely not, can it be?* thinks Clarence. But now, as he looks at him, the chief is just a chief again. Not a gold tooth in sight.

Now the small band of adventurers set off again.

This time the chief, who is grinning broadly at him whenever he can catch his eye, joins Josh at the head of the group. He reminds Josh of a big puppy. If he had a tail, he'd be wagging it, Josh thinks and smiles.

To his surprise, the chief seems to pick up the thought immediately, as he shakes his butt now in an exaggerated way, and panting like a dog, he causes the professors and Jess just behind them to laugh with his antics.

Josh realises now that the chief is telepathic, and as they descend the long stone corridor towards the source of the watery whooshing sound, now getting louder as they approach it, he decides to test the telepathy further and places in his mind an image of the pyramid, with a question mark.

The chief responds immediately! Josh receives back an image of the pyramid from the chief, and he can see within the image a small group moving down inside it.

Of course: it's their little group!

The image changes, and Josh can now see that the chief is showing him something just ahead of them. It is a bright light, and it is flashing, and it seems to be immediately below them... what can he make of this? Before he can answer this puzzle, they have reached the end of the sloping walkway.

Ahead of them, the walkway now levels out and makes a sharp right turn, where it then begins an upward slope. This is the point at which all previous explorers would have to return upwards to the entrance of the pyramid where they started out.

But the chief now grins broadly at Josh, winks mischievously, then reaches out to the wall and runs his hand over a carving. The carving seems to represent a coiled serpent, and the chief has taken hold of the serpent's head.

Suddenly, the wall ahead of them slides open. Dust falls down from the ancient stone track and the entire moving wall is flashing with a bright blue light.

The chief is signing for everyone to step back: clearly there is something about this ancient technology that deserves respect...

Then the blue light stops flashing and dims down to a steady glow. The door is now fully open, and ahead of them are some steps leading down into a huge space.

They can all feel a draught of fresh air.

The steps ahead have a faint fluorescent glow, so that the little group are able to find their way down without stumbling. It's clear that these steps have not been used for centuries, but in spite of that there is no dust on them; just as if they were completed the day before.

No one is speaking now.

The professors are stunned. There is simply no

explanation they can offer for this...

The chief is positively delighted at their response; he has waited a long time for this, and he now makes sure that everyone is safely down the steps...

Jess and Josh are so excited, they glance over at each other. They can't wait to see what is now ahead of them...

Episode Twelve: Inside the Pyramid

Finally, they have reached their destination at the foot of the steps: the interior of the pyramid.

Before them is a breath-taking scene.

A vast space has opened up before them.

They are surrounded by carved and brightly painted walls, which form the inner perimeter of the base of the pyramid.

Somehow, there is plenty of fresh air and light.

Where is the light coming from?

Josh and Jess realise that it is once again the walls themselves that are giving off a soft radiance; enough to see themselves and the massive interior.

Would this have been a refuge from the perils of the jungle in times past? Or was it a place of worship? There is no sign that people actually lived here. It seems more informal, more like a meeting place.

In the centre of the space is a carved stone seat, rather like a throne. It is raised up on a square dais, and on each corner of this dais is a small carved seat, facing out. Would this have been a place where the ruler of this ancient tribe addressed his people?

The professors are in earnest conversation over this very question.

Professor Wadji Wadjiwadj has visited the pyramid once before, but has not penetrated to the interior. The tribal elders, of which our chief is one such, had not permitted entry to the deep interior of the ruin.

Now, it seems, the time is right and the chief has guided them here for a purpose.

What would that be?

Before they have fully taken in the details of this place, the chief is now guiding each of them to a seat. Each person, in turn, is taken to one of the carved seats, forming the corners of the dais. To everyone's surprise, including his own, Josh is led up some steps leading up to the high throne.

He sits himself down, while the chief walks back down the steps and takes his place on the last corner left unoccupied.

So, this is how they are arranged: the professors sit at corners diametrically opposite each other, with Jess and the chief on the other two corners.

There is a moment after the chief has sat down when everyone is a little apprehensive. After all, once they're in place, no one can see anyone else. Each of the four seated on the corners are facing out and away from each other, and Josh, in his high place, is looking out over the heads of the others.

But there is a sense of calm and peace, and Josh is feeling that this is a place of peace and sanctity, like a church or some other place of worship.

The moment they are all seated, there is a sudden and immediate change: the soft yellow light of the walls that had bathed them slowly turns blue, and the carvings and paintings begin to move and dance, revolving around them with gathering speed. Then, to their astonishment, everything goes dark for a moment; only to reveal a starry sky all around them.

The walls have faded away, and it seems to them that they are seated now in a huge observatory or even a spacecraft.

In his throne-like seat on the top of the platform, Josh finds that with a slight pressure from him, the chair rotates now; giving him a 360-degree view, and he has assumed the position of captain of this craft. The craft seems ready, waiting for his command:

Where will they go?

'Wait!

Hang on a minute!

That's not how it went!'

'Oh, isn't it? oh sorry Jess...

How did it go then?'

'Well... a bit like that, but you left out the really important part! You know, when Uncle Clarence, you know...?

'Oh right! Yes, yes, of course Jess, I'm sorry... you know, we writers get carried away sometimes...'

So, yes, Jess is quite right, let's go back a bit, to that important part first, before they all got seated by the chief:

With Josh and the chief leading the way, the little group entered into the huge chamber. Naturally, it was a big surprise to find this vast space ventilated and lit, as if it had been waiting for them. Professor Clarence was particularly awestruck. He was drawn to the carved murals, which seemed to be lit by a soft light from within, somehow.

He grabbed Wadji by the arm and pulled him over to the wall:

'Look here, Wadji old chap. These carvings are pre-Mayan. I mean, just look at the quality of the artwork, I would say definitely pre-Columbian and most decidely pre-Mayan by the looks of it. You see, old boy, there's nothing of the blood-sacrifice here... not a hint of it. It's a good deal more sophisticated, don't you think?'

'Yes, I concur Clarence... I must say, although I've visited the pyramid before, all of this was quite hidden from me.

I had no idea there was a hidden entrance to this space.

Where the chief found the secret mechanism on the wall that let us in, I would have turned right and followed the slope back up to the entrance. Incredible! I've never seen anything quite like these carvings. It's a civilisation quite unique, almost...well...'

Clarence had moved right up to the wall now, and before the chief could stop him, he reached out to touch the murals. Suddenly, there was an arc of blue lightning between his hand and the wall. He shrieked in alarm and jumped back, knocking Wadji over. The chief hurried over, helped Wadji up and was now shaking his head and saying something to him and pointing at the murals. His body language was obvious. It said:

'Don't touch anything!!'

Clarence was unharmed... shaken but not stirred.

'Well, I say! Clearly this was a civilisation that wanted to guard its treasures. Dash it all! That really hurt.'

Clarence rubbed his arm and stepped over to Wadji, who was none the worse for being bowled over.

'Yes, Clarence. The chief tells me that this is a sacred place, still to this day guarded by the magical technology of those early people.

He has been telling me that these people were the wise grandfathers of the later Mayans, and he says they had no part in the ritual sacrifices that followed later.

I know this sounds, well, unscientific, but the chief is saying that these early people were from another planet.

He insists that they were literally visitors from the stars, from another galaxy, and he says the Mayans who followed them much later were their grandchildren... And there's more. He says that much later, there were catastrophic droughts and that famine made the Mayans desperate.

That's when they started sacrificing humans in an attempt to appease the gods. But this, of course, only made things worse, and ultimately led to the collapse of their civilisation.'

Josh and Jess looked over at each other during this conversation and smiled. They saw that the professors were a little rattled by this disclosure of the chief. Their understanding of history had been challenged.

All this while, the chief watched Wadji translating his information. He watched the professors intently; then he took Wadji by the arm and pointed out the central stone dais or platform, and its throne.

He then indicated that by assuming their seats on the four corners of the dais and the upper throne, they would be able to see exactly why this place was created.

So, this is the point at which the professors, Josh and Jess, and the chief take up their positions in their stone seats.

The moment they sit down, the murals all around them change from a soft yellow glow to an electric blue, rather like the colour of the arc that warned Clarence. Now the murals seem to spin and then there is that moment of darkness before the starry sky spreads out around them and they feel as if they are in a spacecraft. Josh finds that a console has risen up out of the floor in front of him, and on this console is a panel of switches, and in the centre of it is a kind of steering mechanism.

'No way, Jose!' Josh shouts out loud. He can't believe what is happening here.

'This is like something from *Star Wars!*' His words reach the others, and Wadji responds:

'Please just stay calm everyone. The chief assures me that we are safe. He says we are being shown something here and it'll only take a moment and we shall not be harmed.'

As he is saying this, Josh has tentatively put his hands on the steering mechanism in front of him. Immediately, there is a quiet whirring sound, a flashing of lights on the console in front of him, and it feels as if the horizon has shifted, as if they are moving off and away. In front of them, the stars begin to speed by. They watch as spiral nebulae approach and pass them. They seem now to be moving at terrific speed. It is way too exciting for anyone to be fearful; and though it was a bit unnerving to be sitting where you couldn't see anyone else, that has suddenly changed.

The Fate Book has floated out of Clarence's bag and

has seemingly divided itself into five separate pages, one in front of each person.

There is now a kind of hovering plasma screen in front of each of them, so that each person's face is shown to every other person. Now everyone is visible, and it's clear how excited they all are.

Then, after a while, they notice something else.

'We seem to be slowing down,' says Clarence.

And indeed they are. Ahead of them, what was a speck has become bigger and bigger, becoming an orb, then a planet not unlike Earth.

They can see landmasses on it, surrounded by seas, and now they are coming in fast and close.

Jess, who all this while has been awed and quiet, suddenly shrieks as they appear to be heading straight down at some speed towards this strange new planet.

'Mom, where are you now that I need you?!'

Episode Thirteen: Back to Earth

Jess is terrified. It's one thing hanging out inside a mysterious ruin being guided by a tribal chief who only a little while before had kidnapped her and then, a short time later was about to become snake-food; and quite another thing to be flying off into space and now approaching a planet in another galaxy.

This is too much! But there is no going back.

With a soft bump, they have landed.

The plasma screens that linked them visually have combined back into The Fate Book, which has then slipped back into Professor Clarence's bag.

Sensing Jess's anxiety, Josh jumps up and runs down to her, while the two professors and the chief are already chattering away, trying to make sense of all this.

Clearly, Professor Clarence is deeply embarrassed at having put his teenage charges in possible danger. He is quite out of his depth here. All his knowledge and understanding, his grasp of science and natural philosophy may be of no use to him now.

His colleague and closest friend Wadji feels much the same way, but at least he is only responsible for himself.

The chief has tried to reassure them both by again insisting that all will be well, that their every footstep is guided.

But still, they are scientists first, explorers second.

They have questions:

Who inhabits this planet? Where is it? Who lives here?

Will the atmosphere of this planet support them?

They are about to find out!

The floor now glows with a strange violet light.

Something they had not noticed before was that it is made of some kind of transparent but durable material, and as they walk across it, it changes colour with each step.

And there is something else: there are soft sounds that go with the colours. The five earthlings stand close together, unconsciously united now for the first time as one unit.

Strangely, or perhaps not, it seems the chief is the most confident of them all. He is still smiling, as if he had expected all of this to happen all along. As if this is what he has been waiting his whole life for.

Jess and Josh are holding hands, looking to Clarence for support. Clarence looks to Wadji, and Wadji looks to the chief. They are now facing the original opening through which they originally entered the place, but to their complete surprise, a door on the very opposite side of the place begins to glow and an almost choral sound comes from it, as it slowly opens, giving them time to turn and face it...

No one appears, though the door is fully open.

Beyond it they can see a brightly lit landscape. The professors wordlessly turn to each other; both relieved that the air is safe and not toxic. Slowly, still huddled close together, the group moves cautiously towards the door.

The chief is the first one out of the door. The others follow him. No one wants to be left alone. They are astonished by what they see next.

'Oh my god!

We can't be, can we?

We're back where we started out!

I don't believe this..!'

Jess's astonishment is reflected on the faces of all the others.

All except the chief. He does not seem at all surprised.

In fact, he is now giggling. Is it because he has

turned blue?

His tribal markings remain intact, along with the porcupine quill in his nose. However, his skin is now a deep shade of blue. But that is not the biggest surprise.

The biggest surprise is that they are now right back in the clearing at the foot of the pyramid, exactly where they had started out. And yet, are they? Something is different.

Everything has a soft yellow-gold glow around it and, as they move, there is the faintest trail of a gold shimmer that follows them.

Josh gets it first. 'Wow, it's the same place, but it's like... I don't know... different? It's more alive, it's more like... complete? Its sort of...'

Josh can't find the words, but each of them is caught up in the wonder of it all. Somehow, their journey has brought them back to a changed Earth.

'My dear friends, I believe we've travelled to the fifth dimension!'

This is the first time Wadji has spoken since they stepped out of the craft/pyramid. He seems confident, excited even.

His eyes are shining.

The chief is nodding madly. He agrees.

It's strange, because each of them is now connected

in a new way. The chief now fully understands their language, and as he speaks, they understand him too, before he has even finished speaking.

'Fifth dimension?' asks Jess.

'What happened to the fourth then...?'

'Well, you see, one leads to the other... The third is, of course space, the fourth is time. And the fifth? Well... I'll explain in due course, Jess. When I understand it! Have you noticed that you don't feel the heat of the jungle now?' asks Wadji.

'Wow, you're right! And the insects aren't bothering me any more either. That's so cool!' says Jess.

Her delight takes immediate form. A kind of colourful winged butterfly form comes out of her and flies out into the trees. She enjoys this new creativity and plays with it.

Focussing on feeling something deeply, then allowing it to take form and shape, and then finally releasing it into the world.

They all do this for a while, literally letting their feelings take form and then take flight.

Although this *seems* to be the self-same Earth they have all known and loved all their lives, something has changed; Big time!

Is it them?

'It's the way we're seeing stuff now, that's what is

different – everything is there, just as it was before, but there's like, soul to it. We're seeing something deeper, and also, there's a kind unity in that, a connectedness. And... oh, wait...I...'

Josh suddenly stops speaking. He is staring, but not at anyone or anything in particular.

He is going inward, seeing something inside of himself.

Something that is disturbing him.

Jess goes over to him.

'What is it Josh? What are you seeing?'

'It's... it's Mom... I can see Mom now... it looks like she's in some kind of danger. I can see four men with her, two of them are friendly, two aren't friendly at all. And those two men are looking for something. They think she has it. It's... a book?

No, wait, it's not just any book. It's... something special.

Fate? Fate Book?' He shrugs, and he now he is back in the clearing.

Wadji and Clarence look over at each other.

A moment ago they were all in a state of bliss, feeling the connectedness of things.

Now, something Josh has sensed and seen has changed that.

Mara is in trouble.

And someone is after The Fate Book.

An edge of anxiety has brought them back to the third dimension with a jarring thud!

Episode Fourteen: The Library

At first, Mara does not notice them. She is deep in a book, thinking that as the library is virtually empty, she will catch up with a little reading. The two men lean on the counter, both dressed in black; both wearing dark glasses. They both have the same swarthy chiselled faces, as if they were carved from the same block. They are scarred and unshaven, although their Armani suits are immaculate.

One of them keeps glancing at the door, the other is intent on holding her attention.

'Yes, can I help you?' Mara looks up and asks in her clipped efficient librarian voice. There is something about the two men that isn't quite right. Something that has woken her up right now.

'You know what we want. Now where is it?'

The other man, still with his eyes on the door, adds, in a kind of lazy hypnotic monotony:

'And please don't say you don't know what we're talking about. That's so cliched and boring and it could make things hurt so much more.'

'Where is it?' his companion repeats. This time his face has drifted up close to hers. Much too close. His breath smells stale and dark like him. There is something of the snake about him, something distinctly reptilian.

Mara isn't afraid.

Not yet.

But she knows she will be, and she knows they won't like her answer.

'Have you reserved a book then? You'll need to at least give me the title, or the author, ISBN number, perhaps?'

And now, quite suddenly, she really is afraid, because the other man has just vaulted right over the counter onto her side and his face is now right up against hers and his breath is as sour and deadly as his companion's.

'The Fate Book. Give it to me. Now!'

She sees out of the corner of her eye that the other man has moved to the door. Keeping his face close to hers, the man has produced a knife. She can feel it's cold steel pressing against her throat.

Mary Mother of God, she thinks. Save me.

Suddenly, the door opens and in comes a woman in a wheelchair. It is as if the sun has burst through the clouds.

'Hello Mara, I see you have some help today.

Nice big boys in suits. How nice.'

The man moves quickly, immediately opening the hatch and moving away to the door. The other is already there, posed to leave. They stare at her for a moment, in a 'we will be back' attitude and then, they are gone.

Mara is grateful for this intervention. She can feel the adrenaline pumping through her and making her a little dizzy. Whether her prayer has been answered or not, she has most certainly been saved.

She wants to rush over and hug the old woman, but she knows it will probably shock her and probably cause her heart failure.

'Oh, Mrs. Stevenson... how wonderful to see you!

I didn't think we'd be seeing you today. Your book isn't due till next week.'

'That's right, Mara. Quite right. Only, you see I'm not sure *'Fifty Shapes of Grape'* is the book for me, my dear... it's not really about vineyards, I find. So I've brought it back early, you see.'

The old woman fixes her eye in a most peculiar way, as if she knows something Mara does not. Then she smiles and leaves. The rest of the day passes without incident, though Mara is shaky and needs strong sweet tea to settle her nerves. She rings security and tells them to be on the lookout for the two men, but somehow she knows they won't be back while she is on the alert.

'The Fate Book?' The man said, as if she should know what it is.

She has never heard of it.

But she knows someone who might have. Her brother, Clarence.

She doesn't know why she thinks that. It's just a hunch.

Mara has a feeling that these dark men are after something Clarence knows about, and that worries her because Josh and Jess are with him. After all, these men have thought nothing of attacking her in a public library.

Mara decides to go home early, which is unusual for her.

She always closes the library at precisely 5 p.m., except for Wednesdays and Saturdays when she closes early at 2 p.m.

This gives her more time to be with Josh and Jess. But today is Monday and she is closing at 3 p.m.

She switches off the lights, locks the library, and drives herself home. She grabs a suitcase and packs a few things, then she locks the house, jumps into her car, and heads for the airport.

She will call her colleagues to explain her absence

once she arrives at the airport.

As she rounds the street heading away from her house, she passes a car heading the other way. Two men, intent on the road ahead, are in that car. She recognises them at once. The dark men in the Armani suits. They are heading in the direction of her house, and they haven't seen her. Perhaps her lifetime of making herself invisible is paying off. She hopes that when they break in they won't make too much of a mess of her house. Then she smiles. Does she really care? No, she doesn't! Now she is beginning to understand how Jess feels about her room. Dear Jess! Thinking of her, she suddenly feels a deep ache inside of herself. The kind of ache only a mother can feel for her child... but she knows that Josh will be taking care of her.

Dear Josh! she realises that he has always assumed the role of the man of the house. Quite willingly it would seem.

As if he knew that would be happening all along, long before he was even born to her... But now Mara feels that she is herself a child again. She suddenly remembers the Book of Kells and the Little People under the waterfall, from all those years ago. Could this be the book they foretold and wanted to be a part of? Somehow, she knows it is. Her adventure has now begun!

Episode Fifteen: Trouble at the Airport

Mara has checked in her luggage at the airport, and now she finds she has butterflies in her stomach!

She casts her eyes up to the boarding screen for the umpteenth time, even though she already knows her flight leaves from gate 27 and she still has an hour before her plane leaves for Guatemala City.

Strangely, she doesn't have a plan.

All she knows is that this is where she needs to be heading, and this is the very flight her brother Clarence took when he left with Josh and Jess less than two weeks ago.

Clarence had promised to call her regularly with updates on where they all were and how it was all going.

In fact, he had kept to his word, as he had called her three days before, but the connection was poor.

All she could see in the satellite picture was a few broken lines and a fleeting image of a smiling Josh and Jess sitting in a leafy place.

Now, suddenly, she can hardly believe her ears, as she

hears her name being called out. How embarrassing!

It's like she's being called to the headmaster's office or something. Thousands of people in the airport terminal hear it too.

'Will passenger Mara Kalikaloos please report to AIRPORT SECURITY immediately... Will passenger Mara Kalikaloos please report to AIRPORT SECURITY immediately...'

Mara feels her stomach knotting up. Why was she being paged? Her passport was fine, not due to expire for some years.

Nothing dodgy in her luggage... She hardly travelled these days anyway. Why her? What could they possibly want with her? A librarian from Dublin, flying out on a whim to see her kids?

'Will passenger Mara Kalikaloos please report to AIRPORT SECURITY immediately... Will passenger Mara Kalikaloos please report to AIRPORT SECURITY immediately...'

She is now about fifty metres from the security kiosk when she sees them, waiting right there, in the kiosk. The two dark men in the Armani suits.

Dear Mary. Mother of God. Save me from them.

She turns and dives into the entrance to the women's bathroom, in the moment they look up and see her.

Her guess is that the men will post themselves outside the loo and wait there for her, knowing she has nowhere else to go.

Her heart is thumping so hard she can feel it in her throat and she is having trouble focussing her eyes.

There are at least five or six other women in the toilet area when she runs in.

No one looks twice at her.

Running people are normal in an airport. There are bags and coats everywhere. Women putting on make-up.

Women washing their hands and faces.

Women brushing their hair. One is even changing her clothes, clearly not content with her travelling outfit.

There is something so secure and comforting for the fugitive Mara in this bustle.

She stands alongside one of these busy women, screening herself from the entrance door. She looks in the mirror and sees her own scared face looking back at her.

Just then, Mara sees a cleaner pushing a trolley into the toilet. It is one of those trolleys that contain trays full of cleaning products and a big trash bag hangs on one side.

The cleaner pushes the trolley to one side, takes off her green tunic and apron, leaving it there on the trolley, and locks herself into a cubicle.

Quick as a flash, an idea comes to Mara. She walks over to the trolley and slips on the green tunic and apron the cleaner had left there. She checks herself in the mirror and trying her best to look and act the part she slowly wheels the trolley out of the toilet.

No one in there has looked twice at her.

She keeps her eyes pointed down and walks straight past the two men in suits, waiting in the corridor outside.

They definitely aren't looking for a cleaner on the run so they completely ignore her. Mara is again invisible.

Luckily for her the cleaner whose role she has taken had been out for a vindaloo curry the night before, and would not emerge from her cubicle for at least another ten minutes. Enough time for Mara to make her way to gate 27.

Just before she enters the corridor leading to the boarding gate, she parks up her trolley, alongside one that is sitting in a corner along with its attendant cleaner. As Mara takes off the cleaner's borrowed tunic and apron, the cleaner with the other trolley, a tall dark and attractive foreign looking woman with a strong resemblance to Cleopatra and wearing sunglasses, looks quizzically at her.

'Oh, I've changed my mind,' Mara says to the woman, as she smooths her dress and hair and walks away from the trolley. 'I've decided it's not the kind of job for a librarian like me.' Then she hurries into the departure lounge at gate 27, hoping the men in suits are still waiting outside the loo.

Once more, she finds safety in numbers as she joins the queue boarding the flight to Guatemala City.

Mara eases herself back in her seat and fastens her safety-belt. For now, she can relax.

By the time the men in Armani suits have discovered her deception and have found another flight heading for Guatemala, she will be well on her way into the jungle, heading for the pyramid and Jess and Josh and Clarence.

Hopefully. If she can find a guide to take her there.

Her heart gradually settles down to its normal pulse.

Wow!

Did all of that really just happen, she asks herself?

Did she, Mara the librarian from Dublin really just outwit two dangerous men armed with knives and bad attitude and bad breath, and god knows what else?

Did she really just do that?

She is exultant. This is way more exciting than checking books in and out of dusty shelves. Why hadn't she thought of doing this years ago?!

She feels a light tap on her shoulder. It is the man in the seat next to her. He is smiling up at her. The eye looking at her is yellow, whilst the other one is a pale violet.

How unusual, she thinks.

He is short, with a scraggy beard and long hair. He seems to be wearing a gown or kaftan. Mara had not seen him checking into the plane, and certainly he would stand out in a crowd: he looks as if he has stepped out of another time, as indeed he has. He is offering her something. She looks down now at his hand, which is small and gnarled with long nails. In it he is holding a silver tray of nougat. To her surprise she takes a piece and pops it into her mouth.

OMG It is delicious! She wants more.

The man seems to know this and when she looks back down, the silver tray is offered to her again.

'Ooooh...thank you! That is just about the most delicious thing I've ever tasted!' she says.

'I have plenty more,' the man answers in broken English. 'Come. Please, you take more, huh? My name, she Morkabalas.'

'Oh, I'm Mara,' she replies.

The man flashes her a bright smile; then as the plane is beginning to accelerate for take-off, he closes his eyes.

Quick as a flash Mara takes another piece of the exquisite nougat, and she notices there are just as many pieces on the tray now as when he'd first offered it to her.

As she puts the nougat into her mouth, pondering this endless nougat supply, she realises that whereas her new friend Morkabalas's one violet eye, is closed, the bright yellow one is now staring up at her. The eye winks at her and closes again.

What a strange man she thinks. But despite this, she feels relaxed in his company, as he seems to give out a very calming energy. So calming, in fact, that Mara falls asleep and the next thing she knows, the plane is taxiing in to land.

Morkabalas is sitting there smiling up at her, offering her more nougat.

What can she do?

What would you do?

She takes two pieces!

Episode Sixteen: Mara Arrives

Mara leaves the plane.

There is such a bustle in the airport terminal, she has never seen anything like it. Here in Guatemala City there is a colourful explosion of every kind of everything.

There are business men, business women, school parties, hen parties, stag parties, political parties, back-packers, front-packers, tourists, farmers, and nuns.

Most of all it is busy and noisy and chaotic, but everyone seems to have a plan.

Mara looks around for Morkabalas. She hasn't seen him since she disembarked from the plane. He has disappeared.

What a shame, she thinks; she will miss that nougat!

Unlike everyone else, Mara doesn't have a plan, and so she is astonished to see a man standing there, holding up a large piece of cardboard with her name on it:

MARA KALIKALOOS it reads. The man holding it

seems to be a tribal Indian. But he is unusually tall and broad.

He is dressed only in shorts and flip flops, and he has markings tattooed on his face and upper body. As she walks up to him, his face lights up, as if he recognises her.

'Hello, pretty lady! You is Mara?' Welcome to Guatemala!

Here: give me; I take luggage for you!'

He takes Mara's bag before she can protest and balances it on his head, as if it weighs nothing at all. Then he flashes her a broad smile and walks out of the terminal, with Mara struggling to keep up with him.

How odd? How did he even know I was going to be here?' she wonders. *Ah well! He looks like a friendly type. May as well go with the flow then.* She shrugs in surrender to it all and scampers off after him.

In a couple of minutes, she is sitting in the back of an old car, painted in loud yellows, blues, and greens. Just like a parrot, she thinks, beginning to enjoy this bright and colourful, unrestrained country.

The parrot car noisily chugs off, with the friendly Indian at the wheel. He is shouting something at her, hardly looking at the road as the car swerves around bicycles piled high with rush cages full of small animals, street vendors selling fruit and vegetables, pedestrians shouting and laughing, and other parrot cars hooting and swerving.

Mara closes her eyes for a moment, as this is all too much too soon, and then she becomes aware that her driver has repeated something and is still awaiting her response...

She opens her eyes, seeing his expectant friendly face leaning out toward her, eyebrows raised.

Somehow, the car seems to know where to go without his participation, as he is not looking at the road ahead at all, and she lets go of worrying about a collision.

He patiently repeats the question:

'Professor Kalikaloos, he your husband..?

'Oh... No, Professor Kalikaloos, Clarence, is my brother.' Mara smiles back.

The man seems relieved.

'Aaaaah! Yes yes yes! This good! You like food? You like for to eat? I take you out for eat dinner one night, maybe... mmm?'

'Mmmmm... Maybe...' she replies, a little hesitantly.

'Aaaaah! Good! Is good! I treat you nice, very nice, good lady!

'What's your name, anyway?' Mara asks.

'My name? Quortaletzl! Quor...ta...letzl!' he replies, alarmingly reaching his hand over to take hers, leaving the cat to steer itself once again. He then surprises her by gently raising her hand first to his chest, then to his lips, and then kissing it oh so gently...

She blushes at this sudden unexpected burst of chivalry.

'So where are you taking me... Quor...ta...letzl?'

'Aaaah! Is big surprise!' He giggles like a schoolgirl, excitedly swaying from side to side, as if the secret is almost too much for him.

He turns on the car radio.

The Gipsy Kings are singing their version of 'My Way' done their way. Mara sighs and shrugs.

Ah well...' she thinks, *there are worse things than being chatted up by a half-naked man in a parrot car that seems to know its own way around.*

She closes her eyes again and surrenders, resting her head against the back seat. The car swerves hypnotically from side to side as it follows the slow bends of the road, which seems to be rising up and away from the city and into the hills.

Now there are now no more buildings and the trees are getting thicker and denser, and in another moment it seems there is almost no other traffic. Except that, behind the parrot car, keeping a steady distance away, is a big black limo.

In it there are two men sitting in the front seats, with

swarthy unshaven scarred faces and dark glasses. They are wearing smart Armani suits.

Seemingly unknown to them, behind a dark glass screen in the back seat of the limo, is an unseen guest:

A small man with gold teeth and a pale blue turban is sitting there, smiling. He knows something that they do not.

In fact, he knows something that none of us knows.

Yet...

Episode Seventeen: The Jungle

The swaying momentum of the car and the tinny staccato of rapid Spanish patter from the radio has gradually rocked Mara asleep.

Somehow she feels safe with this big eccentric driver, who is now tucking into a huge slice of watermelon; holding it in both hands and spitting the pips directly onto the inside of the car's windscreen, where they stick and form a speckled surface he can barely see through.

No matter, the car knows where it is going.

Mara wakes up suddenly, thinking she has heard a gunshot, but it is only the driver loudly breaking wind.

'Ah, sorry nice lady, beg for your pardons. These fruits give me gas!'

He giggles delightedly, pleased that she is back from her sleep.

'It's not far now, pretty lady, is just round bend now... or maybe round next bend after that?' He smiles reassuringly.

On a sudden hunch, Mara glances back. She sees the black limo coming around the bend a hundred meters behind them. She frowns. She remembers something now: that same car was parked behind them at the airport terminal.

A tiny tingle runs up her spine, and did she not just see two men in dark suits in that car?

Quortaletzl, her driver, has noticed her reaction and is peering at both her and the limo in his rear-view mirror.

'Yeah... I see them suit guys in black car, pretty good, pretty lady... now donn youse worry, eh? We got de good guys lookin' out for you; look, I show you!'

He reaches down under his seat and suddenly he is brandishing a baseball bat, painted to match his car in yellow blue and red; a parrot bat!

For emphasis, he wallops the dashboard hard several times, sending a dense layer of watermelon pips around the car.

Is he serious? she thinks.

What if they have guns?

Suddenly they come around a sharp bend where the road opens up into a huge clearing. All around the clearing is a dense jungle.

Quortaletzl leaps out of the car, his baseball bat at the ready.

There is no sign now of the black limo. It must have pulled over down the road. Quortaletzl has already strapped a small rucksack onto his back and has Mara's suitcase on his head and is striding towards the jungle.

He is not wasting any time.

She runs to keep up with him.

The sound coming from the jungle is deafening, after the relative quiet of the car journey. There are chattering monkeys, cicadas, and a host of birdcalls.

Also, some far-off growls and roars...

Suddenly, as they enter the dense undergrowth, they are in a world of dappled green, and now it is quite dark and warm and damp under the towering trees. There is something quite comforting about the protective cover of these gigantic green trees.

Mara thinks of them as big friendly giants.

She casts a final look back behind her as the clearing disappears from view, and she is not sure, but she thinks she has caught a far-off glimpse of a black limo arriving.

She is glad that she is wearing sensible clothing for this new adventure: combat boots and thick socks, which she managed to put on in the parrot car, and loose but strong cotton trousers and shirt. And a hat.

Ahead of her, Quortaletzl is striding along singing

cheerfully. He has produced a machete and is now hacking a pathway through the ever-thickening undergrowth.

Now they are deep in the beating heart of the jungle.

Some minutes and hours go by.

But then, quite suddenly, Quortaletzl has stopped singing and is now listening intently, his head cocked to one side.

Mara is amazed he is able to filter through the cacophony of sounds, but he is now at one with the jungle and deciphering something, his eyes closed. His normally cheerful, even reckless nature, has been traded in for something much more alert and focussed.

He turns, at last, to Mara, who is amazed at this transformation. His face is serious now, intent.

And there is nothing there of the happy-go-lucky flirty watermelon munching driver of the parrot car.

This is a different Quortaletzl altogether. It's as if the jungle has demanded and produced a different man who now lives and breathes in tune with it.

He leans over and whispers into her ear:

'Lady, we is being followed!

Quick now! We need to hide us for a while to see who it is coming up behind us here.'

With that, he takes her hand and pulls her gently under a tree with thick branches and a dense leafy covering, very much like a weeping willow with big leaves. In a moment, they are lying on the ground completely hidden from view.

They don't have long to wait:

In a few minutes, they can hear footsteps breaking twigs and coming their way.

Mara is so tempted to raise her head to look, but her huge companion senses it and pushes her back onto the forest floor; she is forced to watch, at close hand, a trail of ants going about their business of carrying stuff to their nest.

The jungle is such a busy place.

There is always something going on here.

A far cry from the quiet regularity of the library, she thinks.

Suddenly, the footsteps stop right next to them.

Quortaletzl jumps to his feet, and next thing he has someone firmly in his grasp.

Mara looks up and is amazed:

It is Morkabalas.

He is equally as amazed to see her!

Quortaletzl releases his grip once he realises that

Mara and this strange little bearded man in a dressing gown know each other; he is relieved it is not the men in suits.

'Is this man your granfadda...?' Quortaletzl wants to know, looking from one to the other.

Both Mara and Morkabalas find this question very funny, and they laugh out loud. But Quortaletzl stops them with a quick gesture of his hand and pushes them both back down on the ground under the tree again.

Once more, there is the sound of something approaching them through the jungle, but from two directions this time: from the same direction Morkabalas had approached from, and also, strangely, from the trees high above them.

In a moment, the undergrowth peels open to reveal the men in suits!

They look completely out of place in the jungle in their dark Armani suits, and they are both carrying several weapons strapped over their shoulders, including AK47s and absurdly, a rocket launcher.

Less absurd though, is that one of them is using a pair of heat-sensitive infra-red stealth goggles and is scanning the area around him. He suddenly stops and pulls on his companion's arm, pointing down at the tree under which Mara and her two friends are hiding.

He can see them.

'Okay, I can see you guys down there... get out! Now!' he shouts, as they hesitate, aiming his AK47 at them, while his suited companion, sweating heavily, kicks at the three on the ground.

Quortaletzl stands up first, protectively standing between the men and Mara and Morkabalas. One of the men in suits pushes him roughly to one side and grabs hold of Mara, pulling her hair back and putting his face right up close to hers. She can smell his rancid breath and the librarian in her is appalled at his lack of punctuation as he speaks.

'So you thought you could get away from us didn't you you stupid woman? A clever trick the cleaner outfit in the loo but you know what you're gonna do...? You're gonna take us right to the friggin book now aren't you? Oh yeah and please please I'm begging you please don't pretend again that you don't know what the friggin Fate Book is okay?'

Morkabalas's eyes are as big as saucers.

The trip on the plane and now these strange men in suits with weapons and glasses that can find people who are hiding is all too much magic for a hermit from ancient times. But what's really got his attention now is that the man in the suit is talking about The Fate Book, and he, Morkabalas, knows exactly what that is, doesn't he?

But just then there is a sudden increase of noise in the trees above them and the sound of snapping twigs and leaves, and although one of the suits has fired off a few shots in the direction of the sound, the gigantic anaconda is way too big and way too fast and way too heavy, as it drops down from the branches above them and winds itself around and around the men in the Armani suits.

And this time Professor Wadji WadjiWadj is not here to use his snake hypnotism to set them free.

Episode Eighteen: The Fate Book Speaks!

Meanwhile, back at their camp in front of the pyramid, the professors Clarence and Wadji are consulting a large map of the area, while Josh and Jess are hungrily watching the blue chief preparing a meal for them all. He is muttering and mumbling as if he is instructing the food itself.

The blue chief has become an essential member of their little team, and Josh and Jess have become quite fond of him; especially as Jess has now learned to trust him.

Since Josh has received the information about Mara being in trouble, they have decided to postpone any further plans to explore the area in favour of trying to get in touch via satellite phone with Mara, who is, of course, not answering.

Even so, the professors are excited by the new vista of history provided by their experience inside the pyramid.

'It makes history now look like something a child made up after a particularly bad nightmare,' suggests Clarence, as they sit around the campfire the evening after their 'journey' in the pyramid.

'You're so right, Clarrice, erm sorry, Clarence,' Wadji responds. 'I do believe we shall have to make another trip to the pyramid at Giza soon, and see if The Fate Book can give us an update there too. It seems we may have completely misunderstood the function of that wonderful structure. I mean to say, aside from the tantalising hints it has already given us as to the actual dimensions of the Earth itself, and even the relative distances to the moon and sun, we'd now have to consider what kind of awareness the architects themselves had.

We tend to patronise early history, don't we? As if people living back then were primitive and backward, do we not?'

'Absolutely, old boy! I mean, just look at the...'

Clarence is suddenly interrupted by the distinct sounds of gunfire coming from the jungle just ahead of them.

Before they can even think about what to do next, Clarence finds The Fate Book in his hands. He doesn't even know how it got there, from its place at the bottom of his backpack.

But now it is in his hands, and it is open, and he is looking at it, and the others are peering over his shoulder.

All except Josh, who has closed his eyes and is searching his own inner reference systems.

The Fate Book is open and at first shows just a jumble

of lines and colours, rather like a TV set that needs tuning; then there is a sequence of numbers: 1 1 2 3 5 8 13 21 34 55 89 144 running faster and faster, then it settles into clear and distinct moving images. And there it is!

Suddenly they can see, showing up as clear as day, a little group of people in the jungle.

They immediately recognise Mara there. Wadji and Clarence are amazed to see Morkabalas is there too!

How on earth did he, the hermit, the previous custodian of The Fate Book, even get there, from a totally different time and culture?

This is a real puzzle!

The blue chief, looking at The Fate Book over Clarence's shoulder, immediately recognises Quortaletzl, who is one of his own tribesmen and he points at him and laughs with delight at seeing him there, but the biggest surprise to them all is the dark package formed by the two men in suits wrapped up in the coils of the anaconda, (whom you will of course remember, is well known to the chief.)

Did the chief send the anaconda?

Wadji and Clarence stare at him for answers, but he is giving nothing away. He simply hands each of them some food spooned into a large leaf, and indicates that he is ready to go.

They should leave right now, he is saying with his

body language and suggestive hand gestures, before the anaconda turns its victims into paté.

They are all astonished to see that the blue chief has been now joined by a group of Indians who have silently appeared, dead on cue, out of the jungle.

They quickly gather their things and move after the blue chief and his men: first Josh and Jess, then Wadji and Clarence bringing up the rear.

After the incident with Jess, they aren't taking any chances.

The commotion ahead of them in the jungle gets louder as the men in suits are panicking in the tightening coils of the snake, even though Quortaletzl is trying to tell them that struggling will only cause the anaconda to tighten up even more. It is not looking good for them.

There is so much noise caused by the unfortunate suits, that Mara, Morkabalas, and Quortaletzl don't hear the rescue party approaching, and we can only imagine Mara's relief when she suddenly sees her own dear children and Clarence suddenly standing right there in front of her... it really is too much for her!

She bursts into floods of tears of sheer relief, as does Jess, but the blue chief and Wadji waste no time and immediately turn their attention to the struggling victims in the coils of the giant anaconda, who are now turning purple before their eyes as the huge snake slowly but surely asphyxiates them.

Wadji quickly and fearlessly stands directly in front of the massive anaconda and fixes its eyes with a stare. Just as it did before when it had the chief in its coils, the snake immediately drops the men; and with one last reluctant look at its lost lunch, it slowly slips into the jungle.

The terrified men in suits gasp for breath and the blue chief immediately runs up to them and from a bag of healing herbs around his neck, puts something into their mouths.

Clearly, they are in shock and in no fit state to attack anyone right now, but Quortaletzl takes their weapons from them, folds them up as if they are origami, and throws them all into a bag.

Then he ties their hands together with vine rope.

Just in case.

He is talking all this while with his newly-blue chief, who seems pleased with his efforts, and as a reward he goes over to him and spits in his face.

Professor Wadji Wadjiwadj looks thoughtful.

He wants to know what has brought the men in suits here.

'What are they after? And who sent them here?' he asks everyone in general.

Mara then tells him how the men came to her in the

library asking for some kind of book which they called The Fate Book. (the professors exchange looks at this point).

She tells them how they threatened her when she said she didn't know anything about any such book and how they held a knife to her throat and how, at the eleventh hour, she was saved by the arrival of Mrs. Stevenson in her wheelchair.

She tells them that she decided to immediately pack her things, and how she then managed to evade the men in suits at the airport terminal by posing as a cleaner after they had her trapped in the loo.

Jess and Josh think this is amazing.

They look at her now with new respect.

What a cool mom!

Wadji goes up to the men, who are still very shaky after their ordeal, and in spite of their swarthy skins, are now as pale as ghosts.

'Gentlemen. You need to tell us why you come seeking The Fate Book. And if you have any reluctance about revealing that, well, I can assure you, gentlemen, that I am as capable of calling the serpent back as I was in sending it away.'

Of course, the professor is bluffing, but it works a treat.

The monosyllabic one instantly responds; tough as he

is, he does not want to end up crushed and down the throat of a giant snake.

'Look man, we don't know nothing about this friggin' Fate Book thing or even why it's so friggin' important. All we know is that we have a friggin' contract to find it and it doesn't matter who gets friggin' hurt,' he sneers.

'That's it! He's right! Thats juss how it happened!' his companion adds. 'Okay, look, we got this long distance call from some kinda foreign soundin dude and he said *'to look smart about it'* see, that's why we got these friggin' suits!'

Clarence represses a little giggle at this. *Look smart about it!*

These chaps obviously take everything literally! he thinks.

But then he remembers what his sister has told him about their methods and he becomes quite angry, perhaps also remembering how he had to protect her from her violent stepfather when they were kids.

'And so you were told to go to Ireland armed with knives and guns and a rocket launcher and foul language to torture my defenceless sister? Oh, how extraordinarily brave of you: two assassins armed to the teeth against a librarian?

My goodness me!

How impressive!

What men!'

At this castigation from Clarence, the hit-men look a little shamefaced, and taken by a sudden whim, Quortaletzl, who has developed a bit of a crush on Mara, and who earlier on, before the entrance of the anaconda, had to stand by at gunpoint and watch her being mistreated, emphasises the professor's point by whacking a large slice of watermelon with great force into the faces of the men in suits.

'You boys is bastard pigs! Why you wanna hurt my nice lady? Huh? Huh? You is lucky I no give you taste of baseball bat, huh?'

Wadji raises an eyebrow and steps back a pace, but Jess and Josh giggle delightedly.

'Way to go!'

The monosyllabic one, who has been watching Wadji's face intently, spits away the watermelon pips and thinking that Wadji has now decided to call the snake back, pleads pathetically with him, almost grovelling at his feet.

'Look man, please donn call that snake back, man; I swear we really donn know nuttin' about the dude who called us up; he juss said he'd pay up some good bucks when he got this friggin' Fate Book man, I swear...'

Wadji turns away. He is disgusted with all this grovelling and is getting no satisfaction from holding the fate of these two men in his hands. But the jungle has decided that their punishment is not over.

After Quortaletzl's watermelon whacking, the sweet smell of the exploded fruit has drawn some unexpected attention.

Three excited monkeys have dropped down from the trees and are now perched on the hit men. They are chattering and jumping about and eagerly licking the bits of watermelon from their faces: this is a fruit they haven't tasted, and boy do they like it!

Seeing their antics, no one can help laughing at them now; even the men in suits giggle helplessly as the three little hyperactive monkeys tickle their faces with their fur and tongues.

Clarence has seen a further joke in this little scene and is laughing the loudest of all.

'Hahahahaha! Oh, dear God Wadji, look: it's the famous three monkeys, don't you see? There they are.

Hear no evil, see no evil, make no statement... hahahaha!'

Josh and Jess don't get that bit, but they are happy to see the men humiliated by the monkeys; revenge enough for the indignities suffered by their mom.

The blue chief and his men are sorely tempted to capture the monkeys for their lunch, but as they have provided such timeous entertainment, they merely shoo them away and the captives are pulled to their feet.

What's to be done with them now? Where to now?

Mara, though delighted to be reunited with her her family, has some burning questions that she has flown thousands of miles to have answered.

Clarence and Wadji know this all too well.

And they have promised to explain everything.

The first and most pressing thing for now though, is how to get the men in Armani suits off their backs. Clearly, if they are set free at this point, they will be back. They want their money, and they will likely want revenge too.

So, what's to be done with them?

Wadji, the blue chief, and Quortaletzl confer together.

Meanwhile, Josh, Jess, and Mara hold hands and sit down together. They are a close family, but this crisis has brought them even closer together. They are laughing and crying all at the same time and when they recover they are all talking at once. Jess is desperate to tell her mom all about her ordeal with the tribesmen and the snake.

Josh wants to express his relief at finding her safe, and Mara wants to say how much she loves them and how exciting it all is.

Episode Nineteen: More about Morkabalas

All this time, Morkabalas has quietly withdrawn from the hubbub and is sitting alone cross-legged under a big tree with his eyes closed. He has retreated now to his mystical inner world, where everything always makes more sense.

When he, Mara, and Quortaletzl were rescued, he was delighted to be reunited with the professors, especially Wadji, for whom he has been a mentor. They threw their arms around one another like long lost brothers, and for the longest time said nothing.

They simply looked into each other's eyes and connected in the way that people on their level do. The level at which no words are necessary.

After that, he was introduced to the others. When he met Josh, he felt an immediate connection to him: in him he could see the whole purpose of The Fate Book, and a forerunner of the new, intuitive humanity of the future.

Wordlessly, he communicated all he knew to Josh, who eagerly accepted the concentrated fruits of those long years Morkabalas had spent focussing his thoughts.

Beaming with pleasure at finding one so much like him, Morkabalas then did the one thing he knew would definitely please both Josh and Jess. He drew from his bag a small silver tray, piled high with nougat, and held it out to them. Comfort food was just what these young folks needed right now.

They were amazed and delighted to find that the nougat kept replacing itself, no matter how much they ate.

Even after the chief and his men and the three monkeys had also tucked in, the pile on the silver tray looked just as full as it did when it first appeared in the outstretched hands of Morkabalas.

Now the hermit sits quietly under the tree and within him the world turns and reveals itself to him.

He sees the long and painful road men must walk before they wake up to who and what they truly are.

He sees the centuries of strife and war raised by those for whom enough is just never enough.

He sees cities rise and fall and rise again in another place and another time.

Again and again.

He sees lessons learned the hard way when waking up would have hurt far less.

He sees the deeper hurt of those who have not been seen for whom they truly are.

Then he sees things a little closer at hand.

He sees the anger of the hit men come back to haunt them.

He sees the joy of Mara reunited with her family.

He sees the fulfilment of the Indian prophecies.

He sees hope for a new world in Josh.

He sees the innocence of the tribesmen in their Eden.

He sees all this.

He sees the professors having to question everything they know about history.

He sees The Fate Book living on in all people.

Now he feels his work is done, he can go home.

Home.

He takes a deep breath, and as he breathes out, his outline grows fuzzy and shaky. In another breath and another moment he has entirely and completely disappeared.

Meanwhile, the professors have conferred about the fate of the men in suits and of course, Mara and her family have had time to catch up. Clarence explains the significance and workings of The Fate Book to them as best he can, and it's importance, prompted occasionally by Professor Wadji.

He tells Mara that Wadji has recently made him the custodian of The Fate Book, having received it from the mystical Morkabalas, and that there is a tradition of custodians stretching way back into the mists of time.

He adds that Josh already possesses, to a large degree, that which The Fate Book ultimately teaches:

The faculty of intuition.

Wadji adds that this is something already dawning on the whole of humanity, and that it will one day become the default position for communication. Not just between humans, but also between humans and other species.

Clarence and Wadji are both puzzled as to why these thugs had been sent to steal The Fate Book.

Who could be behind that, and why?

They have no ready answers to those questions.

They gather their things, and as they prepare to leave, everyone realises that they have forgotten about someone: Morkabalas.

Then Wadji sees something lying under a big tree.

He recognises it straight away: it is one of Morkabalas's scrolls, tied with a bright red ribbon.

He already knows why it is there and what is inside it.

He picks it up and for a moment he can see the mystic sitting there, in his mind's eye.

'Okay everyone, let's move on then,' he says, his voice a bit shaky. His heart is both, by turns heavy and light. What a strange contradiction.

'But where is Morkabalas?' asks Mara.

'Don't you worry about him, Mara. He has... he has gone on ahead of us,' smiles Wadji, amused by the metaphor; but looking at the professor's face Mara sees that he has a sad smile and there are tears in the corner of his eyes.

She doesn't ask any more questions.

Episode Twenty: The Library

Back at the library now, some time later, Mara was finding life a bit boring. This was very strange for her: normally she thrived on the peace and quiet, the order of her regulated day. The routine of books coming in and books going out, the satisfaction that only someone who uses a big rubber stamp all day can possibly know.

After her taste of danger and adventure in the jungles of Guatemala, life in the library seemed a bit colourless.

Even tedious. She found herself checking the library clock.

A lot. Was it teatime yet? Was it lunchtime? Was it time to go home? This was not good! This was not the old Mara!

Josh and Jess had settled back into their school routine, but they too, were itching for another adventure. Jess checked the letterbox every day, sometimes twice a day to see if there was any news from Uncle Clarence.

Inspired by this last adventure, Josh was reading a lot of books about alternative science, stuff like quantum physics and the golden ratios of the Fibonacci sequence.

Clarence had remembered that this number sequence appeared in The Fate Book just before it showed them the arrival of his sister with Morkabalas, Quortaletzl, and the men in suits. He had mentioned the sequence to Josh, who was now seeing it everywhere in the natural world.

He had also developed a fascination for snakes, especially big ones; and he tried to see if he could stare them out, like Professor Wadji could, at the reptile park.

Back in Guatemala, Quortaletzl was crestfallen when Mara bid him farewell at the airport. The poor man was clearly quite smitten with her, and was somehow convinced that she felt the same way about him.

She didn't, and even if she did, no one would know it.

She had decided years before that she had no place for romance in her life.

A Catholic single mother with a Mayan Indian?

It really didn't figure. She didn't even allow herself to go there. Even though she found herself thinking about him a lot and developing a bit of a passing passion for the taste of watermelon.

The professors Clarence and Wadji had decided to travel onwards to Egypt. After their illuminating experience in the pyramid in Guatemala, they were keen to find out what they could from the pyramid at Giza. Would their view of history be changed there also, with the help of The Fate Book?

The puzzle of how to deal with the stalkers in Armani suits had reached a happy resolution. Quortaletzl had volunteered to drive them to Guatemala City in his self-steering parrot car to hand them over to the police. After all, they were travelling on forged passports, had fired on an endangered species (the anaconda), had attempted kidnapping and extortion at least once, and had smuggled arms and ammunition into the country.

They would be held and interrogated by the authorities and then extradited to the United States once the Guatemalans had dealt with them. At first, they didn't seem to care about this, and put on brave faces.

But by the time they had been securely bound and bundled into Quortalezl's brightly painted self-navigating car and had been subjected to his relentless good humour and been thoroughly coated in spat-out watermelon pips, they felt differently and slowly pleaded with him to release them.

They offered him lots of money.

But he just laughed.

Then they upped the stakes and offered him uncut diamonds and a mobile phone. He laughed even louder, spraying them involuntarily with more watermelon pips.

What use did he have for diamonds and a mobile phone in the jungle? They were about as useful to him as a chocolate teapot!

Still, they pleaded and cajoled with him, finally trying to appeal to his good nature by accusing him of indecency and gross negligence, in handing them over to the police, knowing that interrogation and torture and who knew what else would surely follow.

He did not laugh at this. He pulled the car over and sat there quietly, thinking. The men were worried.

They thought he was now going to finish them off himself.

They had seen the way he looked at Mara, and they also knew how angry he was at how they had treated her.

He got out of the car and stretched himself, breaking wind so loudly they thought he was firing a gun at them, and ducked, banging their heads on the front seats of the car.

Finally, he returned to the car, opened the door, and let them out. This wasn't easy, as they still had their hands and feet tied. He helped them out and sat them down at the roadside. Quortaletzl was strong and well-muscled. He knew how to handle himself.

In his own tribe, he was regarded as a bit of a genetic

anomaly, as he was much taller and bigger and stronger than anyone else.

So now he untied the men's hands; though he left their feet tied for the moment.

'Whattcha gonna do with us man?' whined one of them.

'Listen to me, muchachos. Listen good,' he answered.

'I'm gonna offer you guys another road; instead of that road to the police that is gonna lead you to torture and then a long trip back to the US of A, maybe in body-bags, who knows...'

The men looked fearfully at each other. Quortaletzl wasn't joking, they could tell. He was looking at them like he meant business:

They were listening.

'So, this is the deal boys. Just about a mile from here, in a track through the jungle, is a kind of a mission station.

And donn get excited thinkin' nuns an stuff... huh? This a mission station set up for to plant trees, to replace the trees the loggers cut down and took away, for the super highway that never happened. Yeah brothers, you got it!

You gonna plant trees.

An you gonna get paid for it: but your pay gonna be

food and a bed to sleep in at night. That's it!

And I'm a gonna be watchin you boys.

A lot.

And if you donn plant them trees, guess what?

I'm a gonna call your big ol frenn Rhonda the anaconda an she gonna come give you boys a nice big hug... get it... huh?'

They got it all right. They immediately turned pale at the thought of the coils of that huge snake, which had so nearly squashed them. Though they didn't relish the idea of that kind of work, or in fact any kind of work that didn't involve hurting or killing someone, they preferred the idea of planting trees to interrogation and torture and certain life-imprisonment, not to mention the threat of being hugged to death by Rhonda the anaconda if they didn't comply.

They nodded sullenly in silent assent.

Quortaletzl broke into a huge smile, went to his car and rummaged about in the trunk. In a moment, he had found some scruffy clothes for them, more suitable than Armani suits for the work in hand.

'Here muchachos, take off the suits and put these things on.

They'll give you boots and hats when you get to the mission station.'

Quortaletzl cut the ropes binding their feet and

stepped away, as the men changed out of their Armani suits, which were decidedly the worse for being worn in the jungles and badly creased by a squeezing snake.

And now they stood in mismatched baggy shorts and t- shirts, shuffling about uneasily under Quortaletzl's scrutiny.

He chuckled and tossed them each a slice of watermelon, then brandished his colourful baseball bat, pointing the way ahead.

'Bootiful! You boys is bootiful! Now let's go! Oh and juss in case you're wonderin, nobody gonna be able to find you dere, nobody! Not even your secret boss who sent you here, so donn worry, youse gonna be safe boys!'

He sang cheerfully, now that things were settled. *Yes. This was a good day's work* he thought, as he marched the men through the jungle, his red blue and yellow baseball bat swinging about, to remind them that he meant business.

He found himself thinking about Mara.

What would that pretty lady be doing right now?

Back at the library, Mara has decided to catalogue a pile of books nobody ever reads, on the science of bantam sexing. She needs a challenge she has decided.

With a weary sigh, she heaves the books onto the high

counter and reaches for her pen. Then she starts and drops her pen as a voice breaks the silence and calls to her, seemingly from nowhere:

'Mornin' Mara, and when did you get back from your little journey to the jungles then, me darlin'?'

She glances about her, but no one is in sight. Then the voice speaks again.

'I'm down here, Mara'

She looks out over the counter. It's Mrs. Stevenson, sitting down there in her wheelchair, just out of sight. She is smiling at Mara, her head cocked to one side, and she winks a long, knowing kind of a wink. Then she glances slyly from side to side, making sure no one is listening, and comes closer.

'You know Mara, you're an attractive woman.

You should let someone take you out now and again. D'y'know what I'm meaning? No harm in that m'darlin... all work and no play makes Jill a dull girl, I'm thinkin; no offence, but I've been noticing you're not yourself since you got back from you know who, in you know where!'

Mara blushes. How would Mrs. Stevenson even know where she had been? Let alone whom she had been with, if anyone. How would *anyone* know that?

Mara had been careful to hide her tracks when she left Dublin. Mrs, Stevenson doesn't let up though.

She drifts even closer in her wheelchair and stretches her face up as close as she can, still whispering.

'Ting is, Mara, I managed to save you from them suits that time they trapped you in here, d'you know! D'you really think I just happened in here by accident, me darlin...'?

Course I'm sorry I was a bit late though, my new electric hadn't arrived yet, you see.' She taps the shiny state-of-the-art wheelchair for emphasis.

Mara is now feeling very uncomfortable. Clearly Mrs. Stevenson picks that up; she passes a card to Mara, and starts to slide away.

'We need to talk me darlin' and soon. And don't you worry, I'm on the side of the Little People too, y'know, just like you dear.' She winks again, for emphasis, satisfied at seeing Mara's jaw drop. 'Oh yes. To be sure, we're all looking out for you, if you know what I'm meaning...

Sure hope you do! You'll call on me soon? I just know you will!'

With the sweetest smile and a little wave, she whisks almost silently out of the library, surprisingly fast, Mara thinks, with her eyes fixed on Mara all the way to the door.

Can she be trusted? Is she really on her side, as she says she is? On the other hand, Mara is really curious now.

What harm can it do to visit her? Especially as it is now clear that Mrs. Stevenson may have quite intentionally saved her from being harmed by the men in suits.

And, if the old girl says she already knew they were coming, what does that mean? She needs to find out!

She looks at the card Mrs. Stevenson has left her.

It is a curious card.

There is a drawing of a spiral on one side of it, rather like the kind you see in a shell cut in half. On the other side is her name, in flamboyant cursive lettering:

Rhona Stevenson

Celtic Diviner

7 Sevens Drive,

Dublin 7

Telephone 07777 777777

Mara is genuinely shocked!

All those sevens!

This is not what she'd expected!

The woman knows something. She mentioned the Little People. Mara has never mentioned them to anyone; she has kept that secret since she saw them as a child.

Celtic Diviner?

What is that?

Suddenly she sees in her mind's eye the intertwining nature forms of the Book of Kells. Her heart skips a beat.

Now she can't wait to see this woman to know more.

She decides to call her later, during her lunch break.

In the meantime, she turns her attention to the pile of books on the science of bantam sexing.

Episode Twenty-One: The Visit to Mrs. Stevenson

Mara feels a little trepidation, as she knocks at Mrs. Stevenson's door.

The house is very quiet.

Too quiet.

She feels she is being watched.

The garden is beautiful, but to her, a bit overgrown.

And has she just seen a little form dancing over there in that flowerbed? No, she must have imagined it; if it was there, it's gone now.

The house is reached through a long pathway between two hedgerows. Over the entrance porch is a beautifully carved wooden arch, with intertwined figures and leaves.

Just like the Book of Kells.

The whole effect is one of little folk dancing through the foliage. There is a sweet bell-like sound. She discovers that this is coming from a line of windchimes hanging over there in the porch. They are gently tinkling, but there is no wind. Not even a breeze.

As Mara reaches the porch, a light comes on and the door opens as soon as she reaches it.

She expects Mrs. Stevenson to be there, but she isn't. Though the door has completely opened, to reveal a candlelit interior. Mrs. Stevenson calls to her from somewhere inside the house:

'Come in, Mara! Please, just you make yourself at home now. I've left some tea things out for you. Just follow your nose, me dear.'

Her voice is warm and friendly, and puts Mara at ease straight away. She can smell the lovely smell of fresh baked scones, she is guessing, or maybe shortbread.

She hasn't told Josh and Jess where she has gone.

Should she have? she wonders now, but the delicious smell draws her in and she finds herself in the most gorgeous room she has ever seen.

There are tasteful silk hangings on the wall, standing lamps of exquisite taste lighting up the corners of the room. There are small tables under these standing lamps, and on these tables little treasures are arranged.

Exquisitely lovely carvings and statuettes. Silver candlesticks frame them all, and underlying the smell of the fresh baking there is a floral scent, like fresh gardenias.

Mara feels she could live here forever.

It is enchanting, like nothing she has ever experienced before. She sighs and closes her eyes. It feels like home.

Yet not like any home she has ever had. The tears come unbidden to her eyes. These are feelings Mara has not allowed herself since...

Well, never, really.

She realises then that Mrs. Stevenson has been watching her. For how long she doesn't know. She is a bit embarrassed, especially at letting her emotions run unchecked like that.

Mrs. Stevenson senses what is going through her.

Her response exactly matches Mara's sentiments, as she quietly speaks. Her voice is soft and sweet, and as Mara hears her gentle voice in the ensuing conversation, the tears flow unchecked down her cheeks.

'Sorry Mrs. Stevenson, I... didn't mean to lose control of myself like that...'

'No no no, don't you go apologising now, m'darlin!

You have had to be so strong for so long, you've let your feelings freeze up hard and cold like ice. Let them fly right out of your heart like birds now. You're safe here.

Come now, my dear. We must sit out on the porch

and take some tea. It's a beautiful evening and there's still enough light for us to enjoy the garden.'

Mrs. Stevenson leads the way out through the French doors, onto a long covered porch facing the garden. Even in the fading light it is a beautiful garden, and the smells of the flowers and herbs are intoxicating. Mara can hear the bees and sees that even in the fading light the butterflies are still flitting about. One of them comes over and settles on her head.

'Now sit down my dear and have a scone while they're still warm.'

She has glided over in her wheelchair.

A table has been laid out on the porch with delicate porcelain tea things, and in the centre of it is a high cake tray made of silver, and filled with fresh scones... it's a scene that would remind most people of their grandmother or favourite aunt. Mara has quite given herself over to it, and all resistance melts away now as Mrs. Stevenson gently invites her to sit down in one of the comfortable chairs and she glides over to pour the tea.

In a few minutes, after her second helping of scones with clotted cream and homemade strawberry jam, Mara is ready to hear what Mrs. Stevenson has to say.

'So, my dear, you can quite clearly see now that I mean you no harm. I could easily have eaten you by now if I wanted to... not that you wouldn't be very tasty, I'm sure...'

Mara smiles. The old woman reminds her so much of her grandmother, it's uncanny. Even her mannerisms are the same...

'Soooo, let's see now, Mara. Your trip went well?'

Mara is on the defence again and she blushes. She has quickly moved, in a nano-second, from vulnerable and open to protective and guarded.

'Well... Yes. Thank you, Mrs. Stevenson... I er... I had a lovely time...'

Suddenly, Mrs. Stevenson is no more the kindly old lady; her eyes flash with fire and she is clearly losing her patience.

'Ah, come on now! Don't bullshit me, my dear. I deserve better than that! Those men meant to harm you and I stopped them. Haven't I already told you that? Didn't you get me then? What do I need to say or do to convince you?

Okay ...I know.

You need more proof? Well,

Those men in the Armani suits wanted information about a certain book. Of course, at the time you genuinely didn't know anything about it. But now you do. Are you getting me now?'

Mara can only nod. She finds her mouth has dried up.

Mrs. Stevenson pours her another cup of tea without

being asked. Her face is now softer; it has not lost its kindliness.

'Okay. Then, after the visit of the suits, you went to Guatemala because you were worried about your kids, who were off on an adventure with your brother Clarence.'

Mara is now quite startled and almost drops her cup.

'You were once again attacked by the men in suits once you'd reached the jungle, with your... mmm... Indian friend. ..(she winks slyly now, Mara blushes). Then, you were rescued by your brother and his foreign friend. The other professor. And your children. The men in suits came close to being smothered by a giant snake, I daresay, but then the foreign gentleman, the other professor, timeously arrived and kindly asked it to leave. Your brother then had no choice but to explain to you about the mysterious book in his keeping, which those men were after laying their hands on... Oh, and dare I add that the ancient and original bearer of this book of mystery was there too, and he offered you some of his divine nougat, which you couldn't get enough of... mmm?'

At this point Mara feels a bit dizzy. The woman knows everything.

'Of course you'll be wondering now how I know all this, but you must understand Mara, my dear, that things aren't what they seem! Let me show you.'

With that, Mrs, Stevenson makes a peculiar gesture

with her hand, and a soft light now slowly fills the porch. To her astonishment she sees that the light is being given off by a group of tiny figures. In the centre of this group stand a couple who are slightly larger, and who have a regal bearing. Mara knows who they are. She recognises them from the time under the waterfall, all those years ago when she was just a little girl.

It is the Little People. The sidhe. And are they pleased to see her! Several of them fly up and circle round her head, making high pitched sounds of delight.

Mara can hear the regal fairies speaking, inside her head.

'Welcome our dear friend Mara, how good it is to see you again!

You must not be afraid of Mrs. Stevenson.

She is our friend and yours, and together we work for the light.

These are strange times, and much is hard to believe and harder to understand. Your family are part of a greater plan, just as we are.

To surrender is to overcome... We know you have had to deal with some difficult things, and we know that you humans have to choose between things that sometimes can be difficult to discern.

Just know, dear Mara, that you must always choose love.

When we met you under the waterfall, we told you that we would one day be needing your help. That day has now come. Trust Mrs. Stevenson, as she will tell you what has to be done. Always follow your heart Mara, and know that if you do this, you can never lose your way. Remember: we are always with you.'

With that, the fairies suddenly disappear. The lights in Mrs. Stevenson's porch come back on, as if nothing had happened; and there she is, smiling at her with genuine warmth and love.

'Another scone, my dear? You'll find they're still warm...'

Mara is speechless. For a moment, she can't even think.

She pushes her cup and saucer towards Mrs. Stevenson, who immediately fills it.

'I understand how you're feeling now, Mara. It's like that for me too when I've been with the fairies! They have that kind of effect you see... But just see what they've done for my garden, won't you? They take care of each and every plant with loving care; just as if they're their own children.

The fairies have an essential part to play in the natural cycle, don't you know? Once we humans had a much closer connection with them, but now they've been pushed away into the wilderness and between the covers of story books, and we have no empathy with them in our very modern lives. It's so very sad.'

Indeed, Mrs. Stevenson's face is at this moment the very image of sadness. Mara remembers now how the fairies had stepped in to save her from her stepfather's drunken rage so long ago, by hiding her under the waterfall. She remembers that. And she remembers them telling her that one day they will be needing her help.

That day has now come, it seems...

Meanwhile, Mrs. Stevenson has left the porch and returns in a moment with something heavy on her lap. She drifts over to Mara and holds it out to her.

'A gift for you, my dear...'

Mara takes the heavy book from her. It is the Book of Kells.

Mara is astonished. She knows there is only one Book of Kells, in four volumes, and this is kept in a glass case in King's College Dublin. It is a national treasure of Ireland, only two of the four volumes being displayed at any time...

This is one of the volumes.

Mara looks open-mouthed over at Mrs. Stevenson, then at the book, then back at the old lady. Mrs. Stevenson laughs.

'Watch out, dear! You'll be catchin' flies if you don't close your mouth! And yes, me darlin' it's the real deal. Oh I know what you're thinking. There's only one Book of Kells.

Well guess what? There's another set.

That's the first volume of it, and there are three more.

And only me and the fairies know where they be kept.

Best ask no questions about all that, me darlin'...'

She winks a long slow wink, taking full advantage of Mara's open-mouthed incredulity.

'Folks think that the great book was painted and written and bound in the ninth century... Well, I can tell you me dear, it's earlier than that. Much earlier. The holy monks of Iona, and then those at Kells, kept it safe from them murdering Vikings and buried it. Then, much later, in the eleventh century it was stolen and the cover was torn off it and the book was thrown in a ditch, where it was found and restored. The cover, which was inlaid with precious jewels and gold, and which the elves assisted in the making of, was never found. That same cover has a very much earlier version, in another book.

The Fate Book. In fact, the cover of the Book of Kells, as wondrous and as beautiful a thing it was, was really a pale image of that sacred and mystical Fate Book.

Now here's the thing; the elves and the fairies and the beings of that order of nature have been feeling for some time now that it's right and proper for the Book of Kells to have its proper cover back. You see, my dear, St. Columba was a man who knew the Celtic mind, for he himself had that mind. He knew the old ways and he respected them.

And in his honour the Christian gospels were interlaced with the powers of the natural world and the spirits who move in her, such as the fairy kingdom. At that time, as it is not now, the two were one. There was no separation between nature and the human mind. That is what the Book of Kells would like to say.

And this is what the elves and fairies hope that you might do for them. They want to see The Fate Book. They want to make a new cover for the Book of Kells, and if it is allowed, by seeing The Fate Book, they also want to see if it'll tell them what fate awaits their kingdom...'

The old lady has spoken. She leans back in her wheelchair and closes her eyes, seemingly spent with the effort of her revelations. Mara is gobsmacked. She just doesn't know what to say. She knows her brother Clarence has The Fate Book. And evidently so do the fairies and Mrs. Stevenson.

She looks over at the old lady, who is now looking straight into her eyes. And there behind her wheelchair is the regal fairy couple, watching over her...

Episode Twenty-Two: Jess

Jess watches the skateboarders slipping and sliding and leaping on and off the stairs and ramps in reckless yet coordinated abandon. This is their world, reclaimed from the concrete jungle, marked with each individual's signature in graffiti.

She had come to visit a friend in Croydon, and this inner city buzz was new and scary and exciting and very different from what she was used to in the leafy lanes of rural Dublin. Her friend Katrina had once attended her school in Dublin, then moved away with her Polish immigrant parents here to Croydon, because they said that was where the work was. They had kept in touch.

Now she is getting to know Katrina's friends, who seemingly live out on here on the streets, skating on the edge. Some of these kids are unfriendly and even aggressive. The girls even more so than the boys, it seems to Jess. Many of them hang out in gangs and Jess has learned very quickly in the few days she has been here, to respect their territorial ways.

Just the day before she saw some of them fighting, gang against gang; it was so ugly and violent and so alien to her upbringing. It scared her, made her doubt feeling safe.

Now, when she passes a group of girls in the street, she averts her eyes, knowing now that any eye contact might be seen as a challenge to them, and might lead to attack. Yet back home, the very opposite applies. Not making eye contact would be considered unfriendly and anti-social.

Still, Jess is coping, and is nearing the end of her two-week stay with Katrina and her family. And the few friends she has made here are solid, and she knows that if she visits here again, they will welcome her.

So now she's leaving in just three days, and here she is outside the station waiting for Katrina, who is just coming back from London on the train.

Jess leans against the wall, indistinguishable from any other teenager, checking her mobile phone messages and emails, even though there probably aren't any.

But just now there is a message for her, just three words:

Fate Book Opens

'Whaaaat!

Oh My God!' she gasps, checking the message again:

Fate Book Opens

Jess cannot believe her eyes.

And there is no clue either as to who sent the message.

Strange. No number either. Just three words:

Fate Book Opens

She reads it a third time, and suddenly gets the feeling she is being watched. She knows something is about to happen.

She looks up, scanning the street. Nothing unusual. Just cars, black cabs, buses. A few people.

A man in a long gown stands across the street from her.

He looks a bit like that strange man she met in the jungle in Guatemala. The one who met her mom on the flight there.

The man with the nougat. Morka... something? She couldn't remember the name. Then she looks back and he's gone.

Did she imagine it?

Suddenly, from nowhere, a girl on a skateboard glides up to Jess at great speed and manoeuvres her board so that she stops right up against her. Then, before she can react, another two girls on skateboards come in from opposite sides and block her in, so now she has nowhere to move.

Then two more. She can now see Katrina just coming out of the station and approaching, but Katrina can't see her as she is now completely surrounded by these girls, and so Katrina doesn't see and walks by. The skateboard gang all this time have said nothing, but it's obvious they have Jess surrounded and she is too afraid to say anything or to call out to Katrina, and now her friend, for whom she has been waiting, has disappeared.

The girls, five in all, are obviously from the same gang. They have matching leather jackets and distinctive ear piercings with black skulls tattooed on their necks. Jess is about to pluck up the courage to ask them what they think they're up to when their leader, a taller girl with red and blue striped hair and knock-knees says,

'Shut it!' and shows her a knife.

'Move, bitch!'

She makes her point by shoving Jess along, in the direction of the subway underpass. The other skateboarders still keep her closely hemmed in, so she now has no choice but to go with them. No one passing by bothers to stop and help her, although there are a lot of people jostling down the subway.

As she and her skateboarder escort move down into the damp and smelly underpass, Jess is trying to think frantically of what she can do. She has noticed that the leader of the gang, the stripy-haired girl the others call Missy, the one with the knife, has a smart phone in her hand, and she can also see that there is a map on it that she is glancing at from time to time. Strange. Does that mean that Missy herself doesn't know their destination? Jess thinks now of Josh with all her might and sends him a mental SOS.

She knows he can't help her right now. He is on a field trip to Cairo with Uncle Clarence and Professor Wadji, but she knows that wherever he is, he *will* pick up her distress-call thoughts.

'Help me, Josh! Please, help me!'

In a few minutes, Jess and her captors are up and out of the underpass and on the other side of the station.

There are fewer people about, and two of the girls have now taken her by the arms, one on either side of her. Missy their leader is just ahead of her, while two others follow close behind. Missy stops for a moment, taking a closer look at the map on her smartphone. Then she has brought it up to her ear and is talking on the phone:

'Yeah, 'course I've got her, what you fink?

We're like about ten minutes away I reckon...

Whaaa? We've just frigging come from there man... you're not bloody serious, like we've just come up out of the flipping underpass. Get real dude! So now you're saying you want us to go back down the underpass again?

But there's like frigging well nothing down there... There is? A steel door at the bottom? Oh, alright then... yeah yeah yeah we'll go back down there again. But you'd better have the sodding cash... me an my girls is on the way... You want me to what? Come on! You're not bloody serious? Now you want a photo of her...? Yeah yeah yeah okay, I'm doing it now man...'

Missy angrily leans down and photographs Jess, who manages to scowl back at her as best she can. Then Jess is pushed and jostled back down the underpass again.

Just as they bundle her down the slopes back down the dim and smelly subway again, she is sure she has just seen that man in the gown again. He is standing a little way off, on the opposite side of the road; this time he is looking right at her, and he has just smiled at her, and he is nodding. She feels a surge of hope. And now, she remembers his name:

Morkabalas.

And she remembers the nougat. She could do with some of that right now!

The skateboard gang have been unable to keep quiet all this time, despite their best efforts. Jess has worked out, from their snatched and whispered conversations with each other, that there are twins called Shantelle and Shareen, sullen and solidly built girls with matching dreadlocks and serious skateboarding skills. She recognises them from a few days back, when she was with Katrina. They had been watching them skate under the motorway bridge. Then there is Moosh, the most cheerful of the five.

She is finding it hard to be consistently nasty.

She keeps smiling at Jess then stopping herself as she

sees Missy their leader glaring at her. She could be a friend if things were different, thinks Jess. Pity.

Finally, there is Scaggs, who is always lagging behind a bit, looking about shiftily. She seems to be the most dangerous of the five. She is quiet, has bad skin, dyed black hair, and a dozen piercings in her nose, lips, and ears. She doesn't talk to the others and is always alert. Probably she is on drugs.

Jess suspects she has a knife too.

Jess also thinks she knows their gang name, as she has seen it tattooed on the arms of three of the gang members:

'Chikkin Childrun' emblazoned in bright red letters, alongside the letters *FCK*. Could this be their take on the famous chicken chain?

They are now in the very bowels of the subway and there is no one else about. A dim fluorescent light is flickering. Ahead of them, to one side of the concrete underpass, is a rusty steel door, with the word *DANGER* and a skull and crossbones painted on it, presumably for those who can't read. The floor is wet and slippery here, and there is a dark stain running down the wall above the door, where the water has been dripping. It stinks of wee. Not a cheerful place.

Missy goes over to the door and pulls on it. It opens reluctantly with a nasty squeaky sound as its rusty hinges protest. Shareen and Shantelle help Missy pull the stiff door open. Inside it is so dark you can't see anything at all, and there is a damp smell oozing out of the opening. Jess is pushed inside and almost loses her footing on the slippery wet floor.

Scaggs comes forward with a flashlight and takes up the position in front of the gang, right behind Jess.

'Move, bitch!' orders Scaggs, who pushes Jess further into the dark. She can't see a thing. She can hear the door squeal and bang closed behind her, and the sound echoes into the space ahead, which in the torchlight seems to have opened up into a bigger space. There are concrete steps and rusty handrails leading down, and the sound of running water.

Jess is pleased to see that Moosh is next to her, and has thrown her a furtive smile. This is a dark and terrifying place, and even the tough skateboard girls are showing a little fear too. It is not a place for human beings. Jess is shouting out inside of herself for Josh now, and for the first time since she was kidnapped, she really fears for her life!

Episode Twenty-Three: Josh and Clarence

Josh and his uncle Clarence are also in a dark place.

It is the very deepest darkest place inside of the Great Pyramid of Giza: The King's chamber.

They are standing before a granite sarcophagus, or what has always been presumed to be a sarcophagus.

'It was always thought by early explorers that this was the last resting place of the fourth dynasty pharaoh, Khufu,' Clarence is now telling Josh. 'The puzzle was always: well, where is he then? No record of an incarcerated mummy was ever found.'

'Could early tomb raiders not have taken it?' Josh suggests.

'I mean, like... long before Europeans got here.'

'Possibly, Josh, old chap, possibly. We just don't know for sure. What we do know with certainty is that the pyramid was looted, and we also know that in the fourteenth century a severe earthquake shook a lot of the polished white limestone casing off, and this limestone was carried away and used in mosques and palaces. You can still see it there today. But the remarkable thing is the sarcophagus itself. Take a look. Look over at the precision with which the granite has been carved out on the inside, though the outside has been left quite rough... See here Josh, do you see the chisel marks? Then there's the mystery of the so-called ventilation shafts, which are really not for ventilation at all. So what are they, and why are they there?

What is terribly interesting to me, you see, Josh, is that I discover that these very shafts are oriented precisely toward certain stars in a certain constellation, and one in particular: Sirius, in the constellation of Orion.

Now, we find that this constellation, Orion, has a special relationship to the pyramids, of which this one forms a group, which when taken together correspond to the same layout of stars in the constellation of Orion. Remarkable, eh?

And even the approach to this chamber is all very precise, all very deliberate. There's nothing random about any of it, old chap.

You see, what we're looking at here, my dear Josh, in the King's chamber, is nothing less than an initiation chamber.

I have no doubt that the people who entered here were neophytes, carefully selected candidates who had spent years preparing for this experience: the experience of initiation. Let me tell you, this was not a place for the faint-hearted, and neither was it a burial chamber, like some of the other pyramids certainly are.

Yet, in a way it was a bit of a metaphor for what the ancient Egyptians did for those who had died.'

'You've lost me now. What do you mean, Uncle Clarence?'

'Well, Josh, the Egyptians believed whole-heartedly in the existence of the soul and it's continued journey after death. Much of their rituals are centred on this very notion. And I have to tell you now that what makes this pyramid unique, is that the souls who passed out of this sarcophagus in this very pyramid and into the starry heavens or spirit world, were still in their living bodies, to which they returned after their out-of-body experiences.

You could say that in this sense they were extra-terrestrial, as they literally left the physical plane, and then returned to it again.'

'Why did they do this?'

'Aha Josh, good! A very good question. Why indeed?'

At this very point in the conversation they see torchlight heading into the chamber. It is Professor Wadji Wadjiwadj.

'Ah Wadji, old chap! Your timing couldn't be more perfect!

Josh was just asking me why the ancient Egyptians, the ones who built this particular pyramid, wanted out-of-body experiences. What did they gain from it, he wants to know?'

Professor Wadji gestures to Josh:

'Well Josh, come over here and lie down in the sarcophagus and you shall find out...'

Josh doesn't seem too happy about this!

'No really, you won't come to any harm Josh.

I just want you to be aware of what the neophytes went through, in the process of initiation. Don't lie in there if it makes you uncomfortable. You see, before they were allowed to lie down here, in this sarcophagus; unlike you, the candidates for initiation had already been well schooled in what to expect. They had studied under men who were themselves initiates and had undergone the experience themselves. Then, to be considered worthy of initiation you had first to face a few... mmmm... let's call them challenges.

Today we have no real understanding for these things, but back then they were certainly terrifying ordeals, requiring tremendous courage and fortitude.

It came down to this: You had to face your fears and you had to overcome them. For the ancient Egyptian neophytes there were four distinct trials:

The trial by water, then the trial by fire, the trial by air, and finally the trial by earth: the four elements of the physical world, if you like. These rituals have been handed down throughout the ages in different forms, but they all have the same purpose: to prepare the soul for its journey out of the body and into the spiritual realms.

Once the person has undergone such an experience, it is certain that he will never again doubt the existence of the higher worlds, and he will know also that this is where his true home is, from which he has come, and to which he returns; again and again and again.'

'You mean, like reincarnation?'

'Precisely, Josh!'

'Okay, I get it. But... like, I still don't get why people had to go through stuff like that before they died. Just to really believe there is a spirit world?'

'It's difficult to see that and to really understand it all from a viewpoint of pure reason Josh, but have you heard of NDEs?'

'What, you mean like, near-death-experiences...? Sure, I've heard of those. It looks like loads of people have had them, and there are loads of books about it, and from the stuff I've read it looks like stories of these people who kind of died and came back to life again are often pretty similar.'

'Exactly! But the interesting thing is what a near-death-experience does for the people who've had them: They have no more fear of death.'

'Because they already know what's waiting for them on the other side when they die?'

'That's it! Can you imagine how life-changing that is?

To really know and experience, rather than just trust the reports of others. To not be ruled by fear?

There's then a certainty both about life and death. These initiates then became known as Immortals, because they had now seen the place of the Gods and shared in it with them. For them, for those who entered this very sarcophagus in this very chamber, they would have truly overcome death. The ultimate adventure!'

'Wow! That's awesome!'

Clarence smiles. He is so proud of his nephew and his capacity for understanding. Suddenly, Josh freezes and his smile slowly changes to one of dismay.

'What is it, Josh? What's happened? What have you seen?"

Clarence steps up close to Josh, who has clearly seen something he is not happy about, but whatever it is, it is not here, in the Kings Chamber.

'It... it's Jess... I can see Jess, she's in some kind of trouble.

I can see her in some kind of dungeon... Wait, no, it isn't a dungeon. I think it's some kind of underground place in the city, but she's really afraid! There are people there, who are like, holding her prisoner. Girls, but heavy, nasty girls!

I don't know what to do to help her. She's so far away!

What can we do, Uncle Clarence? She's trapped in there and calling for me. She needs our help.'

Suddenly, Josh looks vulnerable and helpless.

He knows Jess is in terrible trouble, but what can he do? Here he is, thousands of miles away, inside a pyramid.

'Calm down, Josh; let's not panic right now, old chap.

You see, in a way, we're always in the right place. Isn't that right, Wadji?'

'Certainly Clarence, that's true for me. Come Josh, we all need to channel our positive energies now. Let's take a lesson from the ancient neophytes who came here and not give in to panic and fear. That's the real enemy, believe me!

Now, listen to me Josh. Take your time and don't allow yourself to rush away with those dark thoughts; just breathe deeply and think of Jess. Good. Now surround her with your love, your positive thoughts of calmness and safety. She'll pick up these thoughts wherever she is and be able to grow strong through them. Trust the truth.'

The feeling in the King's Chamber has become calm now, and the three allow themselves to become centred and strong. In a few minutes they will start to leave the pyramid, and then they will have to decide how best to help Jess.

Little does he know it right now, but Josh has passed the first trial. More will follow...

Episode Twenty-Four: Jess in the Underworld

Jess knows that Josh has heard her distress-call.

She knows this, because in her mind's eye she can now see his face quite clearly, and she feels herself surrounded by a warm bubble of loving kindness, sent to her by Josh. It makes her feel calm and strong. She also sees images of her Uncle Clarence and his friend Professor Wadji. Are they sending her loving energy too, she wonders?

She knows they are with Josh, so it is quite likely.

The skateboard gang has taken her down some more steps in the damp darkness and the place widens out into a huge underground chamber, through which a river flows quite strongly.

Perhaps this river had once been above ground, and now the concrete jungle above it had driven it below ground.

She had heard of things like this. *Whoever would want to be in a place like this?* she wonders. Her question is suddenly answered.

Directly ahead of them there is a dancing patch of light, and a figure sits there on a kind of earth mound alongside the river bank, guarded by two more girls, presumably belonging to the same gang. It is hard to see the person's face. A hood obscures it, and it is covered in a kind of dark cloak.

The person is sitting close to a small fire. The girls step to one side, allowing Missy to lead Jess up to the fire. She watches as the two girls guarding the figure drop the hood away now, revealing the face of Mrs. Stevenson.

Jess can't believe it!

Is this the kindly old Irish lady in the wheelchair whom she has known all her life back in Dublin? The spinster with the lovely garden who always remembers her and Josh's birthdays with cake and cards? It is clear she has been kidnapped and brought here to this dismal place.

But why and to what end? Mrs. Stevenson looks up. Her face seems ashen, shocked into a frozen expression.

'Jess! Oh, how wonderful to see you, m'dear. I came over from Ireland to visit friends over here and… well… these girls captured me and brought me here to this dreadful place where they're holding me to ransom. And now you too. They'll l only release us if you can give us… them… certain… information.'

'What information, Mrs. Stevenson?'

'Well, it seems they want to know the whereabouts of something called The Fate Book. They want to know who has it. They've sent these tough street girls to get the information. They mean business, Jess. They were sent by the same people who sent those nasty men in suits after Mara in the jungle. They failed to find out, so now it's up to us... you. They know you have the information. You must tell these girls right now who has The Fate Book or you and I will be down here forever.'

The person looks and sounds very like Mrs. Stevenson, but then again, does it? The voice is flat and metallic. It doesn't even have her proper Irish accent. Mechanical and lifeless. Like Darth Vader or something.

Whoever this is has got to be using a voice-simulator, like dodgy blackmailers use on the phone, Jess thinks. And the face is hard and cruel and cold and there are no kindly smile lines. No. This is definitely not Mrs. Stevenson. An icy cold feeling comes over Jess. Who or what *is* this then?

Then the figure leans closer, over the fire, and Jess is astonished to see its face slowly starting to change shape, beginning to melt under the heat of the fire.

She pretends not to notice, to go along with the act for now. Trying not to give in to fear.

The voice continues.

'You must tell them, Jess. Please. Before it's too late for us. You and I could both die down here in this cold dark lonely place. No one would ever know...'

Jess looks up, just in time to see the girls exchanging looks, sniggering at the meltdown of the waxy face. Then she knows.

The figure in the wheelchair sees her look of understanding, knowing now that the game is up, that Jess has not been fooled. There is a sudden change of tactics.

The figure suddenly throws a bag of money in the direction of Missy and her minions and dismisses them all with a contemptuous wave of her hand.

'Thank you, girls. Your work is now done. You can go now. *Look smart*! And close the door behind you!'

Missy grabs the money-bag and turns away and leaves, and the other girls follow her away into the dark.

Moosh comes close for a moment and throws Jess a quick look of apology, and then they are all gone. In the distance, Jess hears them slam the metal door on their way out.

Now she is left alone with this menacing figure.

'Now you come closer Jess. Don't be afraid!

Your mother has not cooperated with us Jess. So now, because of that, she needs a little... pressure. I sent a couple of persuaders, but they failed to persuade her. It left me no choice but to use you, a pathetic teenager, as bait.'

Here the voice suddenly beeps and drops to a deep male tone, then back to its female timbre. The person tries to cover up by coughing. Jess has to stop herself giggling, in spite of her plight.

'Jess, I need you to tell me now where The Fate Book is... I need to know this right now, or else you won't be leaving here. Ever. Do you understand that, child? Ever!'

At this point, the figure stands up momentarily, then remembers 'she' is supposed to be wheelchair-bound and sits down again. Now, if she had any doubts before, Jess really knows this is not Mrs. Stevenson! But why the elaborate hoax? Obviously because whoever this is must know that Jess trusts the real Mrs. Stevenson... sad. Clearly whoever this is doesn't seem to know that the real bearers of The Fate Book are either Clarence or Wadji. Actually, she doesn't herself know which of them at this point.

The bogus Mrs. Stevenson now really seems to be melting. 'Her' face is dropping off to one side now, and she is beginning to look like the painting of 'The Scream.'

How is Jess supposed to take this seriously? Suddenly, the figure seems to have had the same thought and decides to abandon the disguise, opting to move from coercion to desertion. Leaping from the wheelchair, the figure advances on Jess; coming close for a moment with its bizarre one-sided melting face, the metallic voice whines angrily.

'That's it, Jess, you had your moment to tell me!

Now: Enjoy your stay!'

Then it bounds away into the darkness.

Jess hears the metal door squeak and slam in the deep dark distance and the figure has gone...

Episode Twenty-Five: The Underworld

Jess is now left entirely on her own. There is almost no light, only the glow from the dying embers of the fire, which is now only just keeping a ring of red eyes away from her. Rats. Lots of them.

It's cold and it's damp and there are other things scampering about and squeaking in the dark, and she doesn't even want to think about what they might be. It must be hours since she was left there.

Moosh, the only girl in the gang with a shred of pity for her, and probably at great risk to herself, pushed something into her hand before they all left her. Jess discovered it was a chocolate bar; one of her favourites. A Mars bar.

She ate it very slowly, savouring every morsel.

Then she forced herself to save the last third of it for later.

She remembers something strange about that.

When Moosh pushed the chocolate bar into her hand, she glanced around to look at her and for an instant there she thought she saw a little man in a blue turban and a flash of gold teeth. But when she did a double-take there was Moosh again, and then she was gone in a flash with the rest of the gang. Strange... just stress, maybe... making her see stuff, she thinks.

Now something really has changed. There is a soft yellow glow beginning to come from what appears to be a long line of drain covers, high above, in the curved concrete roof of this place. They had not been visible until now. She realises it must be the dawning of the day outside, and the drain covers are allowing, through their tiny perforations, a little of that precious daylight in. Soon, she can see more of the interior of this underworld. It is a gloomy, depressing place, like something from the Gustave Dore illustrations of hell that she had seen in the library. She wouldn't be surprised now if those winged demons flew down upon her! She dared not cry out, in case it attracted the wrong kind of attention. Trying to get help seemed futile.

Her mobile phone was taken from her before she was even bundled into this place.

She looks up suddenly, certain a shadow has just passed over one of the manhole covers above. She keeps her eyes on it, and sure enough, the shadow has passed over it again.

And again!

It's a person, not a winged demon. Jess feels her heart lift!

Does someone now know she is down here?

Once the gang had left, she heard the steel door slamming shut behind them. She knew she would not be able to open it on her own, even if she could find her way back up those awful slippery steps in the pitch dark. She felt she would panic and go crazy when the echoes of that slamming door died down and she realised she was alone with the dark, but then something happened to immediately calm her down:

She saw the face of Morkabalas right there in front of her, smiling kindly, then it faded away and in its place, there appeared a fiery sword, hovering just above her head.

The ring of rats around her retreated at the sight of the fiery sword apparition; which served to keep her from being attacked by them, all night long.

Now she looks up and she sees the fiery sword has gone, its purpose served now that the night is over, and she sees that the light at the manhole is blocked once again by that moving shadow, high up above. Someone must be there, up at that manhole. Jess thinks the manhole must be at least eight or ten metres up from the ground she is standing on.

In front of her, the river is a grey green ooze, and there are things floating on it. The water seems deep and dark and cold...

Suddenly, there is a bright shaft of sunlight, stabbing into the cavern; for a moment Jess is blinded by it. She sees a figure outlined by a halo of light, standing at the edge of the hole way up there. Whoever is there must have taken the manhole cover off and is now peering down the hole into the darkness.

'Hellloooo...? Is pretty little lady down dere...? Donn be afraid, is me! Is Quor-ta... l-eeeee-tzl! Remember me? I friend for your pretty mama...! In jungle... Quortaletztl? You is hear me...?

Hellooooo...?'

Jess finds her heart almost bursting with joy and relief. She can hardly believe her ears and eyes. But this is one person who could not be faked.

'Yes, Quortaletzl, it's Jess. I'm down here! Please, please help me...!'

Then she bursts out crying, both with relief and all the fear she has been holding inside. Up above, Quortaletzl is urgently beginning to lower a rope down through the hole. She can see it quickly dropping, until it's dangling on the ground, not far from her.

'Wait, I coming now! I come down... now now now.'

In a moment, the jovial Indian has slipped smoothly down the rope, and has rushed over to Jess.

He holds her tight, and for a long time he lets her sob against his chest. Looking around, he is appalled by what he sees down there. Who would leave someone in a place like this, he thinks? Even the jungles would be safer and friendlier than this. He is angry. Very angry. But right now, he must think of Jess and her feelings. He holds her away from him for a moment, looking her up and down, making sure she has not been hurt. He is a great big bear of a man and his toothy smile is like the sun shining down on poor Jess. He hugs her again and speaks quietly into her ear.

'Now, is okay now. Jess, is okay. You safe with me now... But first, you must eat and drink something; then, we get you out from this stinking place, huh?'

He quickly produces, from a sling bag a banana, a slice of watermelon wrapped up in a cloth, and a leather bottle of water. She greedily drinks down the whole bottle of water but declines the fruit.

'Let's just get out of here Quortaletzl, please. Now, please? I'm begging you! I don't want to be here one more minute...'

He nods vigorously, understanding at once. Neither does he want to be here one more minute himself. He takes a stick covered in pitch out of the bag, and lights it. There is a sudden flaring of light from the flames, and a bright halo of light surrounds them. Jess is glad also of its warmth.

Quortaletzl notices her shivering and taking a cotton wrap from the bag, he puts it around her shoulders. He is scanning the area, then glancing back at the rope he has just descended from.

Jess looks up at him and shakes her head.

She is definitely not climbing up that. No way, Jose!

She points up the way she came in.

'Up ahead there, Quortaletzl, do you see…?

There's a metal door, just up those steps a way off from here. That's where we came in. I'm sure you'd be able to open it.'

'Okay pretty little lady, come, we go there now, huh'…?'

He gently takes Jess by the hand and they move toward the concrete steps, now just visible in the light from the flaming torch he is holding up.

'How did you know I was here?

I mean, shouldn't you be in the jungle, in like Guatemala or something? And another thing, Morkabalas. I saw him in the street, just before they brought me here! Is he here, too?'

Quortaletzl laughs, moves his hand to her shoulder, and squeezes her.

'Pretty lady, you juss like you mama! So many many question! You guys is juss one big question!'

He is reassuring, this big strong man. Jess feels so safe with him, she hugs him right back.

'Missa Morkabalas, he one clever man. He is know you in danger. He watch watch watch, this many days.

Then he know I come to London, for go visit you mama…'

He taps Jess on the shoulder at this point, and melodramatically puts a big finger to his lips:

'Shhhhhhh... now you no say nuttin to you mama, is big surprise I is coming!'

Jess giggles, in spite of her ordeal. The thought of Quortaletzl romancing her mom cheers her up no end. It's a lost cause, but if there is one man who could do it, it would be him.

'So, Missa Morkabalas, he come to me at airport in London.

He come to me as I climb out from plane, he say: "Big man, you must go help little girl, she in big trouble..."

He know this before it happen. He special man, Morkabalas, you know, he have many big power... many!

He bring me here to Croy-down, he show me hole in ground, then poof, he gone!'

Jess wants to tell him how Morkabalas appeared to her and left the magical fiery sword to protect her, but that can wait till later; all she wants now is to get out of this hellhole.

They have now reached the top of the slimy concrete steps and before them is the metal door. Jess is breathing heavily from the effort.

Quortaletzl stops to let her catch her breath.

He is breathing normally; for him, the real ordeal is dealing with concrete, an alien substance. Jess can see the contempt he is feeling for this concrete jungle, as he glances back toward the river. In the far distance, they can see the rope dangling down from ceiling to floor, and there are thousands of rats swarming up it now.

'Is no animal, no plant here, no nothing. Only rat. Is dead dead dead. Like place of dead. Only, not even ghost of dead is here... is bad place... is verr bad place!' He spits with disgust as they reach the metal door.

With one arm, he pulls on the door, so hard that it comes right off its hinges and clatters away down the steps with an almighty echo. He hurls the flaming firebrand back into the dark, scattering dozens of rats which have been tailing them. They step through the opening, and ahead of them is the damp drippy subway and its solitary flickering fluorescent light.

This time it is he who must draw reassurance from Jess, and she tightens her grip on his hand, giving him a sweet smile as he shrugs and raises his eyebrows at this hostile environment. In no time they have ascended the subway and made the street, and people are stopping in their tracks and staring at this couple just emerged from the underpass.

For the first time, in the light of day, Jess notices Quortaletzl is bare-chested, wearing only tight denim shorts and flip flops. She is grubby and smeared with green slime, and her clothes are torn from being manhandled by the girls. They look as if they have stepped off a zombie movie set. Jess laughs. She doesn't care who thinks what; she is so happy to see daylight, and for a moment she stops and breathes in big lungfuls of fresh air.

Well, as fresh as air can be in Croydon, anyway...

Quortaletzl is frowning, not enjoying this grim place, so far from the leafy greens of the jungle he is accustomed to.

Though he is used to a self-steering car, he doesn't get trams, buses, trains, and unfriendly people.

Or the noise.

'Oi Tarzan, whatya done to Jane...?'

Jess takes his hand, ignoring the shouts, jeers and stares, and leads him away from the station, towards the flat her friend Katrina share with her family. For the first time, she is thinking how worried they must be for her. The last time they saw her was a day and a night ago. They would have called her phone, and got her answering system time after time, not knowing her phone was taken by the gang and was probably even now exchanging hands for the umpteenth time.

In a few minutes, they are pressing Katrina's doorbell, and Katrina's anxious face turns to relief as she sees Jess. There is a moment of shock as she sees Quortaletzl standing there half-naked behind her!

'Oh my god Jess, please don't tell me you've spent the night with this guy! Your mom will kill me... My mom will kill me, and my mom will kill us all!'

'Darling Katrina, now don't you get crazy on me girl, I've had a night in hell. Believe me! And this man rescued me.

He's a real hero and he knows my mom and I think he's in love with her and his name is Quortaletzl.'

'Oh... right... Better come in then!'

Katrina opens the door wide and lets them in; she hugs Jess but she can't take her eyes off this strange man, who is now tucking into his slice of watermelon. and, turning on his heel for a moment, sprays watermelon pips back out of the door...

He flashes her a broad smile and asks,

'Is close now, the Dubbelin town? I visit pretty lady, mama for Jess! I come from Guatemala. From jungle.'

Episode Twenty-Six: Back in the Light

Josh and the professors have left the pyramid and reached the sudden searing heat of the Egyptian sun.

On the way, they have discussed what to do next. First, they will go back to the Cairo Museum, so Wadji can collect a few things. Next, they will change their flights, so as to get to London and then Dublin as fast as they can.

Josh stands quietly for a few moments as they emerge from the pyramid, going within himself again, to check on Jess.

In a minute or two he has tuned in on her and has seen her safe with Quortaletzl. This is a big surprise to him, but he is very relieved and relays this information to the professors.

'Ah! Wonderful news, old boy! But what the devil is he doing over there?' asks Clarence.

'I mean, good lord! He'd be like a fish out of water,

Quortaletzl in Croydon...? My goodness me!'

Wadji is nodding vigorously, a sly smile playing on his lips.

'Mmm...Yes, I think I can guess where the big man is heading to, my friend. I feel this could be, shall we say, an affair of the heart.'

Josh and Clarence stare at him, but he doesn't offer any further explanation. Wadji, it must be remembered, is no stranger to the ways of the heart. Though he is a scholar, he is certainly no gentleman.

In a matter of hours, the three are sitting alongside each other, in a plane heading from Cairo to London; with Clarence and Wadji still tutoring Josh in the subtle arts.

Clarence has already called Katrina's family, who have confirmed that Jess is safe and is with Quortaletzl, and they will be travelling in a day or two to Dublin. Mara has not yet been told of Jess's ordeal; Clarence has sworn them all to secrecy. There is something that needs to be done first, and the news will only distress Mara at this point. It is better she hears everything from Jess herself.

Meanwhile, in Katrina's flat, Quortaletzl has been regaling everyone with his stories from the jungle. Jess has been laughing so much it now seems to her that her kidnapping is just a distant nightmare.

Quortaletzl has told them all about the men in the Armani suits and how he got them working at planting trees.

Amazingly, he tells them that they have both become quite reformed and caring in their own way. One of them has married a local woman and the couple are looking forward to their first child. The other man has become a fierce defender of the 'Save the Forests' campaign and is protecting the local people with the same deadly focus he once did as a hit man...

Quortaletzl has been able to connect with Katrina's family who have a lot of empathy for his feeling of dislocation from the jungles, as they are themselves aliens in this place.

It has been decided that Katrina will travel back to Dublin with them. The kidnapping has brought them all closer, and neither girl feels ready to say goodbye to the other at this point.

Finally, at Heathrow airport; Clarence, Wadji and Josh are reunited with Jess, with Katrina in tow. It is a joyful time.

Finding an unusually quiet corner in the departures lounge, Jess has told them the whole story of her capture:

How, whilst waiting for Katrina she was bundled away by the skateboard gang, down into the dark subway and then into the dark dank depths of the subterranean riverbed.

How she was grilled by the bogus Mrs. Stevenson about The Fate Book and then abandoned there.

How she was about to despair when Morkabalas appeared for a moment, leaving the magical fiery sword to protect her from the rats until Quortaletzl arrived, slipped down a rope and busted her out of there.

Clarence and Wadji smile at each other at the mention of Morkabalas. That's just like him, they think.

There a general sense of confusion over the identity of the bogus Mrs. Stevenson. Clarence is particularly thoughtful about this and ponders it for some time. Who could it be? Clearly the same person who sent the men in suits to attack Mara, looking for The Fate Book. And did that person have an accomplice? Someone who knew him and Wadji well enough to know their family connections?

There were all kinds of questions to be answered.

The unexpected intervention of Quortaletzl is a complete surprise though, and everyone looks to the eccentric Indian for an explanation.

'I come for visit pretty lady in Dubbelin, like I say. Then, when I reach London airport, Missa Morkabalas he come tell me to find little lady girl. He show me bad place in ground. I find girl, bring her out from bad place.

Is simple.

Now I go Dubbelin, see pretty lady...' He flashes a bright schoolboy grin, excited at the thought of surprising Mara.

It would be impossible for this little group to not stand out in a crowd, and so it should be no surprise that they were attracting more than a little attention. From a far place overlooking the departures lounge, a tall dark skinny woman is watching the party. She does not, at any cost want to be seen by them. And so she is heavily disguised with a scarf covering her head and dark glasses cover her eyes and the things she is feeling. Dressed all in black she affects the guise of a widow, as that way people will leave her alone, and will be far less likely to want to engage her in conversation. Or so she hopes.

She has a small travel bag at her side and the label attached to it shows her destination as Dublin.

Her eyes wander back time and again though to one person in particular: Professor Wadji Wadjiwadji.

She is looking at him with a complex mixture of emotions. Love, anger, loyalty, disappointment, devotion, loathing, affection, and even hatred. How can such feelings even live in one place together? It seems that in this person they can and have done for a very long time. She has known him almost all his life and virtually all of his secrets are known to her.

It is Mrs. Kofi.

She sighs.

If only things were different. If only Wadji had paid her more attention over all the years she has served him and attended to his every professional need.

If only he had noticed the care with which she made sure that he was now an internationally respected figure.

It was she who had made him that. It was she who

always reminded him of the papers he needed to submit for his memberships of this that and the other. She who booked his flights and hotel rooms, and looked after his website.

Chose only the most flattering of photographs of him, always those taken in his prime. He was, even now, she reflected, a striking and handsome man.

Perhaps less muscular and virile than in days gone by, but now certainly more distinguished with grey white hair. It was his fault that this was happening: he had courted her and dumped her for someone else after he had confessed undying love for her.

Swine! She wished the crocodile he had famously wrestled to death after falling into the Nile off the back of a boat whilst kissing another woman had killed him instead.

And how tasteless of him, she remembers, to have that same crocodile skinned, and to have had a handbag fashioned for her out of it! With a lapis lazuli catch, set in gold. Still, she is never without it.

She, Lydia, was a beautiful woman back then and even now she still drew admiring looks from men when she walked the streets of Cairo, between her modest home and the museum.

That romance with Wadji was forty years ago, but she felt it as keenly now as she had then. She had kept all of his letters.

How sad that things had come to this.

How sad that, together with an accomplice who had sworn her to secrecy under pain of death, she had concocted a plot to find The Fate Book and had set those men in the Armani suits on Mara. She knew how much it would hurt him to lose that book. She knew it was important to him, and even though he no longer had it in his possession, he keenly watched over it. She knew that from a cryptic note she had found in his diary one day:

The Fate Book, no longer mine.

Now it's someone else's to care for.

That was all. There was nothing else to provide her with a clue as to its whereabouts. But, she would find it. He would never suspect her of taking it. He would think it was the CIA or the Russians or MI5.

How sad that Mara had even looked right at her, not knowing who she was and what she was up to, when she was disguised at this very airport as a cleaner.

And the irony of Mara telling her she was a librarian and not cut out to be a cleaner. Hmmm, as if she, Lydia Kofi, was a cleaner... indeed!

And then, when those idiots in suits had failed her, and had failed to track down The Fate Book; how sad that she then fell even lower by trapping Mara's daughter in the subterranean wastelands of Croydon.

She had come close to succeeding there. She had come so close to getting the girl to talk. So, who had the damn book now? She knew Wadji had passed it on to someone else. It couldn't be that bumbling fool, Clarence. The idiot! How he annoyed her with his Britishness and his stupid mannerisms. But she knew Wadji was close to Clarence's family, and by hurting them she could hurt Wadji.

And then to be let down by poor technology! The voice-phaser had let her down at the crucial moment, and the face-mask, based on photographs of Mrs. Stevenson which she had downloaded from Mara's Facebook friends photos site and then had constructed by her friends in the Moscow Museum of Pathology, was clearly of inferior wax materials.

So Russian.

So now she would follow them to Dublin. This time she had a plan that could not fail.

Ah! The professors and their group are getting up and moving toward the boarding gates. It is time for the vengeful Mrs. Kofi to follow, but to remain unseen, unnoticed...

Episode Twenty-Seven: In Dublin's Fair City...

The party of Professors Clarence and Wadji, Quortaletzl, Josh, Jess, and Katrina arrived at Dublin Airport safe and sound and without incident. Except, of course, for the minor problem of Quortaletzl breaking wind on the plane!

For him, a man of nature, it was perfectly normal to do this. How on earth could one be expected to hold in what nature had designed to be let out? But after several complaints from other passengers, Quortaletzl had been reprimanded and moved to a seat alongside a group of deaf wrestlers, who were unable to hear his intestinal explosions.

Here, he was warmly received.

But, he had to be reprimanded a second time for arm-wrestling one of his new friends with such enthusiasm that he managed to break an arm off the chair and temporarily disrupted the entertainment system on the entire plane.

This then led to a new problem. Quortaletzl got bored and he had no interest in in-flight-entertainment, so he started making animal impersonations.

Firstly birds.

Passengers were alarmed at a series of very loud birdcalls and one of them called the flight attendant over, thinking someone was harbouring birds in the plane. They didn't realise Quortaletzl was making them, as there was no reaction from the deaf wrestlers he was sitting with.

They couldn't hear a thing.

Then he got onto the monkey sounds, and these were so lifelike that people became genuinely alarmed. At this point he was discovered by the flight attendants, and Clarence had to go over to them and explain that Quortaletzl was not used to social conventions on a plane and meant no harm to anyone. In fact, he added, this was simply his way of coping with the confined space of the plane.

'You see, you can take the man out of the jungle, but you can't take the jungle out of the man,' said Clarence sagely.

The flight attendants were sympathetic, after all, and he was quite a charming and childlike person. Meanwhile, Clarence remarked to Jess that if the man's courtship with his sister Mara was to have any success, his consumption of watermelon would have to be reduced in order to avoid these intestinal disruptions.

Wadji, as was his custom, slept soundly throughout the journey, not waking for the evening meal. A smile played about his face as he dreamed. If only he knew what deadly intentions were fixed on him from someone at the back of the plane...

Josh was attempting to explain to Jess what he had learned inside the pyramid about the neophytes who were initiated there, and how he had picked up on her distress, and Jess tried to convey what she had been through in the subterranean depths. They both felt there seemed to be a connection; a resonance between the two events.

From her seat at the back of the plane, Mrs. Kofi watched them all disembarking and she didn't get up until she saw them passing down the stairs leading to the tarmac. Only then did she take her small bag and follow at a discreet distance. She had a taxi awaiting her, and a room reserved in the name of Madame La Fite at a modest hotel in the city centre. She chose that name as it was the name of her favourite French wine, Chateaux La Fite Rothschild.

Mrs. Kofi, as everyone knows, was romantic, if not just a little vicious.

At one time, her name had been indirectly linked to an international scandal, when ten thousand bottles of the noble Bordeaux were seized by police in China. The wine was thought to be fake and linked to an Egyptian smuggling cartel. She was released by the police due to insufficient evidence, and somehow managed to keep the news from Wadji and her family.

And so her plan was to settle into her Dublin hotel and pretend to be a tourist, taking in the sights for a day or two.

She had promised herself a trip to Trinity College,

just to see the Book of Kells. She had always wanted to see it up close. She knew it was also something you did whilst in Dublin. Then she would do what she had spent months planning, in the event of the failures of plan A and B.

Professor Wadji would have to pay for what she'd had to suffer all these years!

Now her taxi driver stood waiting for her in the arrivals hall, with her name scrawled on a placard. Unfortunately for her, he had decided to announce her name as well, in case she missed seeing the placard: 'Madam Left Feet, Madam Left Feet,' he intoned, until Mrs. Kofi walked right up to him and hissed at him to be silent. She looked rather like Rhonda the anaconda at this point. Her unfriendliness did her no favours and the taxi driver refused to accept a tip from her on arrival at the hotel and couldn't help shouting, as he drove off.

'Fekkin stuck-up Frenchy buggers...!'

Not only were these expletives wasted on the doughty Mrs. Kofi, but they weren't even accurate, as she was Egyptian, not French. But this was still not a good way for her to start things in Dublin, as this very taxi driver had connections, including family working in the hotel.

He didn't notice the small man in the blue turban sitting in the back seat of his cab, who morphed into a leprechaun and back into the turbaned figure several times.

Meanwhile, Mara was delighted to see her family again, and was equally as pleased to see Professor Wadji. But, when she saw Quortaletzl standing behind them with a bunch of flowers in his large fist, right there on her doorstep and beaming from ear to ear with the sheer joy to see her again, she was completely nonplussed.

It was left up to Clarence to invite him into Mara's house, while she just stood there red-faced and speechless.

In his usual charming way, though,

Quortaletzl broke through her defences. It wasn't long before the two of them were chatting away like old friends.

After all, no man had paid her this amount of attention... ever!

The big man was bubbling over with enthusiasm. He had never left the jungles of Guatemala; everything he was seeing was strange, bright, and new for him.

So how had he ended up here, she asked?

This child of the jungles? He explained it was due to the charity that funded the re-planting of trees in the damaged forests, which he felt so passionate about, and which he had coerced the former assassins into joining.

That charity had decided that he, this irrepressible child-man of nature, would be the perfect ambassador to promote the cause of the trees, so they persuaded him to travel to London to address some potential sponsors, to show them his passion for the trees.

Of course, he quickly realised it was a short trip from London to Dublin, and the opportunity of seeing Mara was way too tempting for him to turn down. After all, closely behind the jungle and its trees, she was his second passion.

So now his eager childlike face was bright and joyful and full of promise to come. He wanted to see trees and forests and where were the fairies he asked? He wanted to meet them. He had heard all about them and he knew they were there.

Mara was astonished. How did he know about the fairies she asked?

When he was a child, he had been partly schooled by nuns in a mission in Guatemala, he said, and one of these Irish sisters had often told him tales of the 'Leetle Peeple,' as he referred to them.

He knew what part they played in the orders of nature, and he was familiar with similar beings in his own tribal folklore, as stories about them went back into the mists of time.

But he wanted Mara to show him where he could find them, before he returned to the jungles.

So, she immediately called Mrs. Stevenson to arrange a meeting with Quortaletzl... this would be interesting, she thought. What would he think of the feisty old lady and her wonderful garden with its fairy colony?

And indeed, what would they think of him? She couldn't wait to see how they would get on. In fact, she would not be at all surprised if Mrs. Stevenson was already expecting him, and even now she was baking a batch of her wonderful scones. She would want to be there herself, if only for those wonderful treats.

Now, in Mara's quiet study, at the back of her rambling Victorian house, the professors have set themselves up a temporary office. Clarence takes the spot under the window, where he can see out over the garden. There is a shelf full of oddities Mara has collected over the years; some of them are small antiquities Clarence has given her. As he casts his eyes over these familiar objects, a small carving of Ganesh falls onto the floor.

He picks it up and the tiny elephant god seems to glow for a second or is it the light catching the burnished bronze, Clarence wonders?

Or is it a sign?

Meanwhile, Wadji lays out his things on the other side of the room, on the bigger table where the phone and computer desktop stands. This suits him too. Both of them are always needing to catch up on correspondence, emails and calls and now this is exactly what they are doing.

Both on their phones at the same time.

If you were a little bird sitting on the windowsill, you would be hearing something like this:

'Yes, George, you should have the isotope analysis on that Sumerian jawbone in the next day or two and we should be able to date it from that... yes, of course, we'll chat then... mmm?'

'But I tell you, we sent that artefact by courier to the British Museum last week. Why can't you people not function when I leave the Museum? No! Never mind the cost, just call them... imbeciles!'

'Dan, you old cock sparrow! How's the masters coming on? Are you still preparing that thesis on middle-American culture? You are? Well, I've just been there and I can suggest a few new avenues to follow, but I'm not too sure you'll like em, old bean...'

'Look, you'll have to just tell them I'm in Dublin with Professor Kalikaloos. No no no, you're not hearing me, my friend; I said I can't do a conference now.

Yes... You'll have to talk to my secretary Mrs. Kofi.

No... Really? Where is she then?

Strange... she didn't say she'd be away.'

Then suddenly both voices stop.

There is a moment's silence, broken by Clarence.

'My God, Wadji! Look, The Fate Book has just jumped into my lap! And look at that: now it's showing me an image of Mount Kailash, then some caves underneath.

Do you know, I wondered why that little Ganesh statue jumped out at me a moment ago!'

'Oh dear, Clarence, you know I'm not good with caves.'

Wadji has unpleasant associations with caves, having contracted a lung infection from bat droppings. He has never fully recovered.

Just then, the phone rings again.

Clarence picks it up.

'Yes, Kalikaloos speaking... Professor Wadjiwadj?

Yes, he's here, do you want to speak with him? Yes, okay, I'm handing you over. Wadji, it's for you. Something about your friend, Doctor Pradesh?'

'Wadji here. Oh, my dear Kriti! How nice to hear from you, all the way over there in India! Oh. Really? Missing? I'm so sorry to hear that. When did he go there? Nearly three weeks ago? And you say you've heard nothing from him all this time? Yes. That's most strange... mmmm... Yes. Yes, would you hold the line for just a moment, dear?'

He holds the receiver against his chest and leans over to talk to Clarence.

'Clarence. It's Kriti. You know, my friend Doctor Pradesh's wife? I'm sure you remember him from the conference in Delhi a couple of years back?

You know, the anthropologist? The two of you

certainly had a lot to talk about then! Anyway, she says he's gone missing whilst walking in the foothills around Mount Kailash. She says she's not heard from him at all and she's very worried and says she lit incense and asked Lord Shiva for help, and then I came into her head.'

'Good lord, Wadji! Mount Kailash?!' Clarence answers in a hushed voice. 'The Fate Book! It's just been showing me images of that very place, and it keeps showing me some caves around there. Tell you what, old man, this calls for the services of a good tracker!'

Clarence is clearly excited by the prospect of another adventure and he is already offering his services!

He rubs his hands together gleefully.

Wadji rolls his eyes and goes back to his call.

'Yes, of course, my dear Kriti. You can rely on us, my dear. Clarence is a wonderful tracker and has offered his help to find your husband. We'll be there as soon as we can get connecting flights out there.

Of course, my dear, now you must stop worrying. Just leave it to us. I'm sure we can help... yes, yes of course dear, I'll call when we get there... of course... goodbye now. Goodbye.

Mmmmmm... I don't like the sound of this Clarence. Pradesh is a very reliable chap and he always calls his wife regularly when he's away.'

'What was he doing out there now anyhow, Wadji? I

mean, you and I both know this isn't the best time of year to be wandering around there in the snow.'

'I'm really not sure, Clarence. Kriti is so distressed she's talking erratically. Something about Pradesh studying the relics of a lost kingdom, and a map he'd been given by someone, and then again... a pilgrimage? I know Mount Kailash is sacred to several Eastern religions and sects.

And, of course it's said to be the home of Lord Shiva.

I've never actually been to Mt Kailash, but I have, as you know, visited other caves in the Himalayas. But, of course, you know, my poor old lungs won't be happy about this. They don't like caves very much, as you know!

Still, Pradesh is an old friend. I can't let Kriti down. She's so worried about him.'

Wadji looks over at Clarence, who is already packing a few things and whistling a happy tune, the way he always does when he knows he's about to go off and explore. Wadji sighs and shrugs. What can he do? What can he do when both The Fate Book and Clarence have now decided things for him. Then he pauses to think again, remembering something from an earlier call:

'Strange thing, Clarence.

I also just had a call from the Cairo Museum regarding some missing artefacts we shipped to the British Museum.

I told them to talk to Mrs. Kofi and they're now saying she isn't there. She's gone away somewhere...'

'Mmmmm... Gone away? I see. That's odd, old boy.

Not like her at all.

I mean, she never leaves her post, does she?'

Clarence knows this only too well, as he can never get to Wadji without going by her. She is always there!

'Ah well, I'm sure there's a reasonable explanation, old chap. I mean, perhaps she has some sort of a family emergency or problem... or you never know, an affair of the heart.'

Wadji starts to pack a few things in silence. But he is deep in thought and shaking his head. Where can Mrs. Kofi, be? he wonders. Where on earth can she be?

She *never* goes anywhere!

'You know, Clarence, it's strange, and it has made me think. All these years and do you know, until now I've never realised how fond I am of Lydia Kofi. I mean, she's always been there for me, and I've just taken her for granted, I've never stopped to think about how much she does for me, and how much she means to me.'

Wadji is struck with how he feels about Mrs. Kofi.

He has never allowed himself to even look at that. Until now, when he cannot think of life without her. Perhaps he should tell her how he is feeling, he thinks...

Is it too late?

Instead of responding to Wadji's ruminations about Mrs. Kofi, Clarence calls out for Mara. He needs to tell her that he and Wadji have to leave immediately and he knows she is not going to like it! Perhaps she will be too distracted with Quortaletzl's company to be too angry with him?

Episode Twenty-Eight: Mrs. Kofi Meets Mrs. Stevenson

Mrs. Kofi has now found her way to the Book of Kells' display at Trinity College and she is now standing before the bullet-proof glass display case, which houses two of the four books. It is so stunning seeing the books up close that for a brief moment she forgets her plans to avenge herself on Professor Wadji.

The colours are astounding: she has never seen anything quite so glorious. It seems to her that what she is looking at now is beyond the ability of mere human beings. Some Divine inspiration surely lives in this, she thinks.

Let's not forget that Mrs. Kofi has read everything she can lay her hands on about these beautiful books. She has full colour plates of them in her flat in Cairo. She has even discussed them at length with Professor Wadji, who, surprised at her interest in them, gave her many more books and articles about their authorship.

How strange that she and Mara share the same passion.

Now, seeing these original works at close quarters,

Lydia Kofi can no longer hold back her feelings. Not her feelings for the Book of Kells. But her feelings for Professor Wadji, the man she has loved all her life. The man she has never stopped loving. What was she thinking, she thinks?

Wanting to hurt not only him, but those close to him. Mara and Jess. Did she think that would endear him to her, bring them any closer?

Now she knows he will never forgive her. How could he? How could anyone? Who does she think she is, even thinking they could? She has never been convincing in her new role as an avenger. Not even to herself. After all, look at what's happened! Everything that could go wrong, has gone wrong.

Oh, God!

How she misses the wonderful Wadji Wadjiwadj! Does it matter that he never looks twice at her? Does it matter that all the care she takes with her appearance every single day goes unnoticed? Does it matter that he has never complimented her on her efficiency? Not once!

Oh, if only she could turn back time!

If only she were back there in her dusty but familiar office in the Cairo Museum, instead of being here, pretending to be someone else, carrying bitterness and anger in her heart for the man she loves. Unbidden tears flow down her cheeks. Against her will, she has been uplifted.

By the Book of Kells...

That's what real art will do, it seems.

It does not go unnoticed.

'Beautiful, isn't it me darlin'...?'

Mrs. Kofi tears her eyes away from the display and looks down to where the voice is coming from. It is Mrs. Stevenson.

This is a face she knows well, though she has never met its owner.

This is the face whose image had been so cunningly copied and sculpted by her Russian friends into the wax mask she had used to fool Jess. This is the real face of the real woman whom she so dismally failed to fake, in order to extract information from Jess about The Fate Book's custodian.

This, right here, is the real Mrs. Stevenson!

It is too much!

Mrs. Kofi cannot speak.

She looks at the old lady's kindly face.

Then she goes a funny biscuity sort of colour and her eyes swivel in opposite directions and she passes out, narrowly avoiding Mrs. Stevenson's wheelchair as she crashes to the floor.

Sometime later. Mrs. Kofi comes to.

She has been having a terrible nightmare about being melted in a pot full of chocolate faces. They are all faces of Mrs. Stevenson. She wakes suddenly from the dream, only to find the face of the real Mrs. Stevenson staring anxiously into her face.

'It's all right, Mrs. Kofi, you'll be fine now, dearie...

You see, I know all about your little plans, Mrs. Kofi, or is it Madame La Fite? Me nephew Paddy, the taxi driver, called you Madam Left Feet, didn't he, the silly boy?! No no no... don't you try to get up now me darlin'. You rest you there awhile till I've said me say. The security guards here know me very well, you see; and I've told them not to let you run away till I'm quite through with talking to you.'

'You... know... about...?' Mrs. Kofi squeaks, barely recognising her own voice.

'Oh yes. I know, indeed! I have friends, shall we say, in high places.' She chuckles, but it is a chuckle full of humour. Mrs. Stevenson is not the sort to gloat.

'Now here's what's going to happen, Mrs Kofi La Fite. You and I are going now to my lovely comfortable house which isn't far from here, and we're going to have a nice little chat over tea and scones. I know you Egyptians love sweet things, and by God, you could do with some sweetening, woman!

And there's someone I'd love you to meet.'

Mrs Kofi's head is swimming. This is not how things should be going. Not at all!

'I think you'll be fine standing up and coming along right now sweetheart, unless you'd like me to phone the Garda and tell them all about your treatment of the lovely Jess girl? Soooooo... the guards will be helping you outside and over to me little car, which is parked out there. There you are now, one on each side of you.

There.

Lovely.

Thank you, me dear strong boys.'

Mrs. Kofi is frogmarched to the specially adapted car, where she is bundled in forcefully alongside Mrs. Stevenson, whose wheelchair slips in perfectly with Mrs. Stevenson behind the wheel.

'Thanks boys, just follow along behind and stay outside me house, till Mrs. Kofi La Fite and I have had our little chat and a nice cup of tea,' she cheerfully calls out.

In a few minutes, they are pulling up outside Mrs. Stevenson's house, where the still speechless Mrs. Kofi has yet more surprises in store; as with perfect timing, Mara and the ever-smiling Quortaletzl turn up at the same moment.

Episode Twenty-Nine: Mount Kailash

As Clarence had anticipated, leaving Dublin so abruptly had caused a big fallout between himself and his sister, Mara, who, all the while he had been throwing things into his voluminous portmanteau, was going on about how important it was for him and Professor Wadji to meet with Mrs. Stevenson. And how she had promised the old lady that he would come:

'A promise is a promise, Clarence!'

And she was reminding him how typically selfish it was of him to leave like that.

'And it's Christmas, Clarence. You said you'd be here..!'

And how Clarence had always lived in his own little world, and he dare not even *think* of taking her children away with him again, *ever*!

And so on... even as he and Wadji were climbing into their taxi.

Ah well, that didn't go well. What a shame! thought Clarence as they sped to the airport. He didn't like to see Mara upset. And he could have done with having Josh's intuitive input on this trip. There was no chance of that now! *Dear Mara.*

He would try to make it up to her, he thought.

But now they are up in the air again and the plane carrying him and Wadji to Lhasa is leaping about like a grasshopper on caffeine. Just moments before, the passengers had been asked to buckle up, as the pilot said they were about to hit bad weather. Clarence had bagged the window seat, and he was afforded a sudden magical and tantalising glimpse of Mount Kailash, not very far off. It was visible through a filter of snow and cloud cover.

It looked just like its name suggested: a huge dome-like crystal standing majestic above the lesser mountains in the Trans-Himalayan range.

Mount Kailash is considered sacred to four religions:

Bon, Buddhism, Hinduism, and Jainism. Clarence had been doing some research, between airplanes.

He had also discovered that there were several caves in the vicinity of Mt Kailash, which were also held to be sacred and were usually included in the pilgrimages that were made there.

Now, with his stomach lurching, Clarence silently asks for the blessing of any deities willing to help out, and casts a sidelong glance at Wadji, bouncing about next to him, but his friend is, as usual, serene and seemingly oblivious of the state of the erratic air travel, with his eyes closed and a calm expression on his face.

But Wadji has been thinking about something else: his erstwhile secretary, Mrs. Kofi. He has been realising, all through this trip, how indispensable she is to him, and how she always has been. He is thinking how, to his own surprise, he still has feelings for her.

All those years after he dumped her. How foolish one can be in the throes of youthful passion? Did it take her sudden disappearance to put him in touch with those latent and undiscovered feelings?

Of course, he is totally unaware of the catharsis she is undergoing at this moment following her confrontation with the formidable Mrs. Stevenson in the Trinity College Museum.

He has no idea of the danger he would have been in, had he and Clarence still been there, boarding at Mara's house in Dublin.

Who would have guessed what Mrs. Kofi alias Madame La Fite had been carrying, in her small black crocodile-skin bag; the one Wadji had given her all those years back when he had wrestled the unfortunate thing to death, after falling off the back of a boat into the Nile, while amorously engaged?

The one with the gold-plated catch set with lapis lazuli.

Who would have guessed that in this very bag she had been carrying a loaded syringe?

Just for him.

The syringe contained an unusual cocktail of extremely rare chemicals, which once injected into the body, were not detectable. These very chemicals, which she had concocted in Wadji's laboratory late at night when there was no one about, forced the victim to respond truthfully and involuntarily to any question asked to them.

After their confession, the chemicals also ensured they would suffer temporary amnesia,

meaning they would have absolutely no recollection of being questioned, and none at all about the questioner's identity.

Clearly it was Mrs. Kofi's intention to forcefully extract from him the truth about The Fate Book's whereabouts. Her single-mindedness in this regard was quite amazing.

She had researched and obtained these rare plant extracts online, and had even been to a one-day conference on hallucinogenic and psychotropic plants, simply to get her hands on these extracts!

Little did Professor Wadji Wadjiwadj realise how much he owed to the good Mrs. Stevenson's intervention.

Finally the plane makes a very poor touchdown at Lhasa, with passengers involuntarily shouting out loud as they are thrown about like rag-dolls. Wadji finds his thoughts about Mrs. Kofi rudely interrupted by his friend Clarence suddenly coming adrift from his seatbelt and ending up on Wadji's lap. This would have caused almost-certain asphyxiation had

Clarence not clambered back into his seat.

Staring out of the cabin window now, Clarence can see a layer of snow has settled on the terminal building.

This was not the best time of year to be travelling to Lhasa.

April to October would have better, Clarence thinks.

Definitely not December. And definitely not now, a week before Christmas. No wonder Mara had been so upset. She had been looking forward to seeing them all gathered together for Christmas.

Damn shame!

'Ready, Clarence? Look! I can see our reception committee waiting for us.'

It's Wadji, looking perky and all set to leave the plane. With China the official but unrecognised caretaker of Tibet now, everyone travelling there has to have an official guide and driver. It looks like they have several.

Both professors are well known to the Chinese authorities.

Their archaeological services had been required by their government some decades before, in the uncovering of a number of ancient Chinese sites, most notably that of Q'in Shi Huang, the second century BC emperor known for his army of terracotta warriors.

Back then, they were exciting finds indeed!

Even now there is so much still to be excavated.

According to some Chinese writers, the emperor's tomb is surrounded by a river of mercury, and there are still booby traps protecting the entrance to the tomb.

In those days, Wadji had almost sabotaged their chances of being invited to future digs, by getting involved with the beautiful Xan Ku Li, fiancé of the ambitious young Chinese overseer of the site, Lu Kan Xi, who would later be promoted to the rank of General.

And so the young and lovely Xan Ku Li had visited the excavations with some students and officials, all excited about the emerging of the terracotta warriors, and in the enthusiasm for it all, had instantly fallen for his charms.

She had never seen a westerner before. This handsome and sophisticated foreign man had lost no time in exercising his considerable charisma. Who knows where it might all have ended, had not Clarence come between the lovers?

With his flair for languages, Clarence had warned off the exotic Xan Ku Li by suggesting to her in confidence, over a cup of jasmine tea, that although his colleague was indeed handsome and irresistible, he had clearly failed to mention to her that he was the carrier of an infectious and incurable disease, and she would be better off keeping away from him. Besides, he added, she had her husband to-be, Lu Kan Xi to consider.

Even now, the man had his suspicions and was probably looking into deporting the foreign devils who were already far too deep into the mysteries of the Chinese culture.

Clarence was certainly accurate about that last part, for the very next morning several armed escorts quietly manhandled him and Wadji and some hastily gathered luggage into a waiting car, and sped them off to Beijing airport, where they were spirited back to Cairo.

It took years of detente, a change of government, and some skilful negotiation on the part of Clarence, to restore the two professors to anything near their former respectful and scholarly position in the hierarchy of archaeology.

Now, after a four-day journey, with the party only a few miles from Mt Kailash, a swirling snowstorm has reduced visibility to a few yards. Even the team of guides appointed to lead them to Mt Kailash are confused about where they are. They have somehow gone well off the familiar track and have no obvious markers.

The mountains cannot be seen. The wind is howling like a banshee on heat and it is extremely cold.

Professor Clarence 'Stinky' Kalikaloos cannot believe that he had volunteered his tracking skills in a place where tracking is now, in these conditions, about as effective as an ashtray on a motorbike. He is ahead of the party, trying desperately to apply himself.

All he has to work with is a tiny pile of three-day old yak manure, and some spent tobacco from a shepherd's pipe he has salvaged from a snowdrift.

Wadji is looking serenely unconcerned. Perhaps he has too much faith in his old friend's tracking skills.

After all, this is not the first time they have come unstuck.

Suddenly, ahead of him, Clarence sees, or thinks he sees, a man.

A huge man.

All dressed in white fur from head to toe.

Before he can draw the other travellers' attention to this, the figure is upon him.

Clarence realises, all too late, that the figure is in fact a gigantic yeti, who has hauled him up onto his back like he is a sack of potatoes, and in an instant they have both vanished into the snowstorm.

No one saw anything.

No one heard anything.

It was that quick!

No trace of Clarence has been left behind.

After a minute or two of shouting vainly into the storm, Wadji, now a lot less serene, has given the alarm.

The guides have sent a message via one of their own trackers, back to the nearest village.

Clarence has disappeared.

Now there are two professors missing

What is to be done?

Episode Thirty: Mrs. Kofi Spills the Beans...

Mrs. Kofi is feeling very uncomfortable.

Not because she has been bust by the indomitable Mrs. Stevenson.

No.

Not because she knows she is about to face Mara.

No.

And not because she has just seen a huge muscular man emerging from the car Mara has just arrived in.

No.

She is feeling uncomfortable, because, without thinking, she has just done what any woman does when she is about to meet with two other women:

She has nervously reached into her crocodile-skin bag to find some lippy to dab on, only to reach into the wrong compartment, the one where she keeps the loaded syringe.

And she has managed to accidentally jab herself with the needle of the syringe she has kept in there so carefully for Wadji.

Suddenly turning ice cold in discovering her error, she has made things far worse by reaching into the bag with her other hand to pull the needle out of her finger, and in so doing she has now depressed the syringe and injected a great big dose of truth serum into herself.

And that's why Mrs. Kofi is uncomfortable.

And she can't, of course, explain any of this to anyone.

The security guards from Trinity College are sitting in their car at the edge of Mrs. Stevenson's driveway, eating Big Macs and slurping soda, and keeping a wary eye on her.

Mrs. Stevenson is gently but firmly herding the stricken Mrs. Kofi down her pathway flanked by a tall hedge on each side, and bringing up the rear is Mara, the mother of the girl she almost condemned to life imprisonment somewhere nasty in underground Croydon.

Mara is accompanied by a huge strong half-naked savage, who is tattooed and feasting on a slice of watermelon.

Perhaps she will soon be following that watermelon.

Things could not be worse.

Except... wait: there is no sign of Clarence or

Wadji....

Where are they?

Surely, they should be here too?

That would make her misery complete.

Does them not being here make it worse or better?

She is not sure.

But she is starting to feel a little whoozy now...

And now the procession has reached Mrs. Stevenson's front door, which has noiselessly opened for them.

Strange.

There is no one there.

But a glorious smell of fresh baked scones is wafting from inside the house and the place is welcoming, now Mrs. Kofi is feeling quite elated and her hair seems to be standing up on end.

And she feels terrific and all her cells are much more than alive and she feels about forty years younger and she is giggling a little and she just loves everybody now... and yes, yes, oh yes she wants to tell everybody about *everything*!

And stranger still, she can now see fairies everywhere, flying to and fro. They are the most beautiful creatures that she has ever seen.

Mrs. Stevenson pushes her into the house now, with the same gentle firmness, but she can't help but notice that the wide-eyed Mrs. Kofi is now beginning to behave very strangely.

Very strangely indeed.

Has the poor women become hysterical, she wonders?

Before she can decide whether to slap her out of it or not, Quortaletzl suddenly arrives, takes one look at her, and immediately takes charge, grabbing Mrs. Kofi by the shoulders before firing a a stream of watermelon pips from his mouth into her face.

She calms down at once.

Quortaletzl instinctively knows that Mrs. Kofi is undergoing some kind of drug-induced experience.

He has seen people in this state before.

Many times.

After all, there are initiation rites in the forest where he comes from, many of them induced by plants.

But they are overseen by shamans.

He will just have to do.

Still holding her by the shoulders, he is now gently rocking her like a child, looking directly into her eyes.

Meanwhile, Mara has found the crocodile-skin handbag, which has dropped from Mrs. Kofi's arm onto the floor, as she is being rocked by Quortaletzl. As she picks it up, she can't help but notice the now-empty syringe inside it.

She shows it to Mrs. Stevenson.

Aha!

They get it now; the woman is a drug addict.

But looking back at Mrs. Kofi, Mrs. Stevenson has decided that, for now, Quortaletzl is doing fine with her.

'Who you are, lady...?

Why you is here?' he gently asks Mrs. Kofi.

'I am Lydia Kofi!' she smiles back, eager and now under the influence of the truth serum, more than willing to respond to the questioning.

'I've come here to find out from Professor Wadji Wadjiwadj, who now has The Fate Book, so that I can steal it. I have drugs that will make him talk... only... now I've injected myself by mistake. You see, I want to hurt him because he has hurt me!'

The tears start gushing from her eyes, and there is no stopping her now.

'You see, I love Wadji, I always have.

But he doesn't seem to know or care.

And so, when I had persistent long-distance calls from some unnamed person asking me if I knew about its whereabouts, I tried to track down The Fate Book, by hiring a couple of hit men to intimidate Mara. They followed her to Guatemala, but then they disappeared and I never saw them again.'

Quortaletzl smiles broadly at this point. Yes, he knows about this!

'Then, using a voice phaser and a mask, I pretended to be Mrs. Stevenson, and trapped Mara's daughter, thinking she might have information about The Fate Book, but the plan fell flat...'

Now she is crying uncontrollably, and her words, though still coming out, are hard to follow. Mrs. Stevenson decides it is time to intervene.

This is enough!

'Now, now, now, me darlin; it's okay; you just need to calm down now. We all know what it's like to be disappointed and hurt, don't we now...? That's just why people do the crazy things they do, isn't it?

Revenge is never sweet, it's always sour, isn't it?

Now now, you just come over here dear and sit down and I'll pour you a nice cup of tea.

And you shall have a lovely scone and you'll feel better.'

Quortaletzl gently guides Mrs. Kofi to a chair and

eases her into it. For a while she sobs and sobs and sobs and all the hurt comes out of her body. The big man watches her with his head on one side, his face mirroring hers.

Though he has never met her before, he is caring for her as if he has always known her.

Mara, who all this time has only watched and listened and said nothing, is incredibly touched by Quortaletzl's compassion. Even though he knows what Mrs. Kofi has done to her and her family, the big man still cares.

Finally, Mrs. Kofi has stopped crying.

The drugs seem to have lost their effect now, and she is staring about her, as if she is seeing everything for the first time. She starts at seeing Quortaletzl's tattooed face staring down at her. He steps away and gives her some space.

She is exhausted after her emotional outpouring, but cannot remember what she has said, or to whom.

She looks from person to person, clearly puzzled.

'Why am I here?' she asks, though she already has an idea, seeing Mrs. Stevenson and Mara there.

She certainly remembers encountering Mrs. Stevenson at Trinity College, and she remembers being brought to this place. Oh, and now she also remembers accidentally injecting herself!

'Well, my dear, shall we just say that the bird has come home to roost?' says Mrs. Stevenson:

'You've just told us everything.

You managed to inject yourself with some kind of homemade truth drug, which you'd planned to give your boss, Professor Wadji so he could tell you the whereabouts of The Fate Book, so you could then steal it and upset the man and get your own back on him or something and now we know everything...

Have I left anything out, dear?

Good!

I thought not...

Now, will you be wanting some nice sweet tea with that scone...? Mmmmm...?'

Episode Thirty-One: The Yeti

Clarence has been having a dream in which he has found an enormous white bear in the snow, and he has reached up on tiptoes to see if the bear has a 'Steiff' tag in its ear. Then he finds the bear is alive and it grabs hold of him and runs off with him!

Clarence suddenly comes to and sits up.

His first thoughts are that he is alive.

And, to his surprise, he is quite warm and not frozen, though he can hear the snowstorm still raging outside the mouth of the cave.

He seems to be lying on rough bedding of dried plants and rushes in some kind of cave. Not only that, he is astonished to see, all around him in the semidarkness, statues.

Many of them. Ancient carved stone statues. Some of them seem to be Hindu deities; others even more ancient and harder to place.

He remembers now a little bit about his journey here.

Being lifted bodily onto the back of the yeti was frightening.

The creature was immensely strong, and carried him away as if he were no heavier than a goat.

Clearly, the creature had no intention of harming him. If it did, he would surely have been despatched already, and here he was, lying on some rough heather and feather bedding. Why then did it carry him off, and bring him to this cave? His answer comes almost instantly.

He can hear a voice, calling out faintly. A human voice!

Clarence sits up.

He hears the voice again.

It is coming from somewhere, deeper in the cave; just behind the statues. He gingerly stands up. He is bruised and sore after his ordeal, but he stiffly walks in the direction of the voice.

And there, on a raised wooden pallet, is the figure of a man.

He goes toward it. The man hears his steps and weakly tries to sit up.

Clarence is astonished to see the emaciated face of his and his friend Wadji's old colleague, Dr Pradesh!

Pradesh's face lights up at the sight of him, though he is obviously very ill and weak. He is lying on some kind of crude wooden bier, fashioned from branches lashed together and covered in rushes and dried heather.

'Pradesh!

Good God old man, what the devil are you doing here?'

For that matter, what the devil am I doing here?

I mean, what is this place?

Where are the bloody hell are we...?'

Clarence realises then that Dr Pradesh is probably too weak to be questioned. In fact, the man has fallen back and is moving his lips, but not much sound is coming out.

He must have used all of his energy trying to attract Clarence's attention.

Quickly, Clarence reaches for his rucksack, which miraculously managed to stay on his shoulders all the way here. In it, he knows there are some basic supplies:

Rice, beans sugar, water, and a battered old cooking pot, as well as some medicines and bandages and a few essentials he always carries on his trips, including electrolyte powder to treat dehydration.

And forgotten for now, but wrapped carefully in oilskin, in a leather bag at the bottom of the rucksack,

lies The Fate Book.

He takes out his water bottle and leans over Pradesh,

quickly looking him over. The man is uninjured, but is clearly dehydrated. From the look of his clothing and his beard length, he could have been lying here at least two or three weeks. It seems the yeti has done its best to take care of him.

Alongside the bier are traces of nuts, berries, and even something furry, some kind of very dead small animal.

Knowing the doctor is Hindu and therefore vegetarian, Clarence knows Pradesh would not have been able to eat the meat, and so he now casts it out of the cave.

It smells bad.

Turning his attention back to Pradesh, he manages to force some water mixed with the electrolytes between his dry lips. He swallows it painfully.

Now it all makes sense, thinks Clarence.

The yeti must have realised that Dr Pradesh was in a bad way, that he needed help. Was that why it had kidnapped him and carried him here?

Extraordinary!

And where was it now?

Probably rooting about outside in the snowstorm somewhere, looking for food for itself, and its two human guests. Clarence felt deeply touched, that an animal, if indeed it was an animal, would do that for a species totally alien to itself!

He watches as some colour comes back to Pradesh's face.

Then, he gathers some twigs from the floor, surrounds them with a ring of small stones, and makes a fire. Soon, he has a pot of water on the fire, has added some rice, beans and salt, and is whistling away to himself. Pradesh appreciates these homely touches, and though still very weak, he has already recovered enough to support himself on one elbow and whisper some words to attract Clarence, who dashes over and puts his ear close to the man's lips to hear him.

'Thank you, Professor Clarence. I was thinking that I'd die here... when the yeti left, I thought it had given up on me...'

'Well, stab me vitals, it didn't, did it?!

It bloody well came and fetched me, so I could help you, didn't it? Extraordinary! Now don't you talk too much old boy. I'll have us a hot meal in two ticks, and then you can tell me all about how you ended up here, eh?

But for now, you just lie down and rest, eh...?'

Clarence gently pats Doctor Pradesh on the shoulder and returns to his fire. The pot is already bubbling, as at this altitude water boils at a much lower temperature. He is stirring salt into the rice and bean mixture when the entrance to the cave suddenly darkens.

He looks up and there is the yeti. It is covered in thick, pure white fur and it is enormous. At least seven or eight feet tall, Clarence thinks. It has a bright intelligent look on its face. In a moment, it has glanced around the cave and taken in what is happening in there. It stares at him and frowns, baring its teeth for a second as it sees the fire he has made.

It looks from him to Doctor Pradesh and he can see it knows he is being taken care of now. Then, as suddenly as it came, it has left again, leaving a small pile of things at the cave entrance.

Clarence goes over.

It is a handful of frozen berries and a few twigs and leaves.

Tears form in the corner of Clarence's eyes. *For heaven's sake!* he thinks. *There is a ruddy howling snowstorm out there, and the creature has starved itself to forage something to feed them, at great risk to its own life!*

He shakes his head in disbelief and carefully gathers up and puts the frozen berries onto one of his battered metal plates.

Dessert.

He is not even sure that the yeti will eat it, but he leaves a small portion of the boiled rice and beans to one side for it, in case it does return. He puts the twigs and leaves on the little fire he has made and then carefully spoons some warm food into Doctor Pradesh's mouth, bit by bit.

It is slow work, as the man has not eaten much solid

food in days and he is not used to it; but his eyes open up and he looks at Clarence with gratitude.

Now he will live!

While the Doctor is sleeping, Clarence has taken a little time to explore the cave, which is bigger than he first thought.

It seems to have been a refuge for hermits and pilgrims for hundreds, perhaps thousands of years. There are homilies to the Gods wherever you look, carved into the bedrock of the cave. Some of these carvings are even painted, indicating to Clarence's scholarly mind that some of the artists had come here quite deliberately to do this. And if this is so, they can't be too far off the pilgrim route to Mt Kailash.

This is good news!

Some hours later, Doctor Pradesh awakens from a long sleep after his nourishing hot meal, and slowly sits up.

He is feeling much stronger and he is ready to talk. Clarence puts a little more of the dwindling supplies of wood on the little fire, and sits against the bier.

'Thanks again, dear Clarence.

You and the yeti have saved my life.

I think I've been here about three weeks now.

Look over here, I've scratched a mark for each day on the wall of the cave here, so there are nineteen of them; that's just under three weeks then. All this time, I've been looked after by that wonderful yeti. You see, I'd lost my way in the snowstorm, which has been raging without stopping all this time. I know, I know, don't tell me, it's not the right time of year to be travelling!

That's just what my dear wife Kriti kept telling me when I insisted on making the trip here...

But the thing is, Clarence, I didn't want to make this trip along with all the pilgrims, you see!'

He pauses for a minute to catch his breath, and Clarence waits patiently. How ironic, the *wrong* time of year indeed.

'Anyway...' Pradesh continues, 'I found a guide willing to bring me out this way. I was particularly excited about the trip, because I have good evidence to believe that there is, undiscovered somewhere in these parts, an ancient and unknown civilisation. It's astonishingly old, and I think it may reach way back to sometime before the great flood... perhaps even to Atlantis.'

'And...

your evidence?' Clarence asks, his colleague having said the 'A' word; never a comfortable word to mention amongst archaeologists. Atlantis is generally dismissed as myth, though mentioned in some detail by Plato.

'Well, that's the sad bit, my friend...' answers Pradesh

slowly, his eyes looking down at the ground.

'I lost the scrap of parchment, the map to the lost world, in the snowstorm. It's a long story, and I'll tell you the whole thing when I'm stronger, but the fact is, I've been researching for years now.

Briefly then...

Roy Chapman Andrews, the American explorer, who's the model for the film hero Indiana Jones, along with others including the Russian occultist Barchenko, were also looking here and also in Mongolia, for a fabled lost kingdom known as Agarthi, or Shambhalla. In fact, you see, I acquired that map from someone who knew the legendary Roy Chapman Andrews.

Now, no one seems to know whether Shambhalla existed as an ancient, physical kingdom, or whether it is, as the Tibetan Buddhists believe, a spiritual place only accessible to those who are enlightened.'

Clarence has been nodding vigorously at this last comment.

'Yes, my dear doctor, I'm not entirely unfamiliar with that last idea. As you know, your friend Professor Wadjiwadj has been my tutor for some years now, in that regard.

The ancient mystery centres are a speciality of his. I wish he were here now, in fact. He'd be most interested.

But, on that subject, I feel we need to do something right now, to let your dear Kriti know you're safe. And somehow, also to inform Wadji and the guides as to our position.

The thing is, with the weather as it is, I see no way of them making any progress, just yet.

Mmmmm... I wonder though... yes, I wonder...'

He has just had a thought, and reaches into the bottom of his rucksack. He fishes about, then carefully draws out a small soft leather bag. He hesitates for a moment, considering the wisdom of exposing The Fate Book to the untested scrutiny of Dr Pradesh. Considering the nature of their conversation, and the urgency of contacting the others, he makes up his mind, pulls out the bag, takes off its silk wrapping, and in a moment The Fate Book lies in his hands.

He touches the cover, which is slightly warm, considering how cold the cave is.

There is a sudden glow from the book, as if it has lit up from some deep place inside, and then the cover opens.

Once again, a sequence of numbers runs, quicker and quicker, then a series of broken lines and dots coalesce together to form a picture.

A moving picture.

Doctor Pradesh is amazed!

He has never seen anything like this!

Despite the weakness of his body, he has lifted himself up to get a better view of The Fate Book, which is now revealing something familiar; something that he has seen before.

It is the distinctive figure of his old friend Professor Wadji Wadjiwadj.

He is being shown standing knee-deep in snow. With him are several other local men, probably guides. One of them is pointing ahead and shrugging, like he doesn't understand or doesn't know where to go. The other men are standing sullenly and silently off to one side, doing nothing.

It seems clear from their body language that they are not happy, and that their leader, the man with Wadji, is saying they are lost, or that he can't go any further. Or both.

Clarence and Doctor Pradesh look at each other.

Now they understand.

Their friend professor Wadji, whom they had been seeing as their rescuer, is now himself utterly lost.

What are they going to do now?

Episode Thirty-Two: Josh Sees

Josh and Jess and her friend Katrina are sitting up in the tree house. Though it is December and icy-cold and snowy, they are dressed warmly, and holding steaming mugs of hot chocolate, with whipped cream on the top. It is warming them up with each and every sip, and they have cakes too.

Jess is telling Josh how annoyed she is with Mara.

'It's so annoying! I mean, Josh, like, seriously; why wouldn't Mom let us go with her to Mrs. Stevenson's place? Does she think we're like kids or something? Or does she just want to spend time with her new, like...*boyfriend!*' she adds sourly, looking over to Katrina for support.

Katrina has been loving every minute of her time here.

At home in Croydon, she has never felt truly at home, her parents quarrel a lot and it's no fun being there.

That is why she spent so much of her time in the street, skateboarding.

Josh smiles at Jess's complaints.

He has noticed how Quortaletzl's presence has irritated Jess over the last couple of days.

'Aw, come on... I wouldn't worry about our man-child from the jungle too much, Jessie. Anyway, I like him. He's so like, innocent... so harmless. And he's really funny... he makes me laugh. I mean, he knows almost nothing about life outside the jungle! Did you see his face when I was making toast this morning?'

Josh laughs out loud at the memory.

He had popped some bread in the toaster that morning while Quortaletzl was sitting at the breakfast table eating his usual slice of watermelon. The big man watched the toaster, his mouth open in astonishment as the toast popped out into the air, smoking slightly.

He leapt up and was about to throw a glass of water over it, thinking it was on fire, when Josh stopped him, explaining it was okay.

'Yeah, I know I know, he's entertaining, for sure! But, like, it's a bit creepy to me how he lights up every time Mom walks into the room. Almost like, salivating.

Somebody needs to tell him to give up on her.'

Certainly, they have all had to keep a watchful eye on the big man, and it had taken an age to explain the workings of the flush-toilet to him. In spite of that, Josh still found him washing his face in it one day, and had to point out that there was a washbasin for that.

Then, the big man was utterly amazed that water could be magically produced from a faucet at will.

He wanted to know where he could get one, so he could take it back to Guatemala and fix it to a tree.

Then he could show his tribe how he could produce water magically, any time it was needed!

Josh had to work hard on that one, showing him that there were mains water pipes from which the water flowed.

The hardest thing was persuading him to sleep inside; he wanted, in spite of the snow, to sleep outside. No, he would be okay out there with a blanket he said. It took Mara to convince him that the jungle never got that cold and that here he would definitely freeze, and then be of no use to anyone.

The television was the hardest thing. They were all relaxing in the living room and Jess got up to switch it on so she and Katrina could watch an episode of 'Friends.'

Quortaletzel jumped up in astonishment, wondering how they could be looking through a window into someone else's lives. Was it a box, he asked? How could he set free those poor people stuck in there?

And so it went. Aside from his self-steering car, he knew nothing of the modern world and its workings.

It was a relief when he did go off with Mara, Josh thought. Besides... well, he couldn't admit it to Jess, but he was enjoying Katrina's company. She, in turn, thought Josh was wonderful, and kept asking Jess questions about him.

Jess had confronted her on this issue as they lay in bed late the night of their arrival back in Dublin.

Katrina had to sleep head-to-toe in Jess's bed, and Quortaletzl had to be persuaded to sleep on the floor in Josh's room, rather than outside in the snow.

'You really like him, don't you, Katrina?'

Her friend blushed and looked away and fidgeted a bit.

'Well... yeah... I mean you said yourself, he's like the best guy ever or something.'

'No, I said he was like the best brother ever.

That doesn't apply to you. Anyway, look... the thing is, I'm cool about it, Katrina. I wasn't at first, when I saw you guys were sweet on each other. With your sheep's eye looks at each other. But now I'm okay... in fact I'd rather see him with you than some of the other girls around here.'

'Really...?

Oh Jess, I'm so relieved!

I mean, I have to go back home again soon, so I just don't want to, you know, get too serious or anything.'

She blushed again.

Then she suddenly started crying.

'Oh god! I really hate living in that place, Jess. I mean, your getting taken off by those girls shocked me into seeing what it's really like there.'

Jess went over to lie next to her, a comforting arm on her shoulder.

'I know, Kat.

I was thinking about that, too. I don't want to see you hurt out there on the street.'

The two friends hugged for a long time. Then Jess had an idea and spoke up.

'Tell you what; I've just had the best idea.

I'm going to talk to my mom about it, Kat. She was quite shocked when she realised how rough it can be there.

I'm going to talk to her about having you come stay here.

But not like *here, not in this house!* That would be too much for me to cope with, with you and Josh mooning over each other all the time! No, what I was thinking, is this;

Mrs. Stevenson used to have lodgers, and there isn't anyone staying there at the moment... I mean, it's just a thought, we'd have to ask her, of course,' she added quickly, seeing Katrina's face light up.

'There's the danger, though, that you could get really fat on her scones!'

Katrina and Jess laughed together then, and a small pillow fight erupted.

'So, we'll talk to Mom in the morning', Jess said and then promptly dropped off to sleep.

Wow! What an exciting idea! Katrina thought. She was so excited that it took her some time to get to sleep.

The following day the three of them finish their hot chocolate and cakes in the cosy tree house and suddenly there is one of those awkward moments when nobody can think of anything to say.

Suddenly, Josh stiffens. He is seeing something again.

Something inside of himself. Jess knows this and signals to Katrina to be quiet.

'Oh my god...Jess! Uncle Clarence and Professor Wadji are in trouble. I can see them in the snow. They're lost... no wait, they're in two separate places: Wadji is lost in the snow, Clarence is in some caves. In the cave there are like...statues and stuff...

He's with someone I don't know, like a friend of his? Oh, I think that must be like the doctor guy they went out to find. Oh yeah, it's him... and Oh my God, there's this huuuuge gorilla... No wait, it isn't a gorilla, but it's helping them out. Weird! It's white and massive, like a huge teddy bear type of thing. I can't see it now. It's gone out in the snow to get food for them, so it looks like Uncle Clarence is kind of okay, but Wadji stuck somewhere and can't get to him yet. I can't see any more now.'

Josh is back in the tree house now, but clearly what he has just seen has exhausted him. Jess offers him another cake but he refuses it. He is agitated, not knowing what to do next. Katrina has not seen Josh go into an altered state before, and she is looking quizzical. Jess notices.

'It's okay, Kat. Josh has, like, this vision thing. he sees stuff and...'

'Oh my god!' says Katrina.

'My grandmother in Poland has that. They call it second sight over there... what we call *Jasnowidzenie*.

It's normal for us. I mean... not normal, but it's not like, weird or anything for me. I remember, my granny used to tell us stuff she was seeing.'

'Cool... well, this happens with Josh sometimes, and it's always important for us when he does. It usually means we have to help out or something...'

Just then, they hear the sound of Mara's car arriving. The three friends lose no time in getting down from the tree house, meeting Mara as she is about to get to the front door. Jess wants to talk to her about Katrina staying, and Josh wants to tell her what he has just seen.

'Hi Mom! Oh, where's Quortaletzl? Jess asks, noticing he has not returned with her from Mrs. Stevenson's place.

'Oh, well he's just helping Mrs. Stevenson out with Mrs. Kofi. We'll go and pick him up later.'

'And who exactly is Mrs. Kofi?' Josh asks.

'Oh, she's Professor Wadji's secretary and she needed some help. Josh, you're looking a bit pale. Is there something wrong?' Mara asks, looking from one to the other.

Like most mothers, she can sense when something is up.

'Oh well...look, I think we'd better go inside and talk, Mom. It's about Professor Wadji and Uncle Clarence.

I think they're in trouble...'

'And also, I need to talk to you about Katrina...' Jess says.

She has not forgotten her promise to Katrina, and she doesn't want to waste any time presenting her suggestion to Mara, about her boarding with Mrs. Stevenson.

They all bundle inside.

The next hour or so is taken up with them talking over the crisis with the two professors. What can they do?

Mara takes Josh and his gift seriously. She knows they

must act, and she is worried about her brother now, and ever so slightly guilty about the harsh words she had with him when she last saw him. Jess manages to put over her suggestion about Katrina coming over and boarding with Mrs. Stevenson.

Mara thinks it is a good plan, but she is very distracted about her Clarence and says they will talk it over later.

Then she has an idea.

'Actually guys, you know what: let's go and do that right now!'

Jess and Josh are puzzled.

'Come on then guys! We're going to see Mrs. Stevenson right now! And I need to talk to Mrs. Kofi too. She will be keen to help professor Wadji now, I'm sure; and I know she'll have some ideas about what to do.'

They all bundle into Mara's car, skidding away in the snow and ice, and in a few minutes they have pulled up outside her drive. Katrina has not been here before, and she can't help remarking on Mrs. Stevenson's wonderful garden.

'Wow! Look at that garden! It's amazing! This garden has not been affected at all by the snow and ice... it's still got loads of flowers and stuff!'

And indeed, Mrs. Stevenson's garden seems like a little miracle. It looks completely unaffected by the cold weather.

Could this be the influence of her friends the fairies? They have no time to speculate.

Mrs. Stevenson's front door, as ever, opens by itself and she cheerfully calls to them from inside.

'Come in, come in, come in all you lovely people!

I've made a fresh batch of scones and tea, just for you. I know how the young people are always so hungry!'

Clearly, she knows they were coming. Mara isn't surprised. She knows the ways of the old woman. Mrs. Stevenson appears, smiling as always, with that knowing look on her face.

'Ah yes, it's the beautiful children, isn't it? How lovely you are, just look at you! And who would you be, me little darlin..?'

She goes up to Katrina and takes her hand.

'I'm Katrina, a friend of Jess...'

'Ah yes... of course you are... that's so lovely. And a friend of Josh too, of course.

Coming to stay with me now, are you, me darlin...? Well that's lovely! Soooo much better than playing about in the streets with all those rough city types and their nasty manners! I think you'll fit in here very well, my dear. I just know you'll be wonderful company for me too... And I do need some help these days around the house, you see.'

Oh, do come in all of you!

So much to say, isn't there?

We need to talk about Professor Clarence and his friend and how we'll be helping them then. How indeed?'

As usual, Mrs. Stevenson is a step ahead, and she has already told Mrs. Kofi before they came that her help will be needed too. Mrs. Kofi is now strangely tranquil and at peace with herself. Whether that is due to her recent confession or to the dual ministrations of the kindly Quortaletzl and Mrs. Stevenson's healing scone therapy, no one knows for sure.

But she certainly looks wonderful and radiant with the forgiveness offered to her by both Mara and Mrs. Stevenson.

However, she is a little unnerved seeing Jess here, although Jess does not yet know who she is.

Mrs. Kofi is about to step forward to offer her apologies, but she is stopped short by Mrs. Stevenson's wheelchair, which almost runs her over, bustling about at full speed.

'No no no, not now Mrs K... you can talk about all of that later. There's plenty of time for that! No, what we need to do now is to eat those scones while they're still fresh out of the oven, and when we've seen the sense that the magic of flour and cream and strawberry jam have to offer our brains, we'll be able to come up with a plan to save our stranded professors. Now come on Katrina dear girl, you come and help me with the tea things. We need to match them all up first, don't you see...? I know it's the same in Poland, isn't it now? Just like your granny's place, eh...?'

With Mrs. Stevenson and Katrina in the kitchen, Mara immediately gets to work with Mrs. Kofi and Josh.

Mrs. Kofi is at once back to being the efficient and thorough personal assistant she is so good at. Within minutes she has contacted the relevant officials and has obtained emergency visas for herself Josh and Mara and even for Quortaletzl.

She is determined to accompany them to Lhasa. And the big man insists on being Mara's bodyguard, though he has being living rough in the garden with the fairies.

The moment he gets wind of Mara and Josh leaving for Tibet to rescue the professors, he offers his protection and though they all have doubts about him dealing with the extreme cold, he will not take no for an answer!

Mara calls Katrina's parents, who are at first resistant to the idea of Katrina being schooled in Dublin, but then they finally see the sense of her staying at Mrs. Stevenson's and being closer to her best friend Jess. They had already noticed poor results in Katrina's school reports and showed concern for the delinquency in the area, and they know how close the girls are.

Mrs. Stevenson has already shown Katrina her cosy new bedroom, and she has made it as welcoming as anyone could.

Katrina's parents will visit in a few days to meet with the head teacher of the school and bring the rest of Katrina's things.

All being well, Mara, Josh, Quortaletzl, and Mrs. Kofi will leave the very next day, leaving Jess to keep Katrina company at Mrs. Stevenson's.

Mara can see that the old lady would love to go with them, but she finally persuades Mrs. Stevenson that her wheelchair will not cope with the snowy wastes of Tibet, and the girls will need her here more. All that remains now, is to get to Lhasa.

What will happen once they are there is pretty uncertain, but we are reminded of Mara's last attempt to track down her family, with little or nothing in the way of a plan.

Episode Thirty-Three: The Cave

Clarence and Doctor Pradesh are doing their best to conserve their dwindling food stocks. For Clarence, this is much harder than for his colleague, who has had to endure weeks of privation already. They are down to a couple of handfuls of beans and the same amount of rice. In addition to this there is also a large slab of fruit and nut chocolate, Clarence's little weakness, but he is saving that for later.

The yeti has not returned and it is now three days since Clarence arrived at the cave on the shoulders of the huge animal. Things are looking serious.

Although The Fate Book has been consulted several more times, it has not offered any more information.

And there has been no contact from Wadji.

Clarence is now exploring the cave a little more thoroughly.

After all, there is nothing else to do. He is astonished at the wealth and variety of the artworks. The workmanship is refined and exquisite. He has been making detailed sketches of some of the statues, and taking copious notes.

Right now, he is scrutinising a beautiful painted statue of Ganesh, when suddenly he hears what sounds like a distant wind approaching, rushing closer and closer.

Then the floor begins to shake. Gently at first, then violently. Small pieces of the stone ceiling begin to drop on him. He knows what this is.

It is an earthquake!

He rushes to find Doctor Pradesh. They need to get out of the cave immediately.

But it is too late for that.

A huge avalanche has already covered the mouth of the cave with snow and debris, and the doctor has only just managed to slip back inside, after trying to get out.

He and Clarence throw themselves under the doctor's rough wooden bed, the only thing that can afford them some protection from the falling stone.

The tremors continue for some time, then after what seems like an age, but is probably only a hour or two, the shakings subside, and then stop. It is pitch dark in the cave now, with the entrance completely covered by tons of snow and rock.

Both men are uninjured by the falling debris, although the tremors have stirred up a lot of dust, which they are now coughing up.

Clarence, having had the foresight to grab his

rucksack before he dived under Pradesh's rough bed, fishes about in it now, and finds his flashlight. He eases himself out from under the bed and looks about, keeping a wary eye on the roof of the cave, which is crazed with many small cracks, through which dust is still trickling...

Doctor Pradesh follows him, keen to keep within the pool of light thrown out around Clarence's flashlight. This has not been an easy time for the poor man. No sooner has he been resuscitated by Clarence's hot meals, than the cave itself has been shaken to the point of falling in, and the entrance is sealed from any chance of escape.

Suddenly Clarence stops, so abruptly that the doctor walks into him.

'Goodness gracious me... I don't believe it... look at this!

This is....'

Clarence is now speechless, standing there and staring down at what he's seeing in the light from his flashlight.

Doctor Pradesh looks down too. Between two of the most prominent statues, the floor has caved in, leaving a neat geometric hole, which at first seems to drop into the darkest void, but in the flashlight is now revealing down below the beginnings of a wide flight of steps, going deep down into the earth.

'Astonishing, my dear doctor! These steps must have

been hidden for centuries, millennia even... and now the earthquake has uncovered this carefully hidden opening!'

Clarence is so excited he is shaking.

In spite of the ongoing threat of the roof falling in, he is keen to explore immediately. Doctor Pradesh, still weak and frail, is not so sure he can manage such a thing, though he is starting to take in the implications of this find...

Is this what he had been seeking all along?

'Yes, Professor.

It seems clear that this stairway had originally been placed between the two statues and then, at some point a long time ago, it was covered over and hidden. Just look over here, how the stonework had been carefully cut and joined to form an almost seamless joint. Without the disturbance caused by the earthquake, it would have remained concealed, well...forever...'

Clarence has been starin all this time down into the pitch dark depths. Now he can work out that what he sees of the ancient staircase is beautifully fashioned from some kind of pink marble. Vanishing away down there into the dark, there are balustrades and handrails of a different colour, with flashes of paintwork and intricate carving, the like of which he has never seen. He can't wait to get down there!

He has also noticed that there is a faint draught of

fresh air blowing up out of the hole.

'Do you feel that, Pradesh? It's fresh air, old son!

My God, this means there could be another way out of here, somewhere down there...'

Now he is seriously agitated. There is no stopping him.

He grabs his rucksack.

'Coming, old boy...?'

Pradesh has no choice. He can't stay here in the cold darkness of the cave, with the entrance now blocked and impassable. And at any time the ceiling might fall in and crush him. Besides, it is exciting, and the adrenaline coursing through his veins is giving him new strength.

He chuckles. His eyes flash.

'All right, Clarence... let's do this!'

The two men ease themselves carefully down the opening, Clarence leading. He finds the first steps and carefully works his way down the staircase, then pauses and shines the flashlight so Pradesh can follow down after him.

In a few moments, they are standing side by side on a wide staircase which looks like it is curving in a graceful spiral, down and down into the depths.

Clarence notices that as the stair is constructed in a

spiral, it is widening as they go down, as is the space below...

With the limited light from his flashlight, the walls are showing up the most incredible murals, which have been preserved in the dark. There are colours and forms unlike anything he has seen in his long career.

He and Pradesh are silent and still, quietly absorbing the wonder of it all. But then, from above them, there comes an ominous familiar rumbling sound. Everything rattles and vibrates. Pieces of stone and dust begin to fall down on them. Quickly they advance further down the sweeping staircase.

But not a moment too soon!

With a tremendous deafening roar and a crash, the ceiling of the cave they were standing in not a few minutes before, suddenly falls in. Huge stones rumble and bounce down past them, as they crouch as far away from the opening as they can, with their hands over their mouths and noses to keep out the dust.

In a few seconds, it is all over. The noise stops.

The place is now thick with dust and debris.

The marvel though, is that because the ceiling of the cave has now completely collapsed, daylight has broken through, and suddenly the men are able to clearly see the lit-up interior of the space they are in for the first time.

Clarence is astonished. What he can now see completely baffles him. The walls are encrusted with crystals.

They are set into the walls seamlessly, as if they have been pressed into it without force. These crystals are huge, and of many different colours. Having learned his lesson from the walls of the Mayan pyramid, Clarence does not touch them, though he is sorely tempted. With daylight reaching into the deeper parts of this vast cathedral-like space; the symbols and paintings, punctuated by the crystals, are now revealed.

Neither Clarence nor Doctor Pradesh have any prior experience of the things they are seeing. This is clearly from another civilisation, another time, even another dimension.

Somehow there is a purposeful mathematical and geometric sense to all this, Clarence thinks. In fact, he can't help noticing that, just as he focuses on one area of the wall, the crystals there begin to glow. One of them even starts rotating, and there is a gentle, bell-like sound coming from it.

Down below them, where the staircase reaches a vast paved floor, the shaft of daylight is revealing a series of passages going off, like the spokes of a wheel.

It is still some way off, and the two men slowly make their way down, unable to take their eyes off the walls.

Back to Professor Wadji Wadjiwadj.

When Clarence last consulted The Fate Book, he was shown images of Professor Wadji standing knee-deep in the snow. He was with a guide who was pointing ahead and shrugging, and the group of guides and trackers with him were refusing to go on.

It appeared hopeless both for them and for any chance of Clarence and Pradesh being rescued.

'But we *must* keep going, we can't give up now!

It really can't be far now, I'm sure of it...' Wadji is arguing with the lead tracker and guide.

'No. Is no good! Is too much snow, more is coming... no tracks...' The guide shrugs and points ahead, signalling that it is hopeless to continue.

What is he to do? Even now, his friend Professor Clarence may be in mortal danger, freezing in the snow or starving to death. And what about Doctor Pradesh? How he is chiding himself now for not bringing the pair of satellite telephones they normally carry on such trips? It was, ironically Clarence who had left them in Mara's study in Dublin, insisting they were far too heavy and they should travel light in the snow.

Now the trackers and guides are warning that more snow is on the way. They want to return right now to the safety of their villages.

Wadji thinks for a minute.

He has enough food and provisions in his rucksack

for several more days. For himself and two others.

He makes a decision and goes over to the trackers.

'You can go back to your villages now. Leave me here; I'll carry on, on my own. But there's something I want you to do for me. I want you to go back and get help in Lhasa, and to send a party after us once the snow has settled.

Now please take this note with you, and leave someone to wait at Lhasa for a few days. Pass the note on to any parties that may have arrived at Lhasa airport, looking for me or Professor Kalikaloos or Doctor Pradesh.

Do you understand?'

Wadji is acting on a strong hunch. He has a feeling that not having had any contact from them for several days, Mara might have acted on her own accord and put a plan together. Little does he know that this is, in fact, exactly what has already happened. Acting on the message that Josh has received intuitively, Mara, Josh, Quortaletzl, and Mrs. Kofi are at this very moment making their way from Lhasa airport. They are a two day walk away.

So the trackers have now set off, pleased to be going home; leaving Wadji on his own, with extra provisions. He is taking a gamble, but something tells him that it's the right thing to do. After all, how can he relax when his dear friend Clarence has been missing for three days?

Wadji closes his eyes, looking for and finding his still calm place inside. He knows that whatever happens, he needs to stay centred and focussed and not give in to fear.

Suddenly, with his eyes closed, he hears something close by and feels a warm breath on his face. He opens his eyes, and to his surprise, right there in front of himis the huge face of a gigantic snow-white yeti.

The yeti does not flinch. It is looking him directly in the eye.

Wadji stares right back, and in his mind, he receives, telepathically from the yeti, an image of his friend, Professor Clarence. He sees him sitting in a cave with Doctor Pradesh.

The yeti then turns away, and runs on ahead, into the snow.

It stops for a moment, looking back, as if to say:

Well, are you coming then...?

And so it goes. The yeti running on ahead, then waiting as Professor Wadji follows. It is slow progress, as the snow is deep. Finally, the yeti loses patience. Running back to him, it lifts Wadji gently up and over its shoulders, then it takes off with him wrapped across its huge shoulders, bounding through the snow.

Professor Wadji, at first a little alarmed by this passive transport system, realises it's best to give in, as after all, he now trusts the big animal, and is beginning to put two and two together. Did the yeti in fact take Clarence off to Doctor Pradesh, perhaps in exactly this way?

What a remarkable creature! And for it to somehow sense that Clarence and Wadji are connected?

Amazing!

After a time, the big animal slows down and then stops. Wadji can see it sniffing the air. Then it puts him down. They must be near now, thinks Wadji... Yes, there it is! He can see the mouth of a cave ahead, about fifty metres away.

This must be the place.

Suddenly, the yeti seems alarmed. It stands stiffly, then whines strangely... and Wadji can feel it too. What seems like a loud wind coming towards them from the distance, closer and closer, and then the ground begins to shake.

It is an earthquake.

An avalanche of snow and debris falls down, as they watch, which completely blocks the entrance to the cave. The yeti can do no more than respond to its deepest instincts. It turns and runs away into the snow...

And so Professor Wadji Wadjiwadj is left there quite alone once more, it seems.

Episode Thirty-Four: The Lost Kingdom

Clarence and Doctor Pradesh are in Heaven.

Doctor Pradesh is realising that the lost kingdom he had risked so much to find, was right underneath him all the time he was lying there on his back being fed by the mysterious yeti.

Not only that, but this wonderful and mysterious yeti had brought him further help in the form of Professor Clarence, who just happened to be one of the world's foremost authorities on ancient cultures and archaeology.

What forces were at work in such things?

He wishes he were able to reward the creature for its incredible efforts.

Clarence is equally ecstatic. Never in his wildest dreams would he have imagined he would now be exploring a lost civilisation, which was looking to him, more and more like the lost and disputed civilisation of Atlantis.

He had a couple of regrets though, in the midst of this.

One: he had not packed a camera to record these incredible sights, and two, his friend Wadji was not there with him to share in his joy. Also, he is now extremely hungry. He and Pradesh have just eaten the last of the rice and beans. All they have left now is the emergency slab of chocolate.

There is definitely a supply of fresh air, coming from somewhere ahead. And when he is able to gather his thoughts, after all the excitement of finding this amazing place, Clarence deduces that this means there has to be another secret opening into this place.

But how far ahead is that?

And will they be able to last the journey with so little left to nourish them? Would they rather go back, since the earthquake has opened up the roof of the cave? Would that be more sensible now?

And so hunger wins over curiosity. He and Pradesh decide that, in spite of their curiosity about what lies ahead, they need to return to the cave. They need to go back, up the staircase and over that pile of debris formed by the rockfall from the collapsed cave.

So, after negotiating the rubble and at times having to scramble on their hands and knees, Clarence and Pradesh, with a last lingering look back at the ancient kingdom they have just discovered, are finally able to climb up through what was the roof of their erstwhile cave.

How sweet is the fresh Himalayan air as they clamber up and out through the snow!

And how complete is their utter surprise to come face to face with Professor Wadji Wadiwadj, who at that instant is about to look down into the very opening they are emerging from. Having realised that the earthquake that separated him from the fleeing yeti had also closed up the mouth of the cave almost immediately that he had seen it, and perhaps there was a way in from above the blocked entrance, he had climbed up and found the opening.

There is wild and unrestrained jubilation. Three academics are behaving in a most un-academic manner, whooping and hugging each other and even throwing snowballs at each other. They are like children let loose in the park. When they have gotten over their sheer joy at being re-united, Clarence and Pradesh almost fight each other to tell Wadji what they have just found, or more correctly, what the earthquake has revealed to them down below the floor of the cave.

He can't wait to be shown.

But first, he insists, they need food and water. As he unpacks the provisions, Wadji manages to get a word in edgeways. He tells them he was led, and in fact, carried part of the way there by a giant white yeti, which then fled at the onset of the earthquake.

At this news, Clarence and Pradesh look at each other and fall silent, and Pradesh drops to his knees, tearfully offering thanks to his lord Shiva.

Wadji loses no time now in sharing his provisions with the two hungry men, and for a few minutes there is only the happy sound of food being munched. Clarence and Pradesh are particularly delighted to be eating something other than beans and rice. Wadji has thoughtfully also thrown in a handful of dates, which right now are a welcome energy boost.

He expresses his relief at finding his friends after the shock of the earthquake, when the yeti ran off, leaving him there quite alone.

Clarence responds.

'Absolutely, my dear Wadji. Well you can only imagine how astonishing it was for us too, when the earthquake opened up a tantalising view of a vanished world, right there, under our very feet. And just because we decided right then and there to get down there and explore it, we were saved from being crushed by the cave roof falling in a little while later.'

'Yes, indeed, that's remarkable... I can't wait to see it for myself. Of course, we must now also think of a way to let poor Kriti know that you're safe, Pradesh. It's a shame we decided against bringing the satellite phone, Clarence. I'm sure you were thinking the same thing. Also, if we're going to explore the caves below us here right now, I'd suggest we leave some kind of makeshift flag up here to attract the attention of anyone coming this way. Some bright clothing perhaps?

I sent out word with my former guides and trackers to inform any would-be rescuers as to my approximate location when they decided to abandon me... perhaps that will draw someone. I suspect we aren't far off the ancient pilgrim's trail anyhow.'

'True, my dear Wadji, very true! When we go back inside, you'll see plenty of evidence that this cave, or what's left of it, is indeed on that trail. Looks like it has been used as a way-station for a devil of a long time. But I'm thinking that perhaps it's time we consulted The Fate Book again?

Last time I did that it showed you up somewhere on the way, Wadji, and that gave us hope, although your jolly old guides weren't showing much enthusiasm!'

Soon Clarence has retrieved The Fate Book from its place in his rucksack, and in a moment it is open in his hands. As usual, it shows some static and then settles into a number sequence, finally focussing on some images. The scene that now shows itself is at once a surprise and a relief.

They see Mara, Josh, Quortaletzl, and Mrs. Kofi. There is a sudden intake of breath from Wadji. Mrs. Kofi is the last person he is expecting to see. Then they see these three in conversation with the very guides who deserted Wadji.

It appears the guides are showing contrition at having left Wadji in the snow, especially since they now know there has been a powerful earthquake. Anything could have happened to them. The trackers are indicating that they are willing to take the new arrivals to the last place they saw Wadji or this seems to be what they are showing via their body language.

And there is something else that The Fate Book is now also showing them. Even as the guides are speaking to Mara, Josh, Quortaletzl, and Mrs. Kofi; their little group is being watched by the great white yeti. This throws up a cheer from all three men, they have grown fond of the yeti, and it appears the animal has not given up on helping them.

Also, it seems, from the way in which Josh has his eyes closed and is smiling, that he is picking up on the lost professors too. They can't be too far off!

They are much cheered up by The Fate Book's revelations, and immediately they prepare to leave a colourful flag to indicate their position.

In any case, it will be far warmer waiting down there inside the subterranean passages, than out here in the snow.

In a few minutes, they are climbing carefully back down, into the collapsed cave. On the way down, Wadji is shown the statues. Most of them are still intact, as the collapsed cave ceiling has not covered more than three or four of them. Wadji is amazed at their splendour, and their incredible age. Like Clarence, he is sure that pilgrims from the remote past would have come here deliberately to carve and paint the statues.

But now he is even more excited by the hole in the floor of the cave, through which Clarence and Wadji were shown the far more ancient remains of an antediluvian culture.

Now, as the three men descend the beautiful marble staircase, they have extra light to see by.

Wadji has brought with him an additional state-of-the-art flashlight. Mrs. Kofi had insisted on buying it for him a year or two back. Bless her, he thinks. Soon he will be able to thank her in person for her foresight.

He is truly amazed by what he is seeing.

He and Clarence are immediately in an academic huddle with Doctor Pradesh.

What is this? They have no prior reference for this.

At first, Wadji had assumed it was an ancient Tibetan culture, but he quickly realises this is far older than that. The glowing crystals set into the walls are a clue as to their Atlantean origins. Not only that, but the symbols inscribed and carved into the walls are completely unknown to any of these men.

And they are world authorities on ancient cultures.

They are so excited they can barely contain themselves.

Wadji has brought a digital camera with him.

He immediately gets to work photographing whatever he can. Fortunately, thanks again to Mrs. Kofi, he has a high-speed camera, meaning he will not need to use a flash. Bright light might not be a good idea down here, where no light has shone for millennia. In fact, even now, the sunlight that has broken through into the ancient space, due to the earthquake's effects, has already shown some damage to the paintwork on the walls.

The once vivid colours are visibly fading.

Clarence is pointing this out to Wadji, reminding him of that scene from Fellini's film *Roma:* where newly excavated paintings decay even as they are being filmed; when something extraordinary happens.

The Fate Book flies right out of Clarence's bag and attaches itself to a niche in the wall, right alongside a gigantic blue-green crystal.

The Fate Book glows, and immediately the crystal responds to it by lighting up. The light from this crystal is so strong that everything around it is now lit up with a soft blue-green light.

This also illuminates the deeper parts below them, and the three explorers are now able to see huge pillared corridors running off in several directions. Accompanying the light of the crystal, there is a soft sound; not unlike a kind of humming. Very soon, other crystals set into the walls begin to light up and give off a sound of their own. The combined sound and colour has the immediate effect of lifting their awareness. All three of the men are now beginning to receive information about this place and the civilisation that built it, as if all the memory of that time was stored in these gigantic crystals, not unlike the memories of silicone chips in computers.

The Fate Book seems to be interpreting the information for them, as it is showing them scenes from that remote past.

They are being shown a procession of ancient people.

People who once lived and ruled here.

They have a different look about them. Their foreheads are higher, and they seem taller and more elegant.

Certainly, there is a contentment and peace about them.

They can see huge plants and flowers been tended and nursed, fresh water is carefully channelled to them in canals and pools, and all with the conscious intent of these people.

The plants give them food and healing essences. They are being shown the harmonious connections that must have existed in this time. They are being shown that this was a time when people co-existed with nature in a way we have little understanding of today.

The Fate Book then seems to speed up the sequence of time. It is now playing out scenes that seem to be showing the end of this enlightened time. It looks like there is growing dissent in the once harmonious lives of these people.

There are power struggles and destructive behaviour arises. Factions and dissent and decadence follows.

War is being waged. Natural and unnatural disasters follow. The seas rise. There is a gradual mass migration away from here, to higher ground and faraway places that offer them safety.

The Fate Book speeds up even more now to the very end of this once golden age, and they can see the beginnings of things that are more recognisable as modern times.

It is all too quickly over, and suddenly they are back here in their own time. The Fate Book slowly dims down and then it is closed to them. It grows dark and returns to Clarence's bag. The gigantic crystal also begins to dim down, until it has darkened to the original glassy lustre they first saw.

The sounds too, have stopped.

The humming fades out.

Then they are left to their own thoughts.

They have been shown scenes from the past, in a way that reveals how little is really known, or can be known. The professors and Doctor Pradesh are silent for the longest time. It has been a very emotional viewing, as if their own lives have been played out to them. Lives they themselves lived back then, rather than the detached lives of someone else. They are left very moved, and can now scarcely motivate themselves to explore any further. Only their dedication to science and the need to understand their past drives them on to further investigation.

Episode Thirty-Five: Mara and Co.

Mara and Mrs. Kofi have had plenty of time to get to know each other.

Though still very wary of Mara and feeling very bad about the way she treated both her and Jess, Mrs. Kofi has undergone some kind of sea-change since self-medicating with the truth serum she had meant for Professor Wadji.

She has lost all the anger and the feelings of vengeance towards him. The long flight to Tibet, then the journey on foot through the snowy wastes is giving them ample time to talk. They are at first formal and polite with each other.

Josh, sitting next to Mara, is zoning out, listening to his iPod, his eyes closed to them and the world.

Like any teenager on a long flight would be, in the company of two adult ladies. And Quortaletzl, sitting alongside Josh, has fallen into a deep sleep.

'I was married once, you know Mara,' Mrs. Kofi says to Mara.

'You were...? I sort of guessed that from your title, Lydia.'

'Yes, it was a brief affair, you might say. Of course, I only got married to make Wadji jealous. But really, it didn't seem to have much effect on him. And I only succeeded in hurting someone else: My husband.'

'And what became of that? Of him, I mean..?'

'Well, he was very hurt, I think he really did love me, you see. It was so cruel of me, and I see that now. He was nice, very kind, gallant. How blind I was! You see, Mara, I was so in love with Wadji, I would have done anything to get his attention. And so, my husband left after we had a terrible quarrel. I told him I had no feelings for him.

Never did have...

He got very hurt and angry.

He smashed some furniture, shouted and ranted at me, told me I had ruined his life. Then he packed his things.

I never saw him again.

Of course, he agreed to a divorce. It was all very civilised, all done through lawyers; documents and affidavits and papers to sign and then, that was it.

And all through that, Wadji was supportive. He even offered me a job, as his secretary. Of course, I accepted. That way, at least I could be close to him.

I could at least see him, every day.

I could at least still be a part of his life...'

Tears roll down her cheeks.

Mara takes her hand, gently squeezing it. Reassuring her.

Now she understands what drove this woman to do what she did, it makes it so much easier to forgive her.

'And you...?'

'What do you mean?'

'You had a husband, Mara? You must have. You have children; you're a Catholic, aren't you?'

There is an awkward silence. Mara looks at her hands and fidgets.

'Oh... I'm sorry Mara, forgive me for making you uncomfortable. I was just curious. You're so good with your children, it seems like you don't need someone else in your lives. I'm surprised, you see, because I come from a traditional background. For us, there's the mother, the father, the children, grandparents... you know, family values.'

'Look, Lydia, I know you mean well, but this is something I don't like to talk about.

Well, okay, tell you what. I'll talk about it, then it's done, okay? So here it is...

I didn't have a very functional family growing up.

My father died when I was four or five and my mother

re-married. I guess she wanted a father for us. But my stepfather turned out to be a drunk and beat me a lot, because my mom was out working all the time.

My brother Clarence was a couple of years older than me, and he defended me whenever he could.

But he spent as much time as he could out of the house, with his books and his plant and insect studies.

So when I finally got to leave home I threw myself, like Clarence, into my studies.

Then, later, after university, I realised I wanted kids, so I found a willing father. Someone who could just leave me to bringing them up...

That's it really.'

'I see. So you have no contact with the father?'

'No. I don't Lydia. Why should I? Jess and Josh know the score. And now so do you.'

Just then the flight attendant announced they were about to land at Lhasa, and Mara glanced over at Josh.

He still had his eyes closed, but his head was moving in that way which meant he was seeing something again.

Mara lightly touched his arm.

'What is it, Josh? Are you seeing something?'

'Yeah... I'm seeing Uncle Clarence and Professor Wadji...

'And there's another man there too. The one they came out to find. Everyone is safe and they're all exploring some caves and they've left a flag flying to show us where they are. It looks like they've found something really important. They're really excited!'

Mara and Mrs. Kofi are both hugely relieved at this news. Once the plane has landed, the four travellers have their papers checked by Chinese soldiers. The soldiers seem unusually interested in them, and one of them, clearly the one in charge, immediately picks up a telephone and contacts someone. There is a long conversation then, with the soldier frequently looking back at Mara, Josh, Quortaletzl, and Mrs. Kofi, especially Mrs. Kofi. Then he puts the phone on hold and goes up to Mrs. Kofi.

'You frenn Professor Wadji?'

'Yes, I'm his assistant.'

'Why you come here?'

'I've come to assist him. That's what assistants do!'

The soldier doesn't get the sarcasm. He just grunts and goes back to the phone. There is some more conversation.

Finally, the soldier puts the phone down and this time goes straight over to two of his colleagues. They talk briefly, then the other soldiers go to a kiosk and pick up their backpacks and rifles before rejoining them.

'These men go with you now. Escort you. You go now.'

The soldier dismisses them all them with a wave of his hand and walks off. The very same guides and trackers who had left Wadji to his fate then eagerly meet the armed escort and the travellers are then eagerly met in the arrivals hall. They have all been feeling bad about leaving Wadji on his own, although he told them to, and now they are keen to make good, and to take the new travellers to him.

After picking up some provisions and supplies, under the able direction of Mrs. Kofi, the party sets off.

Thoughtfully, she also brings a satellite phone with her.

It is now three days since Wadji was reunited with Clarence and Doctor Pradesh; and nearly a month since Doctor Pradesh woke up to find himself safely in the cave.

Thanks to the yeti.

Mara notices their armed escort keep their distance from the other men, the guides and trackers.

The Chinese regard Tibet as a province of China and their rightful property, but the Tibetans resent their presence.

Theirs is an ancient and proud culture quite distinct

from that of the Chinese, and though there have been points of contact between them, there is an uneasiness to things. Mara also notices that the soldiers who originally questioned them at the airport, are watching them all as they slowly move off on the trail towards Mount Kailash.

Mrs. Kofi has mixed feelings about the journey. There will be some awkward issues to deal with. She will have to come clean with Wadji and Clarence about her shenanigans.

As the two professors left for Lhasa before the doughty Mrs. Stevenson found her out, neither of them knows anything about what she has confessed to. The professors will not be pleased with her when they find out.

Mrs. Kofi knows she now runs a huge risk of losing Wadji.

Not just his respect but her job too.

She has never liked Clarence, but she knows he will have things to say to her about her cruel treatment of his family, and knowing how protective he is towards Mara, she will just have to brace herself for whatever comes her way.

How much easier it would have been just to have walked away from it all when she had her chance.

But that moment has long passed.

Ahead of them the foothills of the Himalayas begin

to undulate upwards, and in the distance the mighty Mount Kailash looms out of the clouds in mystic magnificence.

Quortaletzl, aside from the little bit he has experienced in Dublin, has never seen so much snow and ice before, and is relishing the novelty of it all. He leaps about in the snow like a child, whooping and shouting with abandon, under the wary eyes of the escort.

He has been pelting everyone with snowballs, even the armed Chinese soldiers, who had to brandish their rifles and make threatening gestures to stop him.

He and Josh then settle down to seeing who can throw snowballs the furthest.

There is a moment in the more serious business of the journey when the group stops to make a fire and cook lunch, when Quortaletzl suddenly sniffs the air and gazes into the distance ahead. With his sharp vision, he is the only one in the party who can sense it and see it.

The yeti.

It is watching them too, and knowing Quortaletzl has spotted it, it quickly vanishes into the snow.

Quortaletzl wisely decides to keep this sighting of the yeti to himself so as not to alarm the ladies, and also in case the armed escort is a little trigger-happy and decides to take a pot shot at it.

The yeti shows itself discreetly several more times

during their journey, each time quite deliberately, it seems, only to the keen eyes of Quortaletzl. He has the sense that it is keeping an eye on them and making sure they are staying on the right track.

This is confirmed later, as two days into their journey, Quortaletzl spots a red flag flying in the distance, on top of a long stick planted in the snow. And there beside it, for a brief moment, he sees the yeti.

He feels sure this flag has been left there by the professors. Suddenly, everyone is hopeful of finding them.

But just then, there is a strange sound, like a distant wind approaching and the ground begins to shake.

The aftershock of the earthquake.

Down in the ancient ruins of Atlantis, the professors and Doctor Pradesh feel the tremor also. Cracks are now appearing in the walls, and dust and small stones rain down on them. They look at each other, and without saying a word, they know what they have to do; they need to get back to the staircase and out of there as soon as possible.

Quickly, the men make their way back down the corridors.

On their way down there, they had been hoping to find another entrance or exit, and randomly chose a corridor, one of several that branched off like the spokes of a wheel from the great hall at the bottom of the 'grand stair,' as they liked to refer to it.

After the revelations afforded by The Fate Book passing on the memories of that golden age locked within the giant crystals, the men had decided to explore a little more.

Professor Wadji had been recording as much as he could with his digital camera, and of course, Clarence and Pradesh kept copious notes of the wonderful place. Down the corridor, which was as wide as six or seven people, they saw many more wonders.

The corridors were flanked all along the way with alabaster columns, all magnificently carved with intertwining plant forms and figures. The artwork was stunning and of exceptional quality, quite unknown to them. The closest they could approximate it to, was perhaps the pinnacle of the High Renaissance period. But even that, in Clarence's view, was in a quite different style and a mere shadow of what they were seeing here. The walls were painted in the most stunning colours, and layered over in gold and silver and other metals they couldn't identify. It was as if the walls themselves were shaped and undulated in ways that were organic and alive, as if they had been shaped by thought and intention linked to the highest feelings. At least, so said Wadji, as he looked open-mouthed and incredulous at this beautiful place.

It is hard now to tear themselves away from this treasure trove, but they are running low on flashlight batteries, and so soon they are making their way back up the grand staircase, with the collapsed cave above them.

Just then, there is another strong tremor and several large boulders come bouncing down the stairs. With that, the opening in the roof of the cave widens and a lot more daylight shines down into the space, and then suddenly and to their immense delight, two faces appear at the edge of the hole, where they had planted the red flag up above.

One of them, seeing the three men coming up, shouts down,

'Hey, Uncle Clarence, is that you down there?'

It is Josh! Next to him is the huge round face of Quortaletzl.

Never was a sight more welcome!

'Good God, Josh! Quortaletzl! How wonderful to see you.'

Then the faces of Mara and Mrs. Kofi also appear, just as the trio down below reach the inside of the collapsed cave.

Wadji cannot believe his eyes... and Mrs. Kofi is too choked up to say a thing.

In a moment Clarence is up out of the cave, with his arms around Mara and Josh. Wadji has Mrs. Kofi in a big hug, and she is sobbing uncontrollably. Professor Wadji's face is a study.

It shows a mixture of emotions: surprise, relief, and restrained affection. He has never seen Mrs. Kofi quite like this before.

Quortaletzl sees that Doctor Pradesh is the odd one out, and without hesitation, he gives him a bear-hug and lifts him right off his feet. The astonished doctor is not sure how to deal with this affectionate stranger, but then he sees the armed escort standing to one side, and senses their problems may not be over just yet.

No time is wasted in using Mrs. Kofi's satellite phone to put Doctor Pradesh in touch with his worried wife, Kriti. He has barely made the call, when one of the watching Chinese soldiers steps over and snatches the phone from him, then shouts aggressively at them all to stand together.

He has something to say, or rather, to shout:

'Which one of you Pwofessor Wadjiwadj?!'

'That would be me...' says Wadji, stepping forward.

The soldier pulls him roughly behind him, alongside the other soldier, while brandishing his rifle at the others. Then he searches Wadji and tries to take his camera from him.

There is a tussle over it, as there is so much precious information about the lost world recorded in it. But the soldier wins and Wadji's heart sinks.

'Which one of you Pwofessor Kalikaloos?!'

Clarence steps forward, and without waiting to be asked, he steps alongside Wadji.

'You men, you now pwisoners of Chinese army! You

under awwest!'

'And may I ask, on what charge?' Clarence calmly asks.

'For illegal twespass on Chinese pwoperty...!'

The soldier points vaguely down the hole. It is clear he's not that convinced himself, but he obviously has his orders. He must have been briefed before leaving Lhasa.

All this time, Quortaletzl has been fuming. This trip has been hard for him. Most of all the massive adjustment to a place way colder than even the Irish winter.

He had been equipped with adequate protective clothing.

In fact, Mara had fished out a ski-suit for him which must have belonged to Clarence. It fitted Quortaletzl perfectly.

Clarence must have bought it at a sale and immediately discarded it, and it was easy to see why. It was pretty naff as it was all white and had an integral hood, which was fur-lined and gave Quortaletzl the appearance of an albino gorilla, which would prove useful in attracting the yeti's attention.

He could easily take the rifles off these men, he thinks, but Mara catches his eye and he stops himself.

He feels so frustrated.

Mara had given him no encouragement since he embarked on this trip and he was beginning to feel that his attempts to win her heart were now pointless. He was not one to give up hope, but even the tiniest bit of encouragement would have been helpful.

Now all he was seeing was an isolated and lifeless white wilderness of ice and snow. Nothing at all like the friendly and lively jungle he was used to and now missing so much.

What now?

The Chinese soldiers have now decided to rope Wadji and Clarence together, and have separated them from the rest of the group, much to Mrs Kofi's dismay. She had been looking forward to an intimate chat with her boss and now it was being thwarted.

The soldiers have decided they must all leave immediately, to get back to Lhasa as soon as possible.

One of them takes up position at the head of the group, followed by Mara and Josh (who are not seen as a threat).

Quortaletzl, then Doctor Pradesh and Mrs. Kofi follow them, with the roped-up professors at the rear, guarded by the other soldier.

Quortaletzl was a bit of an unknown as far as the soldiers were concerned. They had no idea what part he played in the dynamics of the group, seeing him as a kind of unofficial playmate to Josh.

And so the group slowly begins to make its way back. There is a general sense of heaviness. Although everyone is delighted to be reunited, the soldiers have enforced a strict silence.

No one is allowed to talk, and so each person is left with their own thoughts.

Mara is thinking about Jess and Katrina. And how wonderful it is that Mrs. Stevenson is playing such a big part in their lives now.

Josh is feeling a bit numb. He had been longing to have a conversation with the professors, and he is itching to know what they had discovered inside the caves. He had not had any visions since the plane, and he was feeling that the whole trip was a waste of time. Sure, they had found the professors and Doctor Pradesh, but now they were being pushed around by a couple of surly soldiers.

Quortaletzl is even more fed up. He doesn't take kindly to being pushed around, and he knows these soldiers are no match for him. Why didn't Mara just let him clobber them when he had the chance and then they could all go home?

And he could return to the jungle...

Now a snowstorm is blowing up fiercely and it is becoming impossible to see the person in front. Suddenly, with no warning whatsoever, he is pulled away by his arm into a snowdrift. It happens so fast, no one notices.

For a couple of minutes, he thinks this might be the end of him. He is being held face down in the snow and breathing is getting more and more difficult.

Then, quite suddenly, he is released.

He stands up gasping for breath and faces his adversary, who still has him gripped firmly by the arms. He is now looking up into the towering face of the white yeti. It obviously likes him, because it is smiling, and dusting the snow off him...

The rest of the party are now a long way off. The yeti hauls him up onto his feet, and the two of them set off, heading in the opposite direction from the rest of the party. Sometime later, with the yeti having kept a cracking pace through the snow, they stop for a rest.

Quortaletzl has adequate supplies of dried fruit and meat in his rucksack. He reaches into it and hands over some dried fruit to the yeti. It sniffs, then eats the fruit, quickly holding out its hand for more.

Quortaletzl has never seen an animal quite like this, and studies it intently as it eats. Its features are humanoid, yet in other respects it is ape-like. It has very long arms and legs with a shorter curved body. What puzzles him is how intuitive it is: how, at this very moment, as he studies it, it is in fact studying him!

Its head is cocked quizzically to one side, and it is smiling in a very human way. Just then it breaks wind very loudly.

Quortaletzl follows suit.

The yeti laughs, making a strange wheezing sound; its whole body convulsing. Then it is quiet. It raises its arm and points into the distance, at a low range of snowy mountains some way in the distance.

As it does so, Quortaletzl receives into his mind an image of a strongly flowing river and woodlands, with a background of thick green undergrowth and bright flowers. He is puzzled, there must be some kind of mistake, for how could such things be here, in these snowy wastes?

Has the yeti simply accessed his memory of the jungle?

There is no time to ponder, as the big creature is now up and off towards the mountains, pausing only for a second to make sure Quortaletzl is following. What choice does he now have? They must be miles away from any tracks or roads, from any sign of human beings at all.

He is losing track of time. Maybe it is an hour or many hours later, he doesn't know; but they have reached the summit of the mountain range and plunge straight over it down a steep gorge.

It is fortunate that Quortaletzl is as strong and fit as he is, because the yeti is now leaping from rock to rock at great speed and is calling out into the gorge.

In a moment, there is an answering call. Suddenly a group of five or six yeti step out of nowhere, where the gorge changes direction! They stare at Quortaletzl.

But they seem to be expecting him, as they humbly step aside and allow him to pass them, and they then fall in line as he continues to follow the yeti.

The snow has quickly thinned out now and has almost disappeared. Then the gorge levels out and opens up. Quortaletzl cannot believe his eyes. He thinks he must be dreaming.

Right in front of him now is an immense green forest.

More surprising to him is that it is warm here, warm enough for him to peel down his ski-suit top.

There is the familiar sound of birds, insects, and running water; and true to the yeti's projected image, ahead of him there is a vast woodland, with a background of thick green undergrowth interspersed with flowers. He is amazed to see familiar species that he knows from the South American jungles: orchids, tree ferns and even lianas...

How could this be?

He remembers the earlier images projected into his mind by the yeti who brought him here, and looks for him, but he has now vanished along with his tribe.

Quortaletzl steps forward, feeling the soft grassy ground under his feet; and then he cannot restrain himself any longer. He pulls off his thick boots and socks, and strips off his cumbersome white ski-suit.

Now he stands only in his shorts and stares up into the forest with the brightest smile.

He has come home!

Rest assured, this is not the last we have heard from him... You shall be hearing about him again very soon.

But for now, we must return for a time to Ireland.

Episode Thirty-Six: Jess

Jess had received a strange message.

It wasn't a phone message, or a text message, or even an email or a Facebook message. No, it was one of those messages she gets from her brother Josh now and then.

She sat now at Mrs. Stevenson's breakfast table and pondered on what she had woken up with, going around and around and around in her head. In fact, it had given her quite a headache.

Since Mara and Josh had taken off with Mrs. Kofi and Quortaletzl, she and Katrina had been taken under the kindly wing of the able Mrs. Stevenson.

Though unfailingly caring, the old woman was also incredibly observant, and the two teenagers found they got away with far less than they would have at Mara's. And of course they had their allocated chores. To start with, their beds had to be made up and their rooms tidied daily.

And there were many other daily kitchen duties, such as washing up and laundry, and the separating out of the rubbish for recycling and composting. Then there were many other tasks to follow those, such as weeding the garden and checking and watering the young plants and seedlings in the greenhouse, using only rainwater.

One afternoon Mrs. Stevenson called Katrina and Jess over and showed them where she had buried several crystal pyramids in the ground, all at carefully calculated points around the perimeter of the garden.

She told them that she had used copper dowsers and the whispered promptings of the fairies to place them, so as to protect the garden and direct the forces of growth.

A garden that flourished and flowered even in the depths of winter.

It was as if, in this way, it was covered over in an invisible, protective dome which kept out snow and hail and heavy rains, but let in light and sunshine and happiness.

And fairies.

During their short stay there, the girls had already learned so much about them: they learned that, freed from the sentimental views of the nineteenth century, the fairies ought to be seen as essential and indispensable elemental beings of nature. Beings who had been allocated their place since the beginning of time.

Mrs. Stevenson explained to the girls that the physical world was interpenetrated by these elemental forces, which were living and aware, and constantly at work. She said that the most physical of these nature spirits were the gnomes, the element of earth. These beings move in the root systems of plants and into the depths of the earth. They also helped the animals.

Then there were the undines, the water spirits, often described as water nymphs or even the mermaids of the sea. They were very shy but could be found in remote brooks and rivers, and in the sea, and are even mentioned by the poet Homer.

Then there were the air spirits, such as Ariel in the Tempest, she said. They moved between the plants and flowers, directing the bees and other insects in the pollination process.

Finally, there were the fire spirits or salamanders, responsible for the blossoms. These could be seen in fire and are even described at the beginning of Benvenuto Cellini's famous Renaissance autobiography, said Mrs Stevenson, where the young artist sees a salamander whilst sitting in front of an open fire with his father. He excitedly points it out to his father, who shows that he has seen it too.

Then, inexplicably, his father strikes him on the head, and when the young Benvenuto asks why he hit him he answers:

'So that you will always remember this moment!'

And so all of these beings work together in nature to perform whatever Mother Nature requires, she said.

Mrs. Stevenson proved her point by mentioning all the many fairy tales the girls would have had in their upbringing. But, she said, there was a terrible danger that people had now forgotten all about them and their place in the scheme of things, and saw them now only as made up tales or stories.

Then she told them about Findhorn, a project in Scotland, where people had worked miraculously with the nature spirits in transforming a bleak wilderness of sand into a nature wonderland of gigantic plants and vegetables.

This was due to a conscious and deliberate cooperation between humans and nature spirits; but in a very modern way. The girls were entranced by this and wanted to know more. Mrs. Stevenson then produced some books she had in her bookshelves.

So now Jess sat at the breakfast table, with her head pounding. Even Mrs. Stevenson's freshly made crumpets couldn't bring her back to herself, and Katrina glanced over at the old lady, who did not fail to pick up the cue.

'Sooo... me dear Jess, I see you're away with the fairies this mornin'? Mmmmm... Let me see: could it be that you've had a little psychic news from your dear brother?'

Jess looks up, startled by Mrs. Stevenson's words.

'Yes, I do know a little about such things, darlin' girl.

Now don't you be fretting away there like a poor little lost bird fallen from its nest. You must share what you've seen with your friends!'

Somehow Jess is still a bit shy with Mrs. Stevenson, as if what she and Josh have is something they can't share. She fidgets and mumbles and turns red and looks from the old woman to Katrina and then out of the window.

'Okay then. So... let's see: you've had a message from Josh. Only it seems you don't fully understand it. And you don't know what to do next and you feel like you're all on your own and you're missing your mammy and your brother and maybe you're thinking the old woman's bonkers and off the planet with her talk of fairies and all that!'

Jess bursts out laughing. She has no choice, with Mrs. Stevenson so utterly accurate and so ingenuously honest.

'Sorry, Mrs. Stevenson. Yes, you're so right... I like, woke up with this feeling, and it's been giving me a headache because I'm not sure what I'm seeing, but I do feel that Josh and my mom and them are in some kind of trouble and I can't get my head around what to do...'

She lets go of a hot bright tear which rolls down her cheek, and is quickly dabbed away by Mrs. Stevenson, who has come up close in her wheelchair and taken Jess's hand, while Katrina puts an arm around her friend. How can she hold back now?

'Yes dear, I know... I know... let me have a look. Mmm... You're seeing Josh and Jess and your mom and the professors being threatened now by foreign soldiers, Chinese I think they are... These men want to take the two professors away. Mmmm... looks like there's been some bad blood there. Our Professor Wadji, let's just say he's been a naughty boy back in the past, and now it is that those birds have come home to roost... I can understand your confusion Jess, there's a lot going on over there now...

Then there's Mrs. Kofi and her shenanigans.

She still has had a chance to spill the beans to her boss lover Wadji about what she put you and your mammy through. This is hard for her, she's really full of it, you see.

And then of course there's your mammy and the puppy-man Quortaletzl, who loves her and still won't see that she's not ready for love... mmm, tricky... this must be hard for you to digest dear Jess, but you know, I can see something else: something really quite strange. There's a wonderful magical creature looking out for them all, and this is very interesting to me, as this gigantic being is from another world.

How am I doing so far, my dear?'

Jess has brightened up. Everything the old woman has said makes sense. Except for one thing.

'What magical creature is that then?'

'Well, I don't really know... It's a funny big furry old thing. A bit like a bear but more like a man... pure white too.'

'Would that be a yeti' Jess replies.

'It may be. I'm sure I've been hearing of such things over there in them mountains. But here's the thing: the creature has been looking out for them all, and that's a strange thing indeed. Stranger things will follow, it would seem... To be sure, there are beautiful and deep things in this world my children, make no mistake!'

Jess is much cheered by Mrs. Stevenson's interpretation of what she has been carrying so painfully in her head, and now she is free of the headache, and tucking ravenously into a pile of fresh warm crumpets.

Mrs. Stevenson swishes off in her wheelchair, humming loudly and smiling to herself. She is enjoying the company of the girls, and Jess reminds her of herself when she was young. She calls out as she leaves the room.

'Oh, and Katrina, don't forget you and I have some baking to do later on me darling!'

Katrina was very happy with this reminder. The old lady was so much like her grandmother, it was uncanny.

The effect of this was that she felt properly at home for the first time since she and her family had left Poland. And now she found that she didn't miss her parents at all. Strange.

So strange that when her mom contacted her to say that she was coming over soon to see her settled in her new school and her new home and of course to meet Mrs. Stevenson, she felt her heart sink. She didn't want to share this new happiness and security with anyone else.

It was a bit like a dream that she didn't want to wake from. And she didn't want her mom to challenge it or even question it.

And she surely would.

She and Jess still found time to get out and do some skateboarding, but she was surprised to find herself looking at her watch and reminding Jess that she needed to get home now to do some baking with Mrs. Stevenson!

It wasn't just the activity of baking and the marvellous smells and the pleasure of it all. It was the company of a woman who chattered constantly about stuff that was really interesting, thought Katrina, and to whom she could in turn, talk to.

And so one day Katrina, perhaps unthinkingly, asked Mrs. Stevenson how she had ended up in a wheelchair.

It was as they were icing a large Victoria sponge cake

and they were chatting and one thing led to another. Katrina had just complimented her on how easily she got around the kitchen in her wheelchair...

'So how did it happen, Mrs. Stevenson?'

Katrina immediately regretted asking, and the old lady stiffened, but then sighed and relaxed again. Perhaps forgiving the teenager's lack of tact as being quite ingenuous and without forethought or malice.

'Well dear... it happened a long, long time ago, and I'm quite okay with talking about it now, especially now I have my lovely shiny electric, you see.

I was married once you know. And my husband was a lovely man, but he had one terrible weakness. He loved motor cars and he loved speed and those are two things that do not mix well.

Pass the strawberry jam down here won't you dear.'

Mrs. Stevenson stopped talking, painfully remembering, as she spread strawberry jam generously over the first sponge layer. Katrina could see she was fighting her emotions. She wished she had not asked.

'Well anyhow, so one day we were driving home after a very rainy day and the roads were wet and muddy and we shouldn't have been driving so fast, but I said nothing and I always wish I had you know... truly I do...'

Katrina could see her shoulders stiffen.

'Yes, and so it happened, and I survived the crash, but my legs didn't and he didn't. It was a long long time ago now my dear...

Sooo...now, we need to spread the butter cream on top of

that sponge now. I'll be leaving it to you, me darling...'

Mrs. Stevenson sped out of the kitchen. As she passed by on her way out, Katrina saw tears running down her face.

She felt awful, but a few minutes later the old woman came back into the room, humming away as if nothing had happened and she complimented Katrina on her baking.

'Well, well, well now see who's outstripped her teacher then! Just look at the lovely sponge cake you've made us!'

Then seeing Katrina's concerned face searching hers, she says,

'Oh it's all right dear, don't you go feeling bad about it...'

Katrina knew what she was referring to and so they both moved on.

Now the three of them are sitting quietly on the porch having a light supper and admiring the garden.

It is a cold but clear evening and for a while they are all enjoying the peace and Mrs. Stevenson speaks first.

'So I've been thinking about what you saw Jess, and wondering what we should do next. Of course, I can't be getting about in the snow in me wheelchair, as your mammy and Mrs. Kofi have said. And it won't do to send the two of you young girls over there, as bold and as brave as you might well be...

Soooo, here's the thing:

I've got in touch with a certain young friend of mine who works at the British Museum. She and your Uncle Clarence and Professor Wadji already know each other, Jess. She was most interested when I told her that the professors had gone to Tibet looking for their lost colleague, Doctor Pradesh. It turns out she knows him too, and she even seemed to have an inkling even of where they might all be!'

'Wow! Mrs. Stevenson, you're amazing!' shouts Jess, hugging her tightly.

'Easy now, me dear, you'll be be breaking we old bones now with those hugs of yours. So then, we had a chat and this young lady is going to get her travelling papers in order, and would you believe she'll be flying out to Lhasa tomorrow? And in case you're wondering how one young woman can be more effective than two feisty teenagers such as yourselves, let me be telling you girls that Ms. Rowena Shardsworth is one tough young lady.

Yes, would you believe, she's some sort of martial arts expert and she once wanted to be a stunt girl?

Before she took up with the museum she survived a whole bunch of them solo expeditions to the poles both the north and the south and up the Himalayas and down to who knows what else. She dresses like some sort of a rock star and bless her if she doesn't give a hoot who cares!

Of course, she's Irish and she also happens to be my niece you see, though we don't let that come between us.

We're friends first, then relatives after that! I don't see much of her these days, with her being so busy galavanting around the world and digging for old stuff in the good earth and all, but her mammy and I were very close, before we lost her to polio, and of course it's true that I had a hand or two in Rowena's education when she was living here.

I think you girls will like her. Oh yes, and I do believe I have a picture of her somewhere. Just a moment now, I'll be fetching it...'

Mrs. Stevenson whisks away and comes back brandishing a thick photograph album. She opens it out on the table, and starts flicking through it.

'Ah, there she is! This picture was taken a year or two ago, I'm thinking; when the dear girl last came over to stay with me. She was writing a doctorate and she said she needed some peace and quiet and lots of good home cooking...'

Jess and Katrina lean over to peek at the album and they are amazed by what they see. Staring back at them is the photo of a young woman dressed top to toe in snow gear with a mop of bright red hair, cascading down her shoulders.

She is tall and strong and her look is bold and challenging.

Her eyes are a clear bright blue and in this photograph she is standing on the summit of a mountain top, with the Irish flag flying just behind her.

She is alone.

There are other photographs.

Rowena in the jungles of Sumatra.

Rowena standing beside an ancient overgrown monument *Somewhere in South America...* Rowena in India, surrounded by smiling children.

Rowena on a trail bike, laden with luggage and technical gear, clearly on an expedition up a mountain somewhere. Rowena in an archaeological dig, looking amazingly cheerful and fit and healthy.

Alone.

Jess feels an instant connection with her, as if she has always known her. This is what she would like to make of herself. Her reaction does not go unnoticed.

'Yes, I thought you'd feel that way about her, Jess.

You're very alike, I think. Rowena is very much her own person and something of a free spirit, I dare say!

Anyway, the dear girl, bless her heart, is going to fly out there in a day or two, on her way to China, and I made her promise me that she'd call as soon as she can, and then we shall all know what's what!'

This conversation cheers up Jess no end. She feels so much better about her mom and Josh now, knowing that the incredibly capable Rowena Shardsworth is on the case.

She can't wait to meet this mysterious young woman!

'Can we see more photographs of her, Mrs. Stevenson?'

'Of course, me darling! Now, let's see. Somewhere in this vast album there will be some picture of the dear girl when she graduated, let's see now…

Ah yes… what about this one then?'

Episode Thirty-Seven: Rowena

The still and cool mountain air is rare in this part of the northern Ethiopian highlands. From the plains, the earth rises up quite suddenly to two thousand six hundred metres and there are cliffs and ravines and areas of barren rock interspersed with grassy meadows.

Mists shroud the place much of the time and it is easy to find the place mysterious and magical and ancient.

There is a brooding melancholy, such as only Africa will offer, mixed up with its splendour and magnificence.

Here now, in the early morning, there are the distant intermittent calls of baboons and wild goats and birds.

This is the mysterious kingdom of Lalibela.

The ancient Christian holy place was carved deep down into the lava rock about the time that Chartres cathedral was built and it is guarded still today, by taciturn priests who do not speak to strangers and will not reveal the secrets they watch over.

It is in the church Bet Medhane Alem, in the north-western cluster of churches, that you will find the eight hundred-year-old Lalibela Cross, which is made of solid gold and reportedly weighs around fifteen pounds. It is said to have been the personal property of King Lalibela, and is perhaps today the most treasured artefact of the Ethiopian church, more holy to them than anything in Jerusalem or Rome.

Other legends even suggest that a mysterious medieval character called Prester John brought the Holy Grail here for safekeeping.

Now in the distance and coming closer fast there is a sound which seems quite out of place here. It sounds like a chainsaw, but now, as it grows louder, it is far too insistent and continuous in its snarl. Soon the sound shatters and covers over any other sound. And now it is at once upon us.

An apparition all colour and noise appears and temporarily it is airborne as it lifts up over the mesa and crashes down on the level plain.

It is a trail bike.

Astride the bike sits a gangly woman, her bright red hair flowing out behind her like fire.

She is dressed in equally bright clothes, a jacket of purple and a crimson scarf, yellow leggings and silver boots with multiple buckles reaching halfway up her thighs.

The trail bike is festooned with flags and stickers and

mud, and packed up high behind its rider are piles of well-secured luggage.

Bags and bedrolls and baggage.

Tents and tarpaulins and tack.

Pots and pans and provisions.

It is all there...

The trail bike narrowly avoids a terrified goat and comes to a reluctant skidding stop, the rider staring at something ahead of her, hidden there but sensed in the mist.

Her intense blue eyes are dancing and make her smile bright and fearless. She eases the bike onto its stand and steps off, standing now with her legs apart and her hands on her hips.

'Okay Abraham, you can come out now! I know you're there! I can smell you from here, you old goat!

There is a moment's hesitation.

Then an old man shuffles out of the mist. He is laughing so hard he can hardly walk. He is dressed seemingly in rags and carries a long stick with a knob on the end of it. It is called a 'knopkierie' in the southern parts of Africa.

'I heard you on that shouting horse before you was smelling me, Miss Rowena... You naughty girl!

She laughs, then runs up to him and does a 'high five'

with him, then, when they have both laughed some more at each other, she slyly produces something from her pocket and dangles it in front of the old shepherd before quickly hiding it again.

'A... *what*... girl, did you say...?'

'Auw... No no no Miss. Rowena, I am forget. You are a mighty queen! Mighty! The sun she is shining from you, it is make me blind! Auw! Too too much!'

He drops to his knees with exaggerated piety and covers his eyes, but then quickly holds out both hands to receive his gift in the traditional African manner.

'Oh, come off it Abraham.... what you won't do for a little baccy eh?'

She hands over the small pouch of tobacco, which the old man gratefully takes, wasting no time in skinning one up.

A small flock of goats surround them now, and it's clear that this is Abraham's flock. One of them, striped in dark brown and white, shows a particular interest in Rowena and comes up close to her, eying her up and down.

'So, how's life treating you, you old devil? Don't tell me, you've taken another wife?'

'Auw... Miss Rowena, I'm too old for another wife. It is very very hard to keep the other ones happy you know...'

He thrusts his hips suggestively.

'Also, you know, Miss Rowena, the younger ones, they want the smartphones and the nice clothes and the sports cars. Things we aren't using here in the mountains...'

He laughs again, shakes his head and squats down, deeply savouring the smoke from his roll-up.

Rowena perches on a rock and smiles, enjoying his enjoyment. For a few minutes neither of them speak.

Here in Africa, there is no such thing as an awkward silence. In fact, it is considered wisdom when one chooses not to speak. But with these two old friends it is also a bit of a game, to see who will speak first.

Time passes and Rowena looks down, giggling to herself.

The stripy goat, still close by, cocks it head at her and bleats along with her as she giggles.

The old man is very sharp and observant, and he has been staring at Rowena now, appraising her. His old forehead wrinkles and he nods slowly as he blows smoke at her.

'Mmmm... I think it's time I find a man for you, my queen.'

'Now don't you get started on that again Abraham.'

'No, but is true. I am seeing this. You are a woman who is needing a man. You know this is true.'

'What is true old friend, is that I'm very happy on my own, So let's have no more on that...

Come on! Tell you what, let's have some coffee!'

Rowena steps over to her trail bike, which is still clicking and clunking from the hot engine. She has a Virgo sense of order and practicality, despite appearances to the contrary. In just a minute she has found the coffee, a tiny percolator, and the wherewithal to make a fire.

Abraham pulls some stones into a little circle and has gathered brush to start the fire.

Soon the delicious aroma of coffee fills the air. Coffee has its ancient origins in these very mountains, she reflects, as she pours for her and Abraham, adding several spoons of sugar to his cup. She knows he likes a good hit of sugar...

Abraham closes his eyes as he swills the first mouthful of sweet hot coffee and gives himself over to it.

His face is a study of utter enjoyment.

Rowena watches him.

She has a soft spot for the old man.

She has known him at least ten years, and first met him some years back whilst engaged on a dig not far from here, on the edge of the Lalibela St George Church site. Back then he had played more of a local role as a church elder, before retiring into the hills with his goats. Whilst still a church elder he would often confer with her whilst she was on her digs there. And now and again he would drop a nugget of useful knowledge or local folklore that she could use to piece together a picture of the mysterious history of the place.

Lalibela was still an enigma in many ways.

The local legends insisted that the buildings were crafted by both men and angels, and that the angels worked their shift at night while the men slept.

Certainly, even today, scientists are baffled by the high level of technological skill in the construction of these churches, and it is clear that they were built quickly, some of them easily within the lifetime of King Lalibela. Mysteriously, he was seen as a 'friend of the bees...'

Abraham is a committed Orthodox Christian, and as such is connected with one of the oldest forms of the religion, originally part of the Egyptian Coptic stream and only recently making itself independent of it.

'How's your coffee, old man..?'

'Auw... thus coffee, she is telling me she is need more sugar Miss Rowena!' And he holds out his cup for more.

She shakes her head in mock disbelief and spoons yet more sugar in to it. Sugar is a treat here. As is most food. The level of poverty here in Ethiopia is shocking, and Rowena has never been comfortable with it. She has tried her best, over the years, to help out with local feeding schemes and the supply of fresh water and medicine, but there are frustrating political hindrances and plenty of government corruption to get in the way.

'Mmm... I have some sugar for you too, Miss Rowena, a little gift...'

The old man reaches into his goatskin bag and fishing about, he finds and produces something carefully wrapped up in a piece of stained but clean cloth.

He hands it over, as is the custom, in both hands.

Rowena lights up.

A gift from Abraham is always exciting.

Over the years he has produced several 'gifts.' Some of them are now displayed in the British Museum, but one or two are still in Rowena's personal collection.

On one occasion he gave her some kind of ancient tool he had found. It completely baffled everyone who came across it, and turned out to made of a metal never encountered before. This had been pounced upon by a strong but vocal visiting group of committed alternative investigators who felt sure that Lalibela was built by aliens. For them, this enigmatic tool, made of exotic and unknown metals, was yet more proof of extra-terrestrial builders.

Another persistent story here, perhaps far more credible, is that Solomon's Ark of the Covenant is hidden here in one of the twelve churches.

It is said that when the temple of Solomon was destroyed, the ark was saved and was secretly brought here, and is even now in the safekeeping of the priests. Indeed, every year, a sacred procession moves through the area, displaying a deliberately fake ark. Beautiful solid silver and gold crosses are carried into the hidden depths of the holy places, some of which are constantly guarded from outside eyes by the inner circle of orthodox priests. Even Rowena has not been able to penetrate this veil, though she has never given up trying.

The actual layout of the twelve churches has also been described by some investigators as having an exact correspondence to the constellation of the Pleiades. Indeed, Professor Clarence 'Stinky' Kalikaloos has been brought here to this very site by his mentor, Wadji, on several occasions. Wadji has always stressed its importance as a sacred site.

Now Rowena holds in her hands the gift from Abraham.

She slowly unfolds the cloth, teasing herself like a child with a new toy. She notices, feeling through the cloth, that the object is heavy for its size, and quite round, with no sharp edges.

Then she can hold back no longer and finally uncovers it.

The crystal now sitting in the palm of her hand is warm.

It appears to be carved from something resembling emerald or jade. It is highly polished and quite transparent, rounded like a cabochon one side, but flat on the other, as if it once mounted into something. Looking through it, there seem to be invisible layers which are refracting the light into rainbow colours. The carving is at first inexplicable.

Rowena cannot clearly see any recognisable form to it. It is certainly not depicting any gods and does not appear to be religious as such. Without further analysis, she is guessing that the stone looks like it could be something like moldavite.

But if it is, what's it doing here, so far from Europe?

The stone radiates a kind of energy.

It seems, in her intuitive sense, to be a key of some sort. The forms carved into it are certainly even and geometric, but there is such symmetry to the work, and such sophisticated workmanship that she can only ponder its place historically.

'Where did you get this, Abraham...?'

He smiles mysteriously and shrugs.

'You like it...?'

'Of course, it's so beautiful Abraham, thank you! But it's a mystery to me...'

He chuckles, pleased at her response.

'I have to tell you old friend, I have no idea what it is

or where it comes from... it's certainly very old...'

This is going to her personal collection, Rowena feels. There is something about this that perhaps she should be sharing with her old friend, Professor Wadji, she thinks.

Then she sees a glimmer deep in the stone. She brings it closer, right up to her face. To her complete amazement she can see someone, right there in the stone, moving about like a living thing.

She knows that person!

It's her aunt, the indomitable Mrs. Stevenson! Her face is clear and sharp and right there!

Just then, there is a very twenty-first century interruption to her musings. It is the insistent ring of her satellite phone, which is attached to her trail bike.

This is Rowena's one modern concession to the perils of being a lone woman in these parts. And now it is ringing loudly, shattering the silence. She goes to it and removing it from its cradle on the handlebars of the bike, she answers it.

'Rowena here... Mrs. who..? Stevenson...? Oh my God, I don't believe this...! I... just... auntie; it's you!'

She looks at the crystal, then at the phone, then at the crystal. There is no doubt about it, the image of her aunt in the crystal is miming in time with her voice on the phone.

'My darling, how wonderful to hear from you... yes, I know the reception isn't great, it's because I'm in the mountains Auntie... Yes, yes I'm in Africa, Ethiopia to be exact... You what? Oh... yes, of course I remember Professor Clarence... yes... and Wadji...? Well of course, we go back a long way, as you know... missing? Really? Both of them...?

When? Oh dear, so you think they're in trouble, do you?

The Chinese...?

Now that's really weird, auntie. I swear you're a witch!

No really, I mean, how would you possibly know the Chinese have just asked me over there to supervise a new dig? You didn't? Wow!

This really is incredible! Well, look, the amazing thing is, I'm due to fly out to Beijing in a couple of days anyway.

I've got a dig happening there... Yeah, yeah, sure!

No problem at all. I'll go via Lhasa and see what's up with Clarence and Wadji!

Okay, sorry auntie, say that again, you're breaking up a bit there... oh... right... okay. I'll call you up in a couple of days when I know more.

Sure, of course I will.

Leave it to me darling.

Love you too. Bye.'

Rowena can't take her eyes off the crystal Abraham has given her. There is certainly something magical about the thing. Not only that, but she has just seen her aunt's image in it, talking to her all the time she was on the phone to her.

'I'm use it for find my goats,'

Abraham is saying to her.

'But I had a dream, and my ancestors come to me in this dream. Yes. Mmmm.

And my ancestors, they're saying to me that I must give this stone to another person.

And this person is you, Miss Rowena.

The ancestors they are telling me that this stone is look for his home. Yes. Mmmm.

This stone, his home is not here, is somewhere far from here; but they say you must take this stone to his home. Yes. Mmmm.

And thank you I am very happy now for more coffee...

Yes. Mmmm... I'm very happy for that Miss Rowena.'

He smiles and holds out his cup to her with both hands.

A little while later the silence of the Ethiopian Highlands is again shattered by the sound of Rowena Shardsworth's trail bike as she takes off across the escarpment. She is heading for her next assignment,

China, but now it seems, via Lhasa. To find the professors.

She smiles as she thinks of her fondness for the old shepherd Abraham. She is intrigued by the gift he has given her, and the way she could see her aunt in it.

What can it mean?

And the mysterious words that Abraham left her with when he handed the precious green stone over:

'You must take this stone to his home...'

Where would that be, she wonders?

And how strange that her aunt should call her right then to ask for her help in locating the professors.

And even more strange that the Chinese have just asked her to run their new dig, and now the profs have had a run in with them in Lhasa.

Mmmm.... wheels within wheels.

She looks forward to seeing the Professors Wadji and Clarence, assuming she manages to find them in Lhasa.

Little does she know how connected all three things are.

And little does she know that as soon as she and her trail bike strapped with baggage and pots and provisions and very good coffee have bounced away into the valleys of the Ethiopian Highlands, scattering goats and birds and baboons, a particular brown and white striped goat which had paid such close attention to her all the while she was there, unseen now by the shepherd at the fire; morphs into a familiar little man with a blue turban and gold teeth.

He mutters to himself and rubs his back now.

'Damn goats always seem to give me a sore back,

Have to stop shape-shifting into those things.'

Episode Thirty-Eight: The Stone Finds its Home

It is now some three weeks since Rowena rescued Professors Clarence and Wadji, as well as Mara, Josh, and Mrs. Kofi. Before she arrived, it had been a very vexing time for them all.

The Chinese soldiers had forced a strong pace on them, to reach Lhasa airport, which was probably a good thing; otherwise they might have perished in the freezing blizzards and their supplies had already run out.

The disappearance of Quortaletzl, when it was noticed, was a crushing blow to the little group.

He had been their unofficial guardian as well as showing an irrepressible childlike enthusiasm for everything, which kept their spirits lifted. Josh was particularly upset about his disappearance, until he 'tuned in' on the big man and saw he was being well looked after, somewhere not so far away.

It was only when the soldiers called a break to the trek that they found Quortaletzl missing.

There were no tracks to follow because of the blizzards, and so they quickly gave up the idea of searching for him, and anyway, as far as the soldiers were concerned, he was of little importance to them.

As far as they were concerned, their orders were simply to bring in the two professors. No one else mattered.

Even Doctor Pradesh was of no account to them, and if they had their way, they would have simply left him, Josh, and the women behind, such was their callousness.

Mara and Mrs. Kofi sensed this and kept a close maternal eye on Josh, and they extended that protection to Doctor Pradesh, making sure he was properly fed when they made their stops. Perhaps it was this very marginalising by their Chinese guards that brought the two women closer and made them such good friends in times to come.

The defining moment in their relationship with the guards came when they were just a day's walk from Lhasa. They had made a final stop to take a hot meal, and one of the soldiers had flung their plates and cups contemptuously into the snow in front of them .

One of the metal mugs bounced and hit Josh on the knee. Without hesitating, Mara got up and walked over to the soldier and slapped him very hard across the face, then glared at him, daring him to respond. In another moment Mrs. Kofi was right there beside her, also staring into the man's face.

This united front of furious womanhood was too much for him, and he backed off and apologised clumsily to Josh, then stumbled away, avoiding the fire in Mara's eyes; his rifle no match for the combined fury of the two women.

The professors, still pointlessly bound together, as they had no intention of escaping and leaving the others to the soldiers, looked on in amazement. They had heard the slap, so loud it was like a rifle shot, and then they turned to see the soldier stumbling away from a smarting slap and the combined threat of the two women. There was a bright red hand mark on the side of his face, which did not fade for days.

Clarence glanced over at Wadji, who looked over at Pradesh, who simply shrugged. 'Served him right' was his unspoken response.

Josh looked over and smiled.

He was proud of his mom and her boundless courage.

The rest of the journey passed uneasily, the soldiers now kept their distance, and soon they had reached the outskirts of Lhasa. Then they could see the airport terminal, and after that everything happened very quickly.

No sooner had the soldiers been met by an advance group of their colleagues just outside the terminal, than a tall, striking woman with flame-red hair and silver boots rushed out of the building and bore down on the professors, who were still roped together. Before the guards could even think of reacting (they were, in any case, exhausted by the trek through the blizzard), she had untied the two men.

Wadji and Clarence knew immediately who it was but were astonished to see her there! They had resigned themselves to spending that night in prison, and were looking and feeling very sorry for themselves.

Rowena Shardsworth took charge immediately! In fluent Mandarin she assured the guards, as they came up to her with their rifles ready, that she had authority over them, quoting their superiors by name and rank and waving some impressive documents from General Lu Kan Xi himself under their frostbitten noses.

Their colleagues in the airport terminal had already been briefed by the fiery Irish woman, and could only shrug and look deflated. Any power they might have had was rendered obsolete, in triplicate.

Wasting no time, she immediately introduced herself to the two women. The moment she mentioned who she was and that Mrs. Stevenson had sent her, Mara lit up like a Christmas tree. How astonishing that the old woman could yet again wield her influence, and this far away!

Rowena assured the professors that the soldiers would now leave them all alone and cause no further trouble, and that from here on, they would be safe with her. Although she was not able to retrieve Professor Wadji's camera, which had been impounded by the soldiers, along with its record of what they had seen in the depths of the caves. All they had now was a book of sketches and descriptions.

Dr. Pradesh had to run for his plane, which was about to leave for Delhi. He hurriedly and tearfully said his farewells, promising to contact the professors as soon as he got home.

There was a shuttle service which would take the rest of them to Lhasa in forty minutes, and Rowena had already booked them into the Sheraton Hotel, where they could all have a hot shower and a slap-up dinner. This was such a heavenly thought to them after the trek through the snowy wilderness, they almost cried with gratitude.

Rowena promised she had good news for them all. First, they had to refresh and restore themselves. She accompanied them on the shuttle to the hotel, checked them into a few rooms, and suggested they all meet her in the foyer. Then they could go to the restaurant where she had reserved a table for them.

Josh was clearly impressed with her, as he couldn't take his eyes off her. From the moment she appeared, he thought she was the most amazing woman he had ever seen. She was like Mara and Quortaletzl all rolled into one. And she was strong, capable, attractive, and feisty. Josh was like a puppy-dog around her, smiling whenever she glanced his way, and constantly thinking of what he could ask her next. The solitary trek through the snow had made him thirsty for social stimulation, so as soon as they were all seated around the dinner table he made sure he was right by her. She sat there, her silver boots up on the table, looking completely at ease.

'So Rowena, how did you manage to get to us so fast? I mean, I know Mrs. Stevenson called you, in... Africa?'

'Yes, Josh, I was visiting a site in Lalibela, amazing place, wonderful energy there. You'd like it. In fact, come with me next time I go. We can get there by trail bike. I always do... Do you ride?'

Josh blushed at her sudden intimacy. This was more than he had hoped for! An invitation? To go with Rowena? And on a trail bike? Wow!

'Er... sure! That would be brilliant... I'd love that!'

He didn't know what else to say at this point, but Wadji saved him, leaning over to engage her in conversation.

'Rowena, my dear. Do you still see Abraham the old shepherd in Lalibela? Such a lovely man. I'm very fond of him.'

'That old rascal? Yes, of course, he was there herding a flock of goats when I visited. Still the same. I don't think he has aged in all the years I've known him, Wadji. He has always been a mine of information. Do you know, that reminds me! On this last visit he casually gave me something while I was making him coffee. Let's see, I've got it here somewhere.'

Rowena jumps up and rifles through her pockets, finds something wrapped in an old cloth, and holds it out to Wadji. He unwraps the cloth, exposing the beautiful green gemstone that Abraham gave her. It glows with un unearthly radiance.

Then several things happen at once: Clarence's ever-present rucksack, which he had placed alongside his chair, opens of its own accord. Everyone sees this, as he is sitting at the head of the table.

The Fate Book, which had been wrapped in silk and managed to unwrap itself, glides over to Wadji, and hovers in the air, over the gem.

Everyone gasps, as the beautiful gem suddenly drifts up onto The Fate Book and attaches itself in the niche in the book's cover, accompanied by a flash of rainbow light and a bell-like sound.

'Well, look at that! The missing crystal! It's just come home to The Fate Book!' shouts an astonished Clarence.

Wadji is speechless. There are tears in the corners of his eyes. Somehow, he always felt that something like this would happen. Morkabalas had hinted years back that something lost would be returned, and then there would be a great change in the way The Fate Book was used.

'Well. There you go! I shall miss that stone, but I suppose you can explain what's going on here, Professor?'

Rowena frowns, her hands opened out in submission to this new turn of events. She is addressing both professors.

'No wait a bit... do you know, I've just remembered what Abraham said when he gave me the stone. He said, *'You must take this stone to his home.'*

Yes, those were his exact words. My God! And you've just said the same thing, Clarence. So, this must be the home of the stone. Clarence, you'll have to explain what kind of a book this is. I think you owe me that, at least...'

Rowena feels she is the only one at the table who doesn't know about The Fate Book, as everyone else seems unfazed by it and by what has just happened.

Everyone except for Mrs. Kofi, who, seeing The Fate Book, and seeing now that Clarence is its unlikely custodian, and counter to her belief, has it in his keeping, turns a whiter shade of pale and drops face-first into her plate of food. Wadji hurries over to her. He gently picks her up, wipes the basmati rice from her face, and whispering to Mara that he will see her back to the hotel, he accepts the room key from her and carries Lydia Kofi out of the restaurant. Josh jumps up to find a car for them, and returns a moment later. It seems the time has come for Mrs. Kofi and Professor Wadjiwadj to have their time together.

The Fate Book has, in the meantime, dropped gently onto the table in front of Clarence. He picks it up, noticing that with the green stone now back where it belongs in its cover, the book has a different feel about it. There is even a gentle hum and a soft vibration running through it as he carefully wraps it in its silk cover and returns it to his rucksack. Who knows what that change will do for it?!

'Well, Rowena my dear,' says Clarence, 'All I can say is that you clearly have a part to play in The Fate Book's custodianship. Wadji and I would be honoured to explain everything, in good time. However, I feel it would be more appropriate to do this somewhere more private. May I suggest you come to our hotel room later? And may I also thank you for your part in re-uniting the stone with its home, The Fate Book?'

'Of course, I can't wait! How amazing! I had no idea you were such a man of mystery, Clarence! I'm gobsmacked!'

The rest of the evening is taken up with Clarence and Rowena exchanging stories of their recent adventures. Josh is spellbound and Mara smiles, seeing her son so taken with this extraordinary woman. It's so good to relax and sit with people who are as connected as they all are. But once again, she finds her thoughts straying. She is thinking about Quortaletzl again.

Where could he be? Is he safe? Will she ever see him again? She feels a little remorse at not treating him as well as she could have, while he was staying with her in Dublin. How wonderful and caring and compassionate he was with Mrs. Kofi, when she was tripping out in Mrs. Stevenson's house. And he didn't even know her! And so what was she, Mara, so afraid of? What was she trying to avoid? After all, they got on so well. Was her old ongoing issue with commitment again?

'Mom... hellooo... ground control calling Planet Mom.

Come in Mom...!' Josh breaks in on her thoughts.

'Oh, sorry Josh, I was miles away. Must be the wine.'

'Mmmm... you were thinking about him again, weren't you? Our friend Quortaletzl? It's okay, Mom. Actually, you know, I really miss him too. He's like a big brother to me. He's such a fun guy to be around. He makes me laugh, and I can't help it; he's so uncomplicated and real! But like I said before, I know he's all right, and I also know we'll see him again soon... okay?'

He reaches over and hugs Mara. She blushes, knowing that for Josh nothing is hidden.

Rowena and Clarence are talking about their impending trip to China, and they are both excited by the prospects.

'...and so General Xi has put me in charge of the whole thing. Yeah, I know, I'm as surprised as you are! I mean look at me, for Heaven's sake, Clarence! I'm the hippie of the archaeology world, and they want me to run the whole damn project! Mind you, this General Xi seems a bit of an upstart if you ask me. I don't know what you and Wadji did to upset him, but he wasn't happy about you guys working with me. In the end, I had to insist on it. He went on and on about Wadji in particular; something about having to watch him with the women.'

'Mmmm... too ruddy right! Bloody old Wadji and his romantic shenanigans.' Clarence rolls his eyes. He knows exactly what Rowena is referring to, but he is far too loyal to his old friend to make further comment.

'Anyway, they're all mad keen to get going straight away. Although the whole thing's become a bit of a media-circus, as if there weren't enough to deal with already. I wasn't going to bring it up right now, Clarence, but I think it's best to bring it out into the open before we get to Beijing. The thing is, they want to have a TV crew on hand to film the whole thing as it's unfolding. In fact, they're looking at fitting both of you up with cameras so the world can see things through your eyes... sort of... yes, I know. She pulls a face showing her distaste for it all.

Clarence rolls his eyes and blows out his cheeks. He is not comfortable with this. This is not the way he or Wadji choose to work. But of course, Rowena knows this.

'Look, Clarence, I know it's not the way we work. God, I mean you know how private I am. I can't bear to have people breathing down my neck either.

But obviously I have to respect the Chinese and the fact that this is huge for them. Really, I mean just think about it, they've never ever opened themselves to the scrutiny of the world before; well, except for the Olympics, of course. But this is different, this is, well, this is for the world really, it's not just their history. They want to share it... That's of course, apart from the fact that a whole shed-load of western technology and specialist equipment donated by the States is going into the project, and that of course, carries a caveat. You know yourself, Clarence, this thing has been brewing for years, decades even. By now there are lots of fingers in the pie...'

'This is true, Rowena. Quite true. Wadji and I already heard rumblings about an impending dig on the jolly old Emperor's tomb when we worked on the terracotta warrior excavation back in seventy-four. I suppose it's a bit ironic that it has taken all these years to develop the tech-support to make it all possible. As for the media involvement... well, it's a bit of a bugger, but I suppose we can live with it, as long as I don't have to lose weight or dye me hair or trim me nails for the camera, eh!'

'Well, actually, Clarence... they want you to carry a bull-whip, wear khaki shorts and a gigantic moustache... no no, only kidding!'

Rowena laughs out loud. She has a distinctive and infectious laugh, and Clarence can't help joining in.

'Sorry, Clarence, I couldn't help myself there... Yes, so as far as the equipment and specialist support teams go, I'll be briefing you and Professor Wadji tomorrow on all of that. You'll be wearing specially designed suits to screen out toxic gases and radiation. Most of all, we need to keep you guys safe from the mercury fumes, and the Chinese have already done some sonar investigations on the general layout of the tomb. More of that in the morning though. I know you must be feeling exhausted from your ordeals. All of you.'

Rowena is right. Josh and Mara are leaning up against each other and are fast asleep. She pays the bill and calls for a car to take them to their hotel.

In spite of his near-exhaustion, Clarence is excited about flying out to Beijing the next day. This is the kind of project he and Wadji have been longing to get their teeth into for years. He's just a little anxious about having to wear an insulating suit, a bit claustrophobic, he's thinking... and the thought of having a camera hitched up to all that... mmm.... damned inconvenient really. Still, have to keep up with these modern Johnnies!

The following day, Rowena makes sure Josh, Mara, and Mrs. Kofi are safely on the flight back to Dublin. The soldiers at Lhasa airport have clearly been briefed and are now very respectful toward them all. In fact, the soldier who was bitch-slapped by Mara now makes a point of escorting them to the plane, all the while smiling and bowing. He even shows Mara a photograph of his children back home, in an attempt to make peace with her.

It is clear that Mrs. Kofi and Wadji have made peace too. Mrs. Kofi is glowing and she is looking quite like a young girl. Mara is pleasantly shocked to see her holding hands with him as they walk along slowly, talking quietly together like lovers, to the boarding gate. Mara also couldn't help noticing that Lydia Kofi only returned to the hotel room she shared with Mara just before breakfast, and then straight after that she could hear her singing 'Climb Every Mountain' in the shower! Certain signs of a reconciliation! She knows Lydia Kofi will be wanting to tell her everything in the plane on the journey back.

And then, Clarence is quite taken aback as Mrs. Kofi suddenly and unexpectedly throws her arms around him and hugs him at the departure gate. She smiles up at his shocked face and says,

'Professor Kalikaloos, I have something to say to you. Something I should have said years ago. Please can you forgive me for being so... well... so crotchety with you all these years. I think you know why. And you didn't deserve any of that. I'm so so sorry.'

As ever, Clarence is a bit embarrassed at this show of emotion. But he is very pleased. Especially that she and Wadji have so obviously made up.

'Oh, don't you worry about that, old girl! Never did take it on y'see... In fact, it never put me off visiting me old friend Wadji. Always knew there was something going on between the two of you anyway! Just look at the two of you now! Marvellous! Damned if I haven't got something in me eye!'

He dabs awkwardly at his eyes with one of his huge handkerchiefs. Wadji has come over now, and takes Lydia Kofi's hands. They stand there looking into each other's eyes, and the rest of the party leave them to their farewell moment.

Josh seems pleased with himself too. For two reasons: Firstly, Rowena made a point of going up to him as they all said goodbye at the departure gate, and reminded him that the two of them had a date with a couple of trail bikes and they would be hitting the hills of Lalibela in the summer, for sure. He blushed as they high-fived on it. What a woman!

Secondly, as he was checking his phone messages, he picked up a message from Katrina. She was wanting to tell him how much she had missed him and how she couldn't wait to see him again. And with that message, there was a photo of her blowing him a kiss. He thought his heart would burst!

Rowena would be flying out with the professors to Beijing the next day. Today she will be briefing them on what they will be facing out there, and of course, she is looking forward to hearing all about The Fate Book.

Clarence waves goodbye to Mara and Josh as they board the plane. His heart is full. He has his family, so what more could he want? And there is the added bonus of a new adventure starting the very next day!

He reflects also on the wonder of Rowena bringing the green stone Abraham had given her, all that way from Africa, and with her not even knowing anything about The Fate Book, not knowing that the stone was destined to be re-united with The Fate Book.

As he and Rowena and Wadji give a final wave as they board their plan for Dublin, Clarence is sure he sees, just behind them, a familiar figure, standing there with them and waving back at him.

It is a small man in a turban with gold teeth.

Episode Thirty-Nine: The General

General Lu Kan Xi paced up and down his office in extreme irritation, muttering Mandarin curses to himself, with the odd expletive exploding out intermittently.

Though tiny in stature, he bristled with energy, and looked formidably fighting fit in his army uniform.

He wore fringed red epaulettes studded in shiny brass stars, a peaked cap, and a perfectly pressed powder-blue jacket with brass buttons, decorated with ribbons and sashes, with matching jodhpurs and polished high leather boots.

Of course, there was a leather riding whip to complete this image of testosterone on legs, and this whip he now used to punctuate his expletives.

Right now he was angry and annoyed and frustrated, which was never a good combination if you were an enemy of his.

Xi was used to getting his way, and this had ensured his rapid rise through the ranks of the Chinese Liberation Army. He certainly didn't start out as a lowly corporal, as more than one ambitious learner-dictators have been known to have.

Instead, he had come from a privileged background, his parents both active members of the communist party and the Politburo and they were leading lights in the modern restructuring of the pro-capitalist though communist, expansionist, revisionist, industrialist programmes in modern China.

He had deliberately chosen to study law and military strategy, and then he went on somewhat randomly to a post-graduate degree in archaeology in Beijing.

He didn't know why, but it seemed like a good idea at the time.

But we know it was fate.

Because it was as a direct consequence of these latter studies that he was fated to meet the young Professors Wadji and Clarence.

At that time, Xi was living the high life with a young and impressionable wife, Xan Ku Li, whom he had courted and married whilst still an undergraduate.

She was impressed with his big brains and connections and his vaulting ambition and his straight teeth and she could see he would go far in the political scrum that was modern China. She had an eye for that kind of stuff.

You may remember that quite a few years before, the hot blooded young Professor Wadji Wadjiwadj had made a huge impression on the lovely but naive Xan

Ku Li, who was at that time the fiance of the possessive and controlling Lu Kan Xi and this it was that had almost sullied the professor's future reputation.

If it wasn't for the timeous intervention of the ever-sensible Clarence 'Stinky' Kalikaloos, who scared her off by convincing her that Wadji had a deadly transmittable social disease, both men might have suffered a dubious fate when the young General-to-be Xi discovered that his wife-to-be Li was falling for the charms of the irresistibly incorrigibly debonair young Wadji Wadjiwadj.

Xi then had both professors spirited quickly out of the country, duplicitously insisting to their faces that he was saving them from being arrested.

On trumped-up spying charges, of course.

And just for good measure, as a backup plan, (for insurance if this plan failed), he had planted a very rare and valuable Ming dynasty fertility vase in Wadji's luggage.

Of course, it had an unconscious appropriateness to it.

He still has it even today, standing on his desk, as a bizarre kind of keepsake trophy. He keeps cigars in it for special guests.

Now, some twenty years later, Professor Wadji Wadjiwadj is again about to cross the General's path.

And this is how:

A month prior to these peripatetic agitations, General Xi had once more been put in charge of the excavations of the tomb of China's first Emperor, having assisted in the excavations of the Terracotta Warriors decades earlier.

This was of course a great honour, but it was a double-edged sword: on the one edge, if he screwed up he could end up naked and destitute and barefoot, planting rice in a paddy field for the rest of his life.

But, on the other edge, if the dig succeeded and revealed the ancient emperor's hoard as well it might, it would bring undreamed-of prestige to the ambitious young general and with it, of course, undoubted further promotions and decorations on his lovely little uniform.

At first, he was so happy he couldn't contain himself. In fact, he was so excited he went out and bought Xan Ku Li a whole new wardrobe, and a new car, and a brand-new smartphone, and a place in Madame Tussaud's of Beijing.

She was rapidly becoming a kind of Chinese Paris Hilton; all she needed now was a chihuahua and a blonde wig.

But then poor General Xi discovered that his exciting new orders contained a poisonous caveat: he was told that because of the sensitive and complex nature of the dig, and its global ramifications, he would have to appoint a westerner to head the team.

Recent scientific tests at the site had found incredibly

high levels of mercury in the soil deep within the tomb mound.

This lent credence to some early Chinese writings that suggested the Emperor's tomb was surrounded by seven rivers of mercury, symbolising the seven rivers of China.

From these ancient descriptions, the tomb of Emperor Shi Huang Di itself appeared to be a hermetically sealed space as big as a football pitch and located deep underneath the pyramidal tomb mound.

And so, to this day, the tomb remained unopened, uncharted and unexplored; one other possible reason may be concerns about the preservation of valuable artefacts once the tomb was opened. For example, after their excavation, the painted surface present on some figures of the terracotta army began to flake and fade. In fact, we now know from direct experience that the lacquer covering the paint can curl in fifteen seconds once exposed to the dry air of Xi'an Province and can flake off in just four minutes!

And so, this was why the proposed new dig was sensitive. There are other chemically-challenging issues; not the least of them being the concentration of mercury on the site and its potentially lethal effects. So, there would have to be effective containment of all the items recovered on site and the quarantining of all workers until they are deemed safe.

This, of course, presented challenges to the Chinese government, but there were a few who saw this as an opportunity for China to be seen as leaders in the field, or put more plainly, a chance to gain political kudos.

But Xi would have to call on Western technological aid and his brief required the appointment of a westerner to lead the team. We now know who that person was and is:

Rowena Shardsworth.

Rowena had only agreed to supervise the project if she was assisted by a team of her own choice. This team included a squad who could handle the containment of dangerous gases and chemicals, and who could constantly monitor the mercury levels on the site.

Fair enough. But then the full thunderbolt hit General Xi. Rowena had insisted on including in her team a certain pair of well-known archaeologists, the Professors Wadji Wadjiwadj and Clarence 'Stinky' Kalikaloos! These are now orders, not options. And this is why he was now so agitated.

You might think his agitated perambulations, which were now punctuated by cursing in Mandarin and slapping a horsewhip about, was all about the history between himself and Wadji, or more correctly, the history between his young wife and Wadji, and of course, you'd be right.

But only partly right.

A far, far more serious consideration now was the threat of a certain scandal being uncovered. A scandal that could bring him down from his privileged position and his elite status and high ambitions and hurl him naked and destitute into a rice paddy.

That scandal had a connection with a certain Mrs. Kofi, and therefore ultimately also with Mrs. Stevenson, Mara, Jess and Clarence, and just about everyone!

The scandal concerned a certain cryptic note scrawled in Professor Wadji's daybook. The cryptic note that his personal assistant Mrs. Kofi had come across, concerning The Fate Book and its new custodian, referred to but not mentioned by name:

The Fate Book no longer mine. Now it's someone else's to care for...

That cryptic note was going to prove central to the scandal, and it had occurred in the following way...

General Xi had called Professor Wadji's office some months previously, to speak to Mrs. Kofi about loaning some important historical Egyptian artefacts for a forthcoming exhibition in Beijing. The call was an entirely routine matter, and as you can imagine, the General was hoping to conduct his business entirely through the highly competent Mrs. Kofi, comfortably bypassing Professor Wadji altogether.

However, little did he know that Mrs. Kofi had been weaving a web, in which she hoped to helplessly spin her erstwhile lover, Wadji Wadjwadj. A web which had been years in the making, patiently fuelled by thoughts of revenge and spurred by his rejection of her, some years before.

Just before Mrs. Kofi ended her call to General Xi, having efficiently made all possible arrangements for the proposed Beijing exhibition, she casually let slip that she'd just come by some confidential information on a most mysterious artefact, which she felt might interest the General.

Knowing General Xi's capacity for anything that might advance his cause on the ladder of professional and political ambition, she wondered if he wanted to know more. Of course he did! And so a plot was hatched between them to locate and steal The Fate Book.

And we know that Mrs. Kofi spearheaded this plot, financed by General Xi's Chinese money. A dastardly and cruel plot, which firstly enlisted the ruthless men in Armani suits who had attempted to track down Mara at her library, and then in the depths of the Guatemalan jungles; as well as a motley group of delinquent inner-city skateboarders who had incarcerated Jess, the innocent niece of Professor Kalikaloos, in a dark and damp underground place. There she was interrogated by Mrs. Kofi pretending to be the familiar Mrs. Stevenson and where Jess would have rotted away, were she not rescued by the intervention of the magical mystical Morkabalas, former custodian of The Fate Book, ably assisted by the muscular melon-eating Mayan man of the jungle and secret admirer of Mara, a certain Quortaletzl.

Of course, the whole thing was a disaster, ending in Mrs. Kofi's involuntarily drug-induced and life-changing confession to Mrs. Stevenson. The General's part in the plot was not revealed, but he now lived in constant fear that it would be. And now it seemed, fate decreed that he had to work with the very people he had tried to sabotage, and still, in spite of all that, he did not have The Fate Book.

And so he is pacing his office now. What is he going to do? Perhaps some kind of little accident could be arranged? An accident that would eliminate the professors? Easy enough. But what about Mrs. Kofi? She needed to be eliminated even more than them!

Now his latest communications were that Rowena Shardsworth, the now-officially appointed head of operations on the Emperor's excavation site, had duly escorted the Professors Wadjiwadj and Kalikaloos from Lhasa to Beijing to take up their positions. She had made sure that the two women and the boy were safely seen onto a plane bound from Lhasa to Dublin.

The three westerners were now ensconced at the curiously titled five-star Shangri-La Hotel. This made Xi even angrier. The fact that these foreigner usurpers were being provided with such sumptuous accommodation was yet more fuel to the fire of the little general's anger and envy. Never mind that, in actual fact, these foreigners were themselves uncomfortable with this luxury. All three of them were far more at home in a tent under the stars.

However, he could not deny that, this way, with the three foreigners ensconced in the hotel, the Chinese government would be able to keep an eye on them, and had already ensured that their guests would be watched twenty-four seven.

If the ambitious and devious General Lu Kan Xi were only presented with an opportunity, and this seemed very likely, he would ensure that some kind of calamity of a permanent kind, could and would befall them.

But wait!

He stops dead and all is still. The noxious General is thinking now of something far more effective. Something ancient, deadly and always successful: the venom of a woman scorned! If he can but endanger Professor Wadjiwadj, surely that would act as a lure to entice Mrs. Kofi? He knew the woman had feelings for Wadji. Why else would she have betrayed him in the way she had?

And if, for example, he is now thinking: if the foreigner she is in love with could be tempted into some kind of... say... life-threatening situation, let's say, for example, that just when the professors have found their way into the depths of the Emperor's tomb, and then a booby-trap was triggered. Let's say that the professors were then entombed down there in the Emperor's tomb... surely then, she would come running to Beijing, and Mrs. Kofi, and then he, General Lu Kan Xi, would have all of his enemies close to him, where he could deal with them.

'Keep your friends close, your enemies even closer.'

The words of Confucius?

Or was it Mao?

Whatever!

This sudden flash of dark genius brought a twisted and humourless smile to the face of General Xi. He had them! *They were as good as dead!* He ejaculated with a triumphant guffaw, slamming his leather horsewhip for emphasis perhaps a little too forcefully on an ancient delicate black-lacquered trinket box on his desk.

It cracked in half.

If Xi were an animist, which of course he wasn't, he would have seen this as a little omen, a warning. He might have seen from reading the pattern of cracks in the lacquer that a favourable outcome was not likely. But he was a communist, not an animist, and believed not in the portents of nature.

No, he, General Lu Kan Xi, believed only in the supreme power of the state.

And so suddenly his mood shifted from the red-black of anger to something perhaps a little lighter. Let's see, what could he buy for his little flower today? He would go take a walk and stretch his legs. Find something nice for her amongst the markets stalls. Mmm... A little gift of some sort... A little silver trinket perhaps? She was just like a child that way, and always excited about any little gift that came her way.

In spite of his intention to surprise his lovely

wife, General Xi was brimming with dark thoughts. Thoughts of how he would snare the foreign professors and Mrs. Kofi in his web. They knew too much, they had to go. Now he was kicking his way down the narrow streets of downtown Beijing, literally booting beggars, old men, dogs, and even bicycles and their precarious cargos. Everyone knew him as the 'kicking General.' They tried now to give way and even hide when they saw him coming. The clamour of traders and food pedlars and gossiping women died down to a whisper as he passed, as his shiny kicking boots cleared a path.

This morning a damp mist hangs about the place and ahead of the strutting generalissimo what seems to be a pile of rags appears ahead of him in the middle of the road, directly in his path. Naturally he raises a boot and kicks out at the pile of rags, but to his surprise and astonishment, his leg freezes before it can connect with the pile of rags. And then the rag pile all of a sudden rises up and at once shows itself to be the bent figure of an old man, whose face is beaming with irrepressible good will.

But then General Xi finds he is stuck in one position, frozen like a mime artist. Strangely, the entire street has frozen too... The old man, however, walks right up to him and eyeballs him, with his face still beaming happily.

'When the elephant is down, even the frog will kick it, eh General Xi? You know, you've got to control that foot of yours, kind sir! Or else, you never know; one day it might end up stuck up your own backside!'

General Xi is unable to respond though he wants to. He wants to dropkick this bundle of smiling rags over the sagging tiled roofs. He wants to but he can't, try as he might...

'Mmmm... tender conscience eh? Hope so, my little General, my little shiny kicking man. You know, the thing is, you start out by rubbing out a couple of people or three, the ones who could show you up for being a bit of a bastard, and the next thing you're an exterminator... but you're still a bastard! Know what I mean? You will only ever see yourself, my friend...'

The old man says all of this with a beneficent smile. Next his teeth turn to gold and he is wearing a pale blue turban and he bows and smiles and then... poof! He disappears! Then, everything unfreezes and the general's foot continues on its interrupted trajectory. But something has changed since the scene was frozen by the mysterious old man, and our vitriolic general is about to get a shock.

Unfortunately for him, his target has been magically substituted, and instead of the pile of rags he had aimed his boot at, he connects full force with a large pile of fresh horse excrement, which now sprays back at him from head to foot.

Astonished passersby snicker and stare, as the spattered and malodorous General Xi has no choice but to return immediately to his quarters to change out of his massively soiled uniform.

He angrily swears vengeance on the old man and even considers issuing a warrant for his arrest; damned if the old bugger didn't disappear into the mist....

As he is donning a fresh new uniform, having spent a good while under a hot shower until he can no longer smell horse shit; the door opens and standing there is his wife, Xan Ku Li, looking utterly radiant!

He immediately forgets the humiliation he has just suffered and allows himself to bathe in her radiance.

If such things had not been outlawed in China as decadent, Xan Ku Li would have won every available beauty pageant, regional or national, hands down. She has the kind of skin which seems to radiate light from inside, and a lustrous waterfall of shiny jet-black hair cascades down her shoulders and frames her lovely features.

We already know she is naive and innocent; and, but for Clarence's pseudo warnings, would have fallen for Wadji's charms years before, when they were all students.

Even now, her beauty is undiminished, fuelled by a sweet, guileless, uncorrupted nature. One could say she is a perfect foil for General Xi, for indeed, she is everything he is not.

Where he is sly and devious, she is innocent.

Where he is ambitious and ruthless, she is shy and kind.

Where he does not care for the suffering of others, she goes out of her way to help those in need.

Though it at one time annoyed him to see her

constantly doing charitable work, he realised this would help his career, so he tolerated it. Even encouraged it. Li is renowned for her international work protecting endangered animals, especially tigers, and is known by many, for this reason, as 'Tiger Lily.'

Her face is now familiar on television and even Facebook users would see her smiling face posed alongside a tiger cub.

She is now one of China's most beloved celebrities.

Beloved of the conservationists, and of the younger generation alike. She represents all that is best in the modern woman; she is beautiful, intelligent, kind, and cheerful. And she is also, of course, General Lu Kan Xi's trophy.

That night, General Xi wakes up screaming, in a cold sweat.

Li anxiously tries to comfort him. It has been the same thing, night after night these last few weeks, ever since he was appointed to oversee the excavations on the Emperor's tomb.

He would wake up from the same nightmare, every time the same story:

He was being entombed alive in the tomb, along with thousands of others.

There was no way out.

They would all die there.

Episode Forty: The Tomb of the Emperor

Professor Clarence 'Stinky' Kalikaloos had lost a massive amount of weight on his trek in Tibet.

Just as well, really.

Otherwise he would be struggling now with the narrow winding corridors he and Wadjiwadj were negotiating.

It was slow going, but exciting!

This was something that had never been attempted before!

Clarence was scanning the way ahead, with the bright LED flashlight on his helmet lighting the way.

The marble paved floor, which sloped downwards, was immaculately clean, as if it had been swept the day before. Of course, he had been briefed about the dangers of booby-traps.

There might be poison arrows hidden behind secret apertures in the wall, trapdoors triggered by stepping on certain stones.

There might be noxious gases set off by their

movements, boulders might drop down on them from above...

Every step they took had to be carefully calculated before it was taken.

Wadji followed precisely in Clarence's steps, trying to stay sharp and focussed.

After extensive ground mapping with sonar equipment, Rowena and her team had finally reached the day on which they were fully outfitted and equipped and they were at last ready to descend into the Emperor's tomb.

Back in the day, the great Qui Huang Shi, first emperor of China, had spared no expense in the building of this project. Thousands of people were involved, and thousands perished. His advisors had insisted that all of those involved in the building of the tomb, especially those present at the end of the project, would never speak of what they had seen down there while it was being built.

So there was only one option:

They would all be entombed with the Emperor! There was no way out! They would all die there!

For this reason, the advance team expected to find many gory and disturbing sights. Rowena, as much as she wanted to be down there with Clarence and Wadji, was essential to managing and directing the crew operating above ground.

This team was split up into those who monitored the toxic levels down there, those who were watching the closed-circuit cameras ever on the lookout for dangerous booby traps and false routes, and those who were monitoring any finds and pre-cataloguing them.

As an expert tracker, Clarence had always been Rowena's first choice as lead explorer, whereas Wadji would be able to assess the nature of the finds and their relative importance.

Both men were wearing what at first looked a bit like beekeeper's outfits, but were in fact sophisticated protective suits, which were electronically climate-controlled and supplied with an internal source of fresh oxygen, completely isolated from their environment.

This oxygen would last a good six to eight hours before it would need to be replenished, so they would not be able to spend more than a maximum of three hours exploring before having to return to the surface.

The rules were unambiguous on this and Rowena had briefed them clearly: as soon as they had reached the three-hour limit, they were to return without any hesitation!

No exceptions!

The suits were also proof against radioactivity, toxic chemicals from decaying matter and hermetically sealed, proof also against their main concern: the threat of mercury poisoning.

Each suit was individually monitored from the team at ground level, and the professors were in constant audio and video contact. In fact, the whole expedition was now being filmed live and broadcast to millions of viewers around the world!

From their home in Dublin, Mara, Jess, Josh, and Katrina were watching this momentous event on TV: the first time in history that an attempt was being made to explore the Emperor's tomb!

From her small flat in Cairo, Mrs. Kofi sat watching the commentary. She had mixed feelings. On the one hand, she was of course thrilled and excited for her boss, Professor Wadji Wadjiwadj. Professionally speaking, of course.

On the other hand, they were now lovers again, and she was feeling things again and acting like a teenager!

She thought, back in Lhasa, when he had carried her back to her hotel room, that it would be incredibly hard to tell Wadji about her pent-up feelings, but she was amazed to discover he felt the same about her. The difficult bit; the plot involving The Fate Book, and the awful stuff about Jess and the kidnapping, and the attacks on Mara by the men in suits she had hired, was far easier than she could have imagined.

Wadji thought it was all so hilarious!

But he also understood the desperation behind it all.

There was a moment where he wept to see what

lengths Lydia went to, just to get his attention. Ironically, he begged for her forgiveness, there in her hotel room, for all the years he had spurned her love and been so utterly blind to something staring him in the face: the love and devotion of Lydia Kofi.

The bit about General Xi's involvement, which she had begged him to keep secret, was a bit trickier to get his head around. If the man was still seriously intent on acquiring The Fate Book, after the plot had already failed twice, Wadji would have to warn Clarence to be vigilant. Though, he is thinking, smiling to himself, Wadji had the feeling that The Fate Book could probably take care of itself, as could his friend Clarence... these things certainly put a little spice in life!

The next day, the professors had flown out to Beijing with Rowena, to begin the great enterprise which was now playing out live in Mrs. Kofi's very living room. For now, the loved-up and revitalised Lydia Kofi would have to accept the image of Wadji on her screen as the closest she would get to him, for a while. For now and the foreseeable future she would have to get used to the idea of sharing him with millions of others...

Back in Dublin, Mara was a little anxious and nervous for her brother Clarence, but he had faced far more challenging dangers in his time.

At least here, on the Emperor's tomb dig, the team was being equipped with every conceivable safety device, and the whole project had been many months in the planning.

Mrs. Stevenson had been invited to come over and watch it all unfold with them in their living room.

Josh and Katrina sat together holding hands, while Jess and Mara busied themselves in the kitchen making tea and heating the scones Mrs. Stevenson had brought along.

The TV broadcast, though live, was interspersed with clips from the preparatory time before the expedition.

Clips were now being shown of Rowena speaking about the steps that had to be taken to keep the explorers safe, and the technology they had to employ, to make the excavation possible. This made Mrs. Stevenson very excited, seeing her beloved niece there on the screen.

She was so proud of her.

She had been like a daughter to her, and hadn't she turned out nice? She turned to look at Josh and Katrina as she said this, just as Josh was kissing Katrina...

Mrs. Stevenson rolled her eyes. Just when she was beginning to think the boy had some sense!

Still, she had to concede, hormones had their rights too.

The TV presenter drones on, covering the background leading up to the present excavation:

'...workers digging a well outside the city of Xi'an, China, in 1974 struck upon one of the greatest archaeological discoveries in the world: a life-size clay soldier poised for battle.

The diggers notified Chinese authorities, who dispatched government archaeologists to the site.

They found not one, but thousands of clay soldiers, each with unique facial expressions and positioned according to rank.

And though largely grey today, patches of paint hint at once brightly coloured clothes.

Further excavations have revealed swords, arrow tips, and other weapons, many of these still in pristine condition.

The terra-cotta army, as it is known, is part of an elaborate mausoleum created to accompany the first emperor of China into the afterlife, according to archaeologists...'

'Mmmm... can I help you with them tea-things, Mara?'

Mrs. Stevenson calls out, now a little bored, not by the TV of course, but by being forced to be a voyeur to the necking going on.

'It's okay, we're just coming through now...' replies Mara, as she emerges with a large tray. Josh and Katrina disengage themselves from each other as the tray is set out in front of them on a large coffee table.

'...Young Emperor Ying Zheng took the throne in 246 B.C.

at the age of 13. By 221 B.C. he had unified a collection of warring kingdoms and took the name of Qin Shi Huang Di—the First Emperor of Qin. During his rule, Qin standardized coins, weights, and measures; interlinked the states with canals and roads; and is credited for building the first version of the Great Wall...'

'Scone, Katrina...? you look as though you could do with one, all this couch rugby...' sings Mara, who is really rather fond of the girl. Mrs. Stevenson giggles.

'...according to writings of court historian Siam Qian during the following Han dynasty, Qin ordered the mausoleum's construction shortly after taking the throne. More than 700,000 labourers worked on the project, which was halted in 209 B.C. amid uprisings a year after Qin's death. To date, four pits have been partially excavated.

Three are filled with the terra-cotta soldiers, horse-drawn chariots, and weapons. The fourth pit is empty, a testament to the original unfinished construction. Archaeologists estimate the pits may contain as many as 8,000 figures, but the total may never be known.

"The tomb was filled with models of palaces, pavilions, and offices, as well as fine vessels, precious stones, and rarities," reads a translation of the text. The account indicates the tomb contains replicas of the area's rivers and streams made with mercury flowing to the sea through hills and mountains of bronze.

Precious stones such as pearls are said to represent the sun, moon, and other stars. Modern tests on the tomb mound have revealed unusually high concentrations of mercury, lending credence to at least some of the historical account.

Chinese archaeologists are also using remote-sensing technology to probe the tomb mound. The technique recently revealed an underground chamber with four stair-like walls.

An archaeologist working on the site told the Chinese press that the chamber may have been built for the soul of the emperor.

Experimental pits dug around the tomb have revealed dancers, musicians, and acrobats full of life and caught in mid-performance, a sharp contrast to the military poses of the famous terra-cotta soldiers...

And now we are crossing live, as our intrepid explorers, the Professors Kalikaloos and Wadjiwadj are ready to descend into the shaft. They are wearing their specially insulated suits, which are fitted with an internal but limited supply of oxygen. These suits are designed to protect the men from any toxic fumes and are also fitted with cameras and radio transmitters. They are now about to enter the shaft linking the Emperor's tomb with the outside world!

Suddenly things become very exciting.

Clearly the news network had leaned heavily on American-style presentation. There is a massive photo-montage of the terracotta warriors and those past excavations up close;

and a huge screen set up next to the entrance shaft to the dig was counting down in LED numbers:

10 9 8 7 6 5 4 3 2... 1!

Then the cameras move in close-up as the professors take their positions on the specially designed gantry that will now drop them, through three successive airlocks, into the tomb.

They look like astronauts, only, they're going down into the unknown, not up!

What are they thinking, there in the depths of their white cocoons? Their special suits and helmets that insulate them from the world?

Clarence is thinking:

Dash it all to buggery! Should have taken another leak before they popped me into this ruddy suit... Ah well, if I've got to go, Iv'e got to go...

Wadji is thinking:

Mmmm... very attractive TV presenter that, must ask her out for dinner when we get back, oh, no wait a minute... I've got Lydia Kofi now! That's even better...

Now we follow them down, white-suited, and helmeted, through the first airlock, then the second, then the third.

A running commentary from the TV announcer accompanies each of these stations, for dramatic effect. Rowena cringes, but what can she do?

Now they stand in a dimly lit hallway, which of course had already been carefully and respectfully entered by the workers who installed the lift shaft and the airlocks.

From here, there is a bronze doorway directly ahead of them, beyond which lies the unknown.

Rowena's voice crackles in Clarence's ear:

'What's up. Stinky? (She is one of the few people he allows to address him by his nickname.)

Now remember, you guys have just three hours of oxygen available in your lovely white suits, no more, before you must return, okay? So no more than three hours in there, then come straight back... make the most of it!

I have a lot of faith in you!

'And Professor Wadjiwadji, and Professor Kalikaloos, I know how much this means to you, and we'd like you to know that the Chinese government and it's joyful and supportive people (this slightly sycophantic part has, of course, been scripted for her by a government stenographer) will always be grateful to you today, on this momentous and historic day, for your brave and selfless efforts.'

Fortunately, the professors' mumbled responses are indistinct at this point. They are neither respectful nor flattering.

But now they stand before the bronze door.

Excitement is mounting, and millions of viewers are watching the drama unfolding.

Wadji is studying the ideograms intently.

He is reading the inscriptions back to Clarence and of course, the millions of TV viewers:

'...and the great Emperor has begun his journey to the other life in the other kingdom... Beware all those who would desecrate his name by entering this hallowed place'

"The flea has no place in the nest of the egret."

Clarence, who has been scanning the area around the bronze door, whilst listening to Wadji, suddenly stiffens, then grabs Wadji and throws him to the ground.

At that moment, a silver arrow flies out of an aperture in the bronze door and over their heads!

'Thanks Clarence, I owe you one, my friend! I should have known not to touch the door...'

Clarence had already learned that lesson from the pyramid in Guatemala, when he had received a mild electric shock from touching the carvings.

'I've got it!

The thing is saying:

'the flea has no place in the nest of the egret'

It's not just a warning.

Look here!

I believe it's a coded instruction on how to open the door...'

Wadji is standing up and is pointing at an ideogram in the centre of the door. Sure enough, he and the viewers at home are seeing it. There is a tiny raised lump alongside a stylised image of an egret. Before Clarence can even step forward to stop him, Wadji has touched it, and the massive bronze door slowly opens!

'Wow! Way to go Uncle Clarence!' Josh shouts back in Mara's living room in Dublin, as he and Jess do a high five.

They can see, through the eye of the camera, the interior of the tomb, as the bronze door slowly opens.

Once again, Clarence and Wadji are back down on the floor.

This time, though, it is Wadji who, acting on his instincts, has fallen to the ground as the door begins to open, taking Clarence down with him.

'Sorry Clarence, I just felt then, that some humility was in order!'

Wadji's instincts prove to be spot-on, as three more silver arrows fly over them, this time from behind them!

'Mmm... why do I have the feeling this isn't going to be easy?' says Clarence. He can feel increasing pressure in his bladder now, or is it just nerves? Avoiding being pierced by four arrows may have had something to do with it.

The two men stay on the ground, wriggling on their bellies toward the opening.

The lights illuminate an area inside the tomb which seems to be richly decorated, and right there, looking incredibly life-like, are two terracotta swordsmen with their swords raised.

Wadji carefully shines his flashlight at them, to make sure their sword-arms are not hinged, to inflict damage.

Beyond the terracotta swordsmen there is a long corridor leading to a set of steps. The steps seem to be going downwards, towards the burial chamber.

The professors carefully stand up, checking the area all around them. They inch forward, now standing upright again, past the terracotta swordsmen.

They are so lifelike, Clarence swears he can see their eyes following him as he passes under their swords.

In fact, they *are* following them, those eyes! Some kind of mechanical system in the statues has been activated!

Suddenly, Clarence holds out an arm to stop Wadji from stepping forward. He has seen something suspicious: a small pyramid of sand on an otherwise spotlessly clean floor, and it is getting bigger.

Clarence can now see why: a tiny trickle of sand is falling from the ceiling above them... Uh oh! Once again, he grabs Wadji, and they nimbly take two or three paces off to one side.

In the nick of time too.

With an almighty rumble, which millions of viewers around the world can hear on their surround-sound TV systems, a gigantic granite train-sized boulder comes crashing onto the floor, onto the very spot where the professors were standing a moment before.

And they have only advanced about twenty meters beyond the bronze entrance door.

'We're both okay, don't worry!' shouts Wadji into his headset, as the room fills with fine dust. The gigantic boulder has rolled away to one side. For centuries, it has been waiting for its moment, poised up in the roof, and now that has been witnessed by millions!

Up above, at ground-control, Rowena is pacing nervously.

Should she abandon the project now, while there is still a safe exit? She is already thinking, somewhat anxiously, that she does not want to endanger the lives of these two men.

Three booby traps have already been activated, and they are hardly beyond the entrance.

What should she do?

God, she's no good at this kind of thing!

Her headset crackles.

It is Clarence this time.

Even before the dust has settled, the two men have advanced to the edge of the steps, and are now climbing downwards, down and down towards the entrance to the Emperor's tomb.

'Hello there Rowena, dear girl.

Just avoided a bit of a mmm... shafting! And then we had a bit of a mmm... shall we say *rock* concert down here, but ermm. Well, Thank god, it's over, for now!

We're going down the steps now, the dust in the air is clearing, and you should be able to see where we are...'

There is no stopping these men!

The cameras attached to their helmets show the most beautifully decorated walls appearing just ahead of them. The workmanship is indeed fit for an Emperor.

Viewers at home are gasping!

This kind of magnificence has seldom been seen before, and never by so many. Clarence and Wadji stand for a moment, taking it all in. Glancing up at the roof where the granite boulder fell from, Wadji has just seen a new threat.

What seems to be a dark shadow is moving out of the hole left by the boulder: a gigantic nest of scorpions has been dislodged from up there, and they are now swarming down the walls!

Fortunately, the men are protected from them by the thick artificial skin of their insulated suits, and the creatures scuttle away towards the dark recesses of the corridor.

What next?!

From the safety of their living room, Mara and her family had been on the edge of their seats.

This is reality TV at it's awful best!

They could not take their eyes off the drama unfolding on their TV set; when the arrows were let loose, Jess involuntarily ducked, and then, as the gigantic train-sized granite boulder crashed onto the floor, narrowly missing the professors and rolling away out of sight of the camera, they all shouted out loud.

As if that's not enough, they are now seeing a huge swarm of scorpions emerging from the hole.

'Mary Mother of God!' exclaim Mara and Mrs. Stevenson in unison, and Mara drops her freshly loaded scone.

Katrina rushes out of the room to relieve the pressure on her bladder, and Josh stuffs a whole scone into his mouth.

This is too much. More comfort food is needed. Now!

Surely the professors will be called back now, to the safety of the surface? Surely to God! thinks Mrs. Stevenson.

In fact, Rowena has just done that very thing.

She has asked the professors to turn around. To return.

Already an hour has gone by since they left the safety of the lift shaft.

This means they only have two hours of oxygen remaining before they must turn back and return along the path they have taken.

There are no options on this. Everyone, including the Professors Clarencce and Wadji, know the rules.

Rowena has just spoken with General Xi, who shrugs.

He and his government have too much invested in this project to give up now, but the eyes of millions are on this dangerous saga, and he knows Rowena will want to pull the plug on it.

Masterful in his cunning, he leaves the responsibility with her. He makes her feel she is the one in charge of the crisis.

But there is, as we all know, a sub-plot brewing.

He wants the professors down there.

He wants them to be exposed to as much danger as possible. He wants them trapped, so that he can lure Mrs. Kofi into the web he is weaving.

But he must play the game without showing his hand.

Rowena's voice crackles in the professors' headsets:

'Look guys, I'm feeling now that this is getting way too dangerous. I'm pulling the plug on this.

You need to come back.

Do you read me?

Do you copy?

I order you to return immediately!

Professor Wadji?

Professor Clarence? Stinky?

Please, answer me!'

But there is no answer.

Not from either of them.

And there is no camera recording where they are now.

There is now just an empty space where the professors had been standing and all radio and TV contact with them has been broken.

They have disappeared.

Episode Forty-One: Fired Clay...

Lying some three metres below the original floor level, Clarence is quietly cursing himself. Of course, he knows now that the scorpion swarm was a fiendish distraction.

Because he had his eyes on them, he didn't see what was staring him right there in the face.

That change in the colour of the jointing material of the paving slabs should have alerted him, but it was too late!

A cunning pressure-sensitive trapdoor, set off by the slightest footstep, had suddenly dropped him and Wadji without warning down into some dark space below.

He can hear Wadji groaning next to him in the dark.

His helmet flashlight had smashed on impact, but he could see, from the light thrown upwards by Wadji's still-intact head light, the opening through which they had dropped.

Fortunately, he still has another flashlight in his rucksack...

'Wadji! Are you alright old chap?'

Wadji answers immediately via his helmet microphone, though a little hoarsely:

'Yes, Clarence... I'm okay. That fall just knocked the wind out of me. Thank God for the cushioning effect of these suits... though I think we've broken our radio contact with Rowena now...' Wadji answers.

'Mmm... dashed nuisance, too!... We seem to be lying in water. No wait... my God Wadji! I just got some light on it. It's not water, it's, it's... d'you know, it's... it's... ruddy mercury...?!

Thank God for these ruddy suits we're cocooned into, eh?

Otherwise we'd be snuffing it now, wouldn't we, old bean...?'

'Too true... And there's something else, Clarence... we're actually moving in the stuff, we're drifting off in a river of mercury; look, you can see we're now moving away from that trapdoor up there that we dropped through...'

Sure enough, they are drifting along now, in the mercury.

Wadji raises his head, training the headlamp ahead of them.

He can see that they are now lying in a narrow canal, hewn out of solid granite, and incredibly smooth!

Who else in history can claim that they have drifted down a river of mercury, and have lived to tell the tale?! he thinks.

They are around three metres down from the original floor level and the canal they are lying in is curving in a slow arc away from them and dropping very gently.

They drift slowly onwards and now find themselves moving through a tunnel. Clarence has a twinge of claustrophobia as they go through it, but then the tunnel opens up into an entirely new and marvellous space.

The professors are speechless.

Nothing could have prepared them for what they are seeing now.

They have floated on the river of mercury into a huge open space, richly carved and decorated. All around them are terracotta figures, also brightly painted and decorated, as if they have just arrived there. It is as if they, the professors, have gate-crashed a party of stoneware revellers.

Their flashlights are now showing something quite unbelievable. Wadji rummages about and has found another flashlight in his bag, and the extra light is showing up the sheer splendour of the place. There are terracotta dancers, performers, acrobats, and athletes, all engaged in some chosen activity, and frozen forever in it.

There is a ring of soldiers standing guard around them, and right there, seated at the far edge of the stone group, is an effigy of the Emperor himself, in all his imperial might and regal glory. Somehow, his clothes are as bright and fresh now as when the architects of this place installed the tableau more than two millennia before.

Rich silk robes hang on this statue. Clearly no expense has been spared to authenticate his appearance.

He is sitting on a golden throne, flanked by his advisors.

Weirdly, they all seem to be looking at Wadji and Clarence now, as they drift into this dreamlike mime tableau, and the two professors even find themselves a little embarrassed by their undignified entrance, even though the figures are obviously just made of fired clay.

The edge of the mercury river is now only a few feet up from the surface of the floor.

Clarence is on the alert.

Well, as much as he can be whilst drifting on his back in a bath of mercury. His eyes settle on something suspicious.

Just ahead of them is a kind of fine trip-wire suspended almost invisibly over the river.

He quickly shouts out a warning into his microphone and points this out to Wadji, but it's too late!

Just as Wadji tries to raise himself onto the dry bank of the river, his foot has connected with the wire... now the two men quickly but cautiously ease themselves onto the bank or edge of the bizarre liquid metal river, expecting anything.

What will happen now?

The tiny droplets of mercury still clinging to their suits slowly trickle back into the main flow.

They carefully stand up, the pair of them in their white cocoons and helmets; a bizarrely modern contrast to this ancient courtly tableau.

The trip-wire must have triggered something, thinks Clarence. His alert and worried eyes wander around the huge room they are standing in, looking for a response.

In every way, it is a reproduction of the interior of a palace.

This is where the Emperor would have entertained his special guests, and taken advise from his courtiers.

Suddenly Clarence realises something:

He and Wadji are the special guests!

And have they now arrived to be entertained, or...?

Wadji has obviously had the same thought.

Just then, two high backed stone chairs move out towards them, on rails, and stop a few paces away.

The chairs face the throne. The professors decide to decline the invitation.

They now stand back to back, defensively scanning the area around them with utmost scrutiny, watching, waiting...

There are three high bronze doors leading into the chamber, one behind the Emperor's throne, one directly opposite it; and another opposite the river, which flows from east to west.

And they can hear something now: it's a high pitched whistling sound, cutting through the silence and echoing around the chamber.

Wadji nudges Clarence and points.

Clarence follows his gloved finger.

He can't quite believe it, but the sound is coming from a terracotta flautist standing in a group of musicians.

Then, all at once, music emerges from that whole group.

Strings, drums, woodwinds!

All seemingly playing together now!

A mechanical orchestra is entertaining them!

This is probably the first sound to fill this chamber in two thousand years or more.

And they are thinking now, that if they have been

expected, they had better take care.

Just then, with that very thought, the tall bronze door behind the Terracotta Emperor slowly opens on ancient brass hinges.

To the amazement of the two men, a whole group of terracotta warriors now silently arrives on rails fixed to the floor. Somewhere an ingenious mechanical contrivance has been set in motion by that trip-wire and now:

It's Showtime!

Clarence and Wadji are transfixed!

The group of terracotta warriors stops now, just behind the Emperor. Half of them have moved to his left, the other half to his right. All this while the music continues to play.

Clarence marvels, what genius thought of all this?

And with such perfection, that the music would still play, even now, with such clarity and precision, some millennia after the Emperor's interment.

But the show is not over.

Not by a long way!

The bronze doors behind the Emperor have now closed.

There is a pause.

Wadji and Clarence are still keeping their eyes peeled.

Wadji has noticed something new.

Glancing down, he sees that the level of the mercury in the river has risen slightly and seems to be moving faster.

Also, the music has changed again. Now there are the sounds to announce a new arrival, they are guessing.

And then, with incredible grace and elegance something makes a stunning and regal entrance.

It is a golden boat, floating down the river of mercury.

The boat is in full sail.

The mast and jib seem to be made of pure gold.

The sails are bright red, with ideograms painted on them.

In the boat there are several sailors and robed dignitaries.

But this time, these figures are carved not of clay, but of wood, clearly to keep the weight down.

At the prow stand a group of three archers, their bows strung taut. Sailors artfully tend to the sails and tiller.

And there at the stern of the boat is a funereal bier, and upon it lies the carved wooden effigy of a small child, all in exquisite detail, dressed in royal robes.

It is known that the Emperor took the throne whilst only a teenager, and ruled somewhat ruthlessly, tolerating no criticism whatsoever for just fifteen years and he was then succeeded by his son.

Was this some kind of tribute to him, in advance?

Or is this a metaphor for the fact that he, the first Emperor, took over as Emperor at the tender age of thirteen, thus altogether forsaking his childhood and forever mourning it? There is no written record to explain any of this.

Clarence and Wadji are open-mouthed in awe!

The boat sails past them with slow and stately dignity now, and in a few minutes, it has moved gracefully on and out of sight, behind the throne and onwards.

But there is more…

The music has changed yet again, and there is something far more festive to it, more joyful and energetic!

The next minute, rose petals begin to fall through concealed apertures in the ceiling, cascading down and covering everything in a beautiful pink and red shower of petals.

How on earth have they kept the rose petals so fresh?

ponders Wadji, picking up a handful and studying them.

Of course, he is unable to smell them through his insulated suit, but he imagines the chamber must now be permeated by their wonderful fragrance, which it certainly is.

At the same moment as the fall of the rose petals, a group of beautiful terracotta dancers in the central space rotate gracefully together, on a circular table fixed to the floor.

Then the bronze door in the wall opposite the Emperor's throne opens, and the Empress enters, carried in a sedan chair by four strong men gliding in on hidden rails in the floor. The sedan chair is made of solid gold and ivory and is festooned with rich silk hangings, to match the exquisitely detailed wedding dress of the Empress.

She is beautifully dressed in silks and looks incredibly life-like as she moves past the awestruck professors and stops alongside the Emperor's throne.

Then, from the same door a line of terracotta servants files slowly in, carrying trays piled high with fruit and meat and delicacies, all delicately moulded and painted, and looking as lifelike now as the day they were made.

Once again, hidden mechanics have been set in motion, and the show goes on and on and on.

This is clearly a wedding feast being played out and

the two professors, are the uninvited guests.

A vast replay of the wedding feast of China's first Emperor.

If only this was being filmed, thinks Clarence.

Without him knowing it, it is!

Even though the radio signal to the outside world has been interrupted, the entire tableau is still being recorded by the cameras fitted inside the professors' helmets.

What they are seeing now will one day be recovered from the cameras in their helmets, and will one day be seen and enjoyed by millions.

Now the stone servants slowly withdraw, reversing back through the door they entered from, leaving the Empress sitting in her golden sedan chair alongside the Emperor.

The door slowly closes.

All is still for a time.

Wadji, although entranced by this magical mechanical display, has been carefully taking note of things, studying every part of the chamber and everything in it. Looking for a way out.

He notices that the door behind the Emperor's throne leads to a sealed chamber, but he sees that within this chamber there are no other openings.

He also sees that the second door, on the opposite side of the throne, the one through which the servants have just entered and withdrawn, leads into a small chamber; but again, like the other one, it is completely sealed, with no other openings leading into or out of it.

What now? How will they escape?

Then there is a sound opposite them, from the third door.

They have clearly saved the best till last.

To their utter astonishment, the massive bronze door, easily four metres wide and around six metres tall, slowly and majestically opens inwards.

Out of the chamber beyond, a huge terracotta horse, three times the normal size, with an ornate saddle of spun gold and silver and studded with precious jewels, and whose counterpart clearly belonging in life to the Emperor, moves out of the tomb in stately glory and into the Imperial chamber.

Tiny terracotta birds, strung on wires, and hidden until this moment, fly out and over them, and now, beyond the bronze door, in the light of their flashlights, they can see revealing itself before them the very tomb of the Emperor.

The inner sanctum.

They know this is the tomb, as it showed up in the sonar scans done by the Chinese some months back.

They also remember, from these scans, that the tomb has two openings leading into it.

One of them leads back here, into what they now call the Imperial chamber, and the other opens into a vast central space, which was unknown and indecipherable on the scans due to the incredible thickness of the walls.

This is it!

This is their chance to escape!

A slow procession of monks in dark clothes, presumably priests and holy men and mourners, files out of the space ahead of them in the tomb.

Wadji grabs Clarence's arm, and they quickly negotiate around the slowly moving figures, heading in the opposite direction, so that in a moment they are right inside the chamber housing the tomb, while the procession continues.

Ahead of them is an incredibly ornate structure, the sacred tomb of the Emperor itself. It is mostly black and red in colour, but there are decorations of pure gold and ivory on it, inlaid with precious stones and pearls.

It is magnificent!

Again, there are several armed terracotta archers framing and guarding the doors leading into the tomb.

Wadji and Clarence carefully look over every part visible to them, as the priestly procession now stops inside the Imperial chamber.

Behind the funeral procession, they can see a door leading out, and presumably into the much larger room they know to be there from the scans.

It is closed.

Suddenly, without warning, two of the terracotta archers, holding drawn bows, swivel in their direction and let loose their arrows.

This time the arrows are made of gold, and they whistle with tremendous speed over the heads of the professors,

who have already flung themselves onto the floor.

They did this with great alacrity the very moment they saw the figures begin to swivel in their direction.

And then, at the very same instant, there is an ominous rumbling sound from the Imperial chamber.

All of a sudden, the floor shakes as a huge pile of soil drops down from the ceiling of the Imperial chamber directly onto the stone chairs, which the professors would have been sitting in had they not declined the invitation.

The guest chairs are now buried in about a ton of damp soil.

'Well, stab me vitals!

They've bloody well thought of everything!

If that's what they think of their guests we'd best thank 'em for the lovely show and take our leave, eh Wadji, my man?'

Clarence whispers into his microphone.

Wadji smiles.

They had already agreed to keep as quiet as possible, just in case another booby trap is set off.

Which it has!

Twice!

Clearly the ancient Chinese builders of the tomb complex had pre-empted an intrusion from this door.

The glazed archers with golden arrows were ready and patiently waiting for them: all two thousand years and more! And just for good measure, if the guests had accepted the offered stone chairs, they would now be buried alive.

Fortunately, the professors are in audio contact with each other, but of course the fall through the trapdoor had damaged the radio connection with ground control and has effectively cut them off from the outside world.

Or has it?

While lying on the marble floor in case of further

arrows, Clarence and Wadji check the status of their oxygen supply. There are dials cleverly projected onto the inside of their helmets. All it takes is the activation of a small button on the outside of the helmet to see these dials.

The read-out they are now both seeing is not encouraging.

The needle on the oxygen dial is edging into the red area.

This means they now have less than an hour before their oxygen runs out.

Not good!

Something needs to happen!

Soon!

Wadji points at the door, on the opposite site of the tomb room, and waves his arm for Clarence to follow.

He has decided to go for it.

They carefully tiptoe toward it, looking every inch like a couple of mad beekeeper's escaping a swarm.

Which is more or less what now happens.

The soil dumped on the stone guest-chairs has also released underneath it, an ancient an impressively large hornet's nest that was obviously quite deliberately encouraged to be there.

The angry insects, disturbed from their two millennia hibernation, swarm and buzz, and sensing the body-heat generated by the professors, they head straight for them, like a big black muttering cloud of bad temper.

'Run!' shouts Wadji, as he now abandons caution and legs it for the door. Clarence needs no encouragement.

On a whim, or perhaps it is just sheer desperation, Wadji frantically turns the huge ornamental knob in the centre of the door.

It opens!

With a squeal that somehow confuses the cloud of angry hornets, who suddenly retreat, the door swings inwards,

and the professors dash into the dark space beyond the door, slamming it and the hornet cloud closed behind them.

They can hear several arrows slamming into it from the other side.

Of course, there were more archers waiting, weren't there?

They stand there for a moment catching their breath and getting their bearings. There is something strangely familiar about the space they are now standing in.

They are both feeling that now.

It is vast, and shaped like the interior of a pyramid.

Where have they seen this before?

They stare at each other as they suddenly realise!

It is the same interior as the pyramid in the Guatemalan jungles. The one they took a ride in with the blue chief, and Josh and Jess. Even the walls have the same soft glow, and they can see a stone dais in the centre, with a throne on top of it, and four further seats carved into the corners of the dais.

Clarence reaches into his bag, and draws out The Fate Book, which is already pulsing with a soft warm light, just like a heartbeat.

Meanwhile, some time much earlier, when she saw the empty space where they were before they dropped through the trapdoor into the river of mercury, Rowena tried frantically to connect with them, calling out over and over...

Nothing. No reply.

It's no good, they've gone.

She picked up her phone and immediately called an emergency meeting with General Xi.

While she waited for him, she ran through everything she has at hand. All the data ever collected about what lay below her, in the tomb. Everything.

Meanwhile, the cameras remained fixed on a blank wall in the mausoleum, until the flustered TV presenter came back on, with her hair skewed and lipstick covering her chin, to tell the anxiously awaiting world that they had lost all audio and video contact with the professors, but she insisted it was probably just a temporary technical malfunction and communications would shortly be restored.

Then a couple of minutes later, an advert for deodorant specially created for adventurous men came on, followed by some clips from earlier moments in the broadcast, just to fill in the time.

No one knew what would happen next...

'I'm bloody going down there, General, get me a spare suit!'

Rowena shouted at Xi as soon as he walked into the control room, without waiting to see his response to the emergency.

He is strangely cool, too cool, Rowena thought.

The cooler he looked, the hotter she got...

He strutted about the room, a supercilious smile on his face; playing with his tiny moustache, flicking his polished horse-whip about.

Things were just where he wanted them to be!

'Come now, Rowena, you must be patient.

We just don't know enough yet; the professors may

be safe.

And you, you are project leader, you could be putting yourself, them, and the whole project in even more trouble by going down there alone...'

Of course the General was right, but for the wrong reasons.

'Who said anything about me going down there alone? You're coming with me, you little bugger...!'

The General turned pale.

This was not in the plan.

No not at all.

So far, everything was going well for him.

The professors were trapped down there and that was just as it should be, and soon the world, including Mrs. Kofi, would know that there was no hope for them...

The web was being spun!

But now this ridiculous red-haired woman wanted him to go down there with him to attempt a rescue!

Never!

'No, I can't allow this, Miss Shardsworth!

Forget it! It's irresponsible and unprofessional!

There's too much at stake! The government of the People's Republic have invested far too much time and money in this project, for you to act like some kind of spoiled child.

You'll have to wait a little while longer, at least for us to know more of the facts. We want facts now.

Facts!'

She wanted to hit him.

She wanted to punch him in his silly smiley little face!

She wanted to take that horsewhip of his and shove it somewhere where the sun didn't shine! Instead, she said,

'But meanwhile, General, the fact is they're using up precious oxygen down there even while we speak... surely you can allow...'

Just then, there was a sudden crackle in Rowena's headphones. The voice of Clarence!

'Rowena?

Rowena... do you copy, old girl?

My God! It's Clarence!'

'Yes, Clarence, I copy!

Oh, thank God it's you!

What's happened to you?

Where are you now?'

'Well... we've taken... bit of a tumble my dear.

Ruddy... trapdoor! sshh... kkkk...

dropped into a ri… of mercury... shh... kkk.

Dashed nuisance!

Anyway... we... sshh... kkrrr.

out of the chamber... sh... shhh...

Think... found... sshh... kkkrr...

brrr... kkk.

another… kkrrr... way... shhh...'

The signal broke up gradually and finally cut off altogether, and Rowena slammed her fist down on the table in sheer frustration.

What did he say?

That they had dropped through a trapdoor, for god's sake?!

Into a river of... mercury?

Oh my God!

Her worst nightmare!

And did he say they had found a way out?

Where?

How annoying that she had lost radio contact again, with these crucial questions unanswered...

Damn! Damn and blast!

Rowena paced angrily, ignoring the General and his waxy smile, then she dropped into a chair at the control room, putting her hands over her eyes, trying somehow to draw inspiration out of herself.

Facts, facts, facts!

Okay, so let's check the data, she thought.

She had just seen the oxygen dials, transmitted to her from the suits.

There was now under two hours of oxygen left to them, and the suits could not be refilled without removing them.

Actually, one hour and forty-two minutes and counting...

Fact: The cameras down there still showed an empty space where the professors had been.

Fact: The radio was silent.

What to do?

Fact: Ultimately, the General was in charge of the

project, and she knew she had no choice but to follow his orders.

But at least having heard Clarence she knew the professors were alive, though where they were now was still a mystery.

Should she just listen to her instincts and put on a suit and go down there, right now?

But she didn't know where they were...

The little generalissimo was right, damn him!

She could get lost or hurt down there on her own, and the cowardly little rat wouldn't even dream of go down there with her.

What to do now?

Think, Rowena! Think!

She looked up from where she had been sitting, with her hands over her eyes, aware that someone was standing there, right behind her.

The lovely smiling face of 'Tiger Lily,' Xan Ku Li looking down at her.

'You look so worried, Rowena.

Please, tell me!

What can I do for you now?'

Back in the tomb, and sometime later now, the

professors finally are able to take a breath, though it seems they're going to be running short of those soon.

They are marvelling now at the interior of the pyramid, into which they have escaped from the swarm of hornets.

'My God, Wadji, look at the thing, will you? It's identical! Surely it must have been constructed around the same period as the Mayan one!'

'Quite so!

This is very exciting, Clarence. It means we may have stumbled onto an ancient but advanced technology, which might have allowed travel to any part of the world in mere moments – a kind of pyramid teleporting system; all that was required was another pyramid like this, to go anywhere you wanted in no time at all.

And for all we know there were probably dozens of them in existence back then!'

'Oh, my giddy aunt, Wadji, look up there, we have company...!' says Clarence in a shocked whisper, pointing up at the throne on the dais.

To their amazement there is a figure sitting there.

Around him is a strange soft blueish glow.

It is the Emperor himself, dressed in full regalia.

And now he stands up and has raised an arm to greet them.

The professors are shocked out of their wits.

It is one thing seeing a bunch of terracotta warriors moving about and even dodging their arrows, but another thing altogether dealing with a real live ancient Chinese Emperor.

Suddenly, there is a loud booming laugh that echoes around the vast interior of the pyramid, and with that, the figure of the Emperor shape-shifts, before their very eyes, into a huge Michelin man!

'Got you, boys! Hahahahah! Just look at your scared little faces! You thought I was the Emperor for a minute there, didn't you?!

Surprise surprise: ce moi! mon petite shu's...'

It's the Djinn!

He has shape-shifted back into his familiar form, complete with a turban and gold teeth, and here he is now, bowing deeply and standing right there before them.

'Good day, gentlemen!

Congratulations on reaching this place!

My dear Clarence, I really am most impressed.

You'll remember, I'm sure, that I offered you my services oh so long ago, and you haven't called on me once. Not once. What a Trojan you are!

All this time I've been looking out for you and yours,

but rules are rules and I've not intervened.

Not once.

Though... I might have mentioned... something to your chap Morkabalas, something about your niece being in danger once or twice.

That's allowed you know!

Yes, I'm very impressed, Clarence.

I would have thought floating on your back down a river of mercury would have done it, then having a few shafts aimed and fired at you by men with feet of clay, not to mention plagues of hornets and scorpions, and a few tons of topsoil?

Mmmm... but then, what can I, a mere spirit, possibly know about the limits to human endurance and frailty?'

Clarence can't pretend he isn't happy to see the Djinn, and hadn't even thought of calling on him, even though they now have less than an hour of oxygen left in their suits.

Wadji knows about the Djinn, but knowing Clarence's connection with him, looks to him for a response.

'Dash it all, old bean! I say!

You've come in the ruddy nick of time!

You must have heard me sphincter calling, I think!

Yes, things are looking just a bit tight... we're running out of air, y'know... just a few minutes left to us now... and well... there you are...bloody nuisance!

So, I'm asking you now…

Can you help us out, old boy?'

'Actually, I can!

You will need The Fate Book of course.

You will find the restoring of the green stone to its cover has given it new life and, well... a few neat new tricks!

But, my dear and valued friend, in just two ticks from now you'll be having some welcome visitors from above, then you can fly this baby you know how to you know where.

Josh and his family will be waiting for you there, and then... well, tut tut tut... I've already said too much, I won't spoil the surprise.

My only advice to you at this point is, always fly first-class if you can, and carry clean extra underwear, just in case, oh and make sure you have a good story when you come back.

You'll need it!

With that, he bows with a flourish and vanishes in a puff of blue smoke, just as a bronze door on the opposite side of the pyramid opens and there, in their insulated white suits, stand their rescuers.

Rowena Shardsworth, the General Xi, and his wife the lovely Xan Ku Li, who must be credited for talking her husband the general into overcoming his fear and coming down here.

They are staring about them in unrestrained wonder.

What is this place?

What's it for?

They are about to find out!

So how, dear reader, did they manage to get here so quickly, you are most likely asking?

Let's go back a bit while our new arrivals in the pyramid take a moment to orient themselves, and find out...

When Rowena had reached a point of despairing impasse, when she knew the professors were dangerously low on oxygen, and realised she could not rescue them on her own, Tiger Lily appeared in the control room.

Tiger Lily aka Xan Ku Li, beloved of young Chinese social networkers and darling of global conservationists.

She stood there behind Rowena's chair, watching her with the utmost kindness and compassion, as she sat there despairing with her hands over her eyes.

'You look so worried, Rowena.

Please, tell me;

What can I do for you?'

Rowena turned around to look up at her.

Tears streaked her cheeks, deep lines scored her forehead.

Her bright red hair stood up where she had been pulling her hands through it.

Frankly, she looked a mess.

'Oh God! They're stuck down there, Li, and I can't do a bloody thing about it. Xi won't let me go down there on my own, and he won't come with me either...'

Without hesitating, Li turns on her heel, marches straight up to her husband Xi, who is smirking in the shadows, and launches into a tirade of Mandarin.

She berates him for standing by whilst people are dying down there through lack of oxygen and proper care, she calls him a coward and a disgrace to his gender.

She reminds him that he has a responsibility for each individual life on this project, however foreign and reprehensible that life is to him.

And finally, she deals her trump card:

She will never speak to him again if the three of them don't all put their suits on right this minute and go down there to bring back the professors, right now.

That does it!

Some noble part of the little general, in some deep place, buried alive in its own personal tomb, buried under the layers of ambition and status and sheer ego, wakes up.

Immediately, three spare suits and helmets, already primed with oxygen and ready to go in an emergency, are requisitioned.

Tiger Lily insists on accompanying the General and Rowena, and she will not take no for an answer.

Just as well, really, as who knows what might happen if he decides to renege on this noble part of him, freshly awakened?

The suits are a little too large for Tiger Lily and the General.

In fact, the two of them look rather like little old ladies do, when they peer over the top of the steering wheel of their cars. Just their eyes and the tops of their heads are visible.

In spite of things, Rowena giggles to see the upstart General, peering up at her in his helmet, his eyes just visible.

He and Li look like little children in a theme park, about to fly off into virtual pretend space.

Rowena has already assessed the layout of the tomb, based on the sonar scans she has. She has found a short cut to the huge space that the professors are now standing in, breathing the last of their suited air.

She quickly briefs the General and the lovely Tiger Lily, and in a moment they are traveling down the lift shaft, passing through the three airlocks.

This time, there is no media accompaniment, no commentary on their journey.

In fact, a ring of heavily armed Chinese soldiers stand around the control centre at ground level, with strict orders from General Xi to allow no one through the cordon at any cost.

Also, until they return from their rescue mission, no news and no inquisitive intervention of any kind will be tolerated. A blanket ban has been imposed.

No questions will be asked and no answers will given; not to anyone at any time until General Xi returns.

Meanwhile, the three suited rescuers have reached the entrance hall, where the professors had started out.

Rowena takes a second to get her bearings.

She knows that just ahead of them is a slope downwards, toward the bronze doors that Wadji had activated by puzzling out the riddle of the flea and the egret. Beyond that lies the corridor where they were bombarded with arrows, the gigantic boulder, and the scorpion plague.

They won't be going that way.

Instead, behind them, and quite close to the lift shaft, is an ancient wooden door, studded with brass nails.

A simple door, free of any decoration or embellishment, except for the huge bronze padlock locking it.

Rowena knows, from the sonar scans, that this door leads to a spiral staircase leading down directly into the vast pyramidal chamber directly below them. She is wildly guessing that this is where the professors have ended up.

This route was deliberately not chosen by Wadji and Clarence, simply because they did not believe it would take them to the Emperor's tomb.

So now, the three rescuers stand before the door. Rowena, as capable a tracker as Clarence, with the added bonus of woman's intuition, carefully investigates the area around the door. She is very aware that, according to her calculations, the professors have only around forty-five minutes of oxygen left. She examines the padlock, turning it over and looking at its clever workmanship.

Then, she reaches for her sling bag. The General and Li think she is going to use something to pick that lock.

She gestures for them to stand back from the door as she reaches into her bag.

Next thing, there is an almighty bang, and Rowena

stands there in the drifting smoke, looking pleased with herself, and the damage done to the padlock by her smoking magnum. Desperate times require desperate measures.

The padlock now drops off, Rowena swings open the door, quickly makes sure it is safe to proceed, and gestures for the others to follow. In a few minutes, they have made their way down the spiral staircase and reached the bottom.

Ahead of them is a bronze door. This time there are no padlocks or riddles required, and Rowena pushes the door open.

They are inside a vast pyramid and ahead of them are the two professors, waiting for them.

Meanwhile, back in Cairo, Mrs. Kofi's flat is strangely empty. In fact, her television is still on, still showing the commentary on the events leading up to the descent into the Emperor's tomb.

But Mrs. Kofi is no longer there.

She is already on a plane bound for Beijing.

The moment she saw the TV pictures of an empty space where the professors had been before they dropped out of sight down the trapdoor, she was up and packing her things. She had called the airport in Cairo and found a flight leaving in a few hours. She had left a message with her relief staff at the museum, explaining that she was going to Beijing and even leaving them the flight details.

Then she called and checked into the Shangri-la Hotel in Beijing, where she knew Rowena and the professors were staying.

She threw clothes and toiletries into her flight bag, pausing here for just long enough to make sure, as a lover would, that she had a few outfits there which she knew would please the discerning eye of Wadji. And then she retrieved the crocodile skin handbag; the bag which represented so much to her now about her new life.

Didn't she read somewhere that crocodiles represented renewal?

Certainly, she and her beloved Wadji had now made a new start and there was no way anyone would take him away from her now that she had found him again!

(TO BE CONTINUED...)

Peter lives in Surrey with his beautiful wife Debra, and their two magical cats, Jasper and Little Bear. He likes to travel to exotic places where the sun shines, the food is good, and he can write to his heart's content...

To find out more about Peter and his books, go to
www.petervanminnen.com

OTHER BOOKS IN THE FATE BOOK SERIES:

The Fate Book 2: The Tigers Nest: out soon!
The Fate Book 3: The Secret Archives: out soon!